THE BLACK MASK LIBRARY

THE EARLY YEARS (1920–26)

The Man in the Shadows: The Complete Black Mask
Cases of Terry Mack *by Carroll John Daly*

THE SHAW YEARS (1926–36)

Blood on the Curb *by Joseph T. Shaw*

Black Harvest: The Complete Black Mask
Cases of Jules Tremaine *by Norvell W. Page*

Boomerang Dice: The Complete Black Mask
Cases of Johnny Hi Gear *by Stewart Sterling*

Dead Evidence: The Complete Black Mask
Cases of Harrigan *by Ed Lybeck*

Laughing Death *by Raoul Whitfield*

Luck: The Complete Black Mask Cases of
Oscar Sail *by Lester Dent*

Murder Maze: The Complete Black Mask Cases of
Jerry Tracy, Volume 2 *by Theodore A. Tinsley*

The Price of a Dime: The Complete Black Mask
Cases of Ben Shaley *by Norbert Davis*

Somewhere in Mexico: The Complete Black Mask
Cases of Jerry Frost, Volume 1 *by Horace McCoy*

South Wind: The Complete Black Mask Cases of
Jerry Tracy, Volume 1 *by Theodore A. Tinsley*

THE LATER YEARS (1936–51)

Dead and Done For: The Complete Black Mask Cases
of Cellini Smith, Volume 1 *by Robert Reeves*

Dog Eat Dog: The Complete Black Mask Cases
of Cellini Smith, Volume 2 *by Robert Reeves*

It Happened at the Lake *by Joseph T. Shaw*

Let the Dead Alone: The Complete Black Mask Cases
of Luther McGavock, Volume 1 *by Merle Constiner*

Murder Costs Money: The Complete Black Mask
Cases of Rex Sackler, Volume 1 *by D.L. Champion*

Murder on the Midway: The Complete Black Mask Cases
of the Human Encyclopedia, Volume 1 *by Frank Gruber*

IT HAPPENED AT THE LAKE

A

Mystery

JOSEPH T. SHAW

cover by John Drew

BLACK MASK

2022

Table of Contents

It Happened at the Lake / *3*

An Interview with Joseph T. Shaw / *273*

It Happened at the Lake

1

THE GIRL WITH the stringy bob said, "Yeah," pulled the plug from the switchboard, let it plop back into its slot. Her glance swept half across the big city room, sought out a tall, rangy young fellow, leaning, half sitting on one of the many flat topped desks. He looked bored with idleness.

Chattering typewriters of the pre-noiseless variety, voices in one-sided telephone conversations, calling, dictating, talking, furnished a volume of sound that seemed a tangible substance.

"Mr. Ran-dolph!" The operator's voice was slightly nasal; its tone rose in sing-song above the noise. "Big Bo-oy! the See Ee-e wants to see-e you!"

The tall young man smiled a little embarrassedly, detached himself from the desk with the easy motion of flowing muscles, and strode long-legged the length of the room. He stopped at a door in the glass paneling that closed and sound-proofed that end, laid one hand uncertainly on the knob. Lettering on the glass read: Mr. MacArthur, City Editor.

The man at the half-moon desk inside, without glancing up, jerked an arm in peremptory gesture. Randolph went in.

He paused a little behind MacArthur's shoulder. As he watched the city editor's frantic efforts to keep pace with the incessant demands of the ringing Continental phones and the plopping pneumatic cylinders, his eyes lost their somewhat vacuous expression and grew shrewd and speculative.

For his height, Randolph was a well set up youngster. The close fitting shirt beneath his opened coat showed thick pectoral muscles and a lean, flat stomach. His waist was narrow. Well tailored trousers and coat, not too new, were moulded over capable appearing legs and arms and heavy shoulders. He looked built for both speed and power.

The jaw was rugged; mouth humorous, with straight nose and good forehead. The grayish-blue eyes alone were baffling, with a naive frankness of expression that seemed, nevertheless, forever on guard.

The city editor's right hand cradled a phone; the left reached automatically for a newly arrived cylinder. The slight turning movement gave the tail of his eye a glimpse of the broad shoulders and six feet of height that dwarfed his own pudgy, perspiring form.

MacArthur grabbed another phone, barked into it, "Hold everything a minute." He scraped a pad across the desk, scribbled on it as he talked, although what he wrote and what he said were unlike. His spoken words were clipped, hurried.

"Managing Editor says he's sending you up here for a try-out. Didn't tell me if you were hired or what. I'm betting th' idea's a Boy Scout one-day take-over. Aw right; I'm giving you a try.

"Beginning today, Burke's throwing one of his weekend parties up at his big place 't Crossley Lake. Go out there. Get a story. Take a candid camera and get some pictures. Thirty seconds for questions and try to make 'em sensible."

"Mind telling me who Burke is?" Randolph asked mildly and without enthusiasm.

The city editor shot him a quick look. The beginning of a smile twitched his lips. He turned it into a hard, poker expression.

"Ross Burke is one of our—er—best known lawyers. Made

a big rep for himself in court practice. Wealthy. Lavish entertainer. Famous for his parties. Avoids publicity and objects to
having his picture taken. Get pictures. Get anything. And get
th' hell outa here."

Resentment surfaced young Randolph's eyes for an instant,
then was gone. His lips still held their smile.

"No," he said, slowly shaking his head, "I don't think I would
want it."

The swivel-chair creaked shrilly as MacArthur whirled
around.

"Heh?" he barked angrily. One hand groped toward a phone
that was now behind him. "You don't want—"

Randolph's big right hand, in deprecatory gesture, moved
slowly through the air not far from the city editor's purpling
face.

"Your job. Too much blood pressure."

MacArthur gauged the breadth of that hand, mentally calculated the height above him of Randolph's innocent appearing
grin. A bleak smile twisted his lips as he reversed the movement of the chair.

"I can take it. You cubs never can. Go see Morrison. He'll
give you the dope."

"How about the invitation?"

MacArthur came about again.

"The—*what?*"

"Perhaps I should have said invite. To the party, you know."

Puzzlement narrowed the lids over the city editor's pale blue
eyes; then growing anger caused them to sparkle.

"Will you tell me," he howled, "why they inflict a thing like
you on an editor who's trying to keep his family from starva-

tion and keep circulation up! Invitation hell. Th' only invitation you'll get is a chance to beat a load of shot over the garden wall. If you don't do it I'll break down and cry. See Morrison, damn it! Now *will* you get outa here!"

He turned his back, this time with an air of definite finality, raising both hands above his head to express the futility of mere words to measure his disgust. As they came down, one automatically groped in the pneumatic receiving box; the other caught up a phone.

"Let 'em come!" he yelled.

Randolph took up the slip of paper which the city editor had torn from the pad and then apparently had forgotten. As he looked down upon the galvanic motions of the pudgy man, his expression was capriciously amused. He closed the door softly behind him and stepped into the roar of the city room.

From the photographic department, he obtained a candid camera, several rolls of films and containers for handy mailing, which he had stamped and addressed. He drew twenty-five dollars of expense money from the cashier. As he strode back along the corridor toward the city room, he added the bills to a sizable roll whose denominations were tens and twenties.

Randolph paused by the switchboard while the girl did legerdemain with her battery of plug switches then leaned back and looked straight up at him. He glanced away from her slowly widening eyes, nodded across the room.

"Will you tell me, Miss, which is Morrison?"

She came to normal pose, with a jerk and a little unladylike grunt.

"Sad-faced, oldish guy 'way over there in the corner."

Randolph thanked her, moved away.

Morrison was typing steadily and expertly at his desk. He was sitting bolt upright, frowning down at his work while his long, bony fingers played with the keys without wrist motion and with the skill of a pianist. At Randolph's approach, without looking up he suspended a hand above the keyboard, motioned toward an adjoining desk and chair and resumed his swift measure.

Randolph sank slowly into the chair and stretched long legs before him. He let his glance wander over the room then return until he had Morrison under the corner of his eye without appearing to look directly at him.

He saw a man who was probably ten years younger than the forty-odd he appeared. Thin, graying hair straggled carelessly above a high, bony forehead. The nose was straight and prominent. The long face narrowed to a pointed chin and tight-lipped, bitter mouth.

Beneath the eyes, in the hectic spots on the sallow, sunken cheeks, in the lines between cheek and lip, dissipation had placed its stamp. The features, their form and set, moulded a fixed expression of disillusionment, of disappointment without resignation.

The roller whirred as Morrison tore the sheet out. At his hoarse call a copy boy came, took the sheets Morrison had typed, rolled them to fit the cylinder he carried and stepped over to shove the cylinder into a tube. Morrison's chair scraped on the floor.

"Lookin' for me, kid?"

Randolph turned with his amiable smile and got slowly to his feet. Morrison's head went backward as his eyes followed Randolph's upward. There was no answering smile on his saturnine features. His eyes were dark and watery, a little filmed, slightly unclear; but through their opaqueness fires burned.

"Mr. MacArthur told me to see you."

"Uh-huh. What about?"

"He wants me to cover a week-end party at a country place. Burke's—Ross Burke. He said to get the information from you."

"Why don't he bury his own dead!" Morrison growled irritably. He had been looking at Randolph casually, remarking his unusual build and appearance of hard fitness. His scrutiny grew more keen as he glanced at the youth's smiling face whose frank candor was somehow flattering.

"Burke's a louse," he grunted. "But he's got the dough and flies high. His money controls everything around him. That means you can't get to him if he don't want you. Tough assignment, kid."

Morrison stood up, disclosing a lean form of nearly Randolph's own height. Unexpectedly he smiled at Randolph. Altogether you did not want to see it from him at the moment. It seemed an admission that he was relinquishing something to which the younger man might be heir. Perhaps it was ambition; faith in a career. Randolph's eyes did not show that he caught such impression.

"You will tell me where to go and what to do, Mr. Morrison?"

"Sure, sure. But we can't talk in this damned racket. When you starting?"

"As soon as I know what it's all about. This is sort of new to me."

"Uh-huh. Got your expense?"

"Yes."

"We'll go over to Jack's. I'll take a highball for breakfast while I give you the dope. Couldn't talk on an empty stomach, this time of day anyway."

Morrison led the way to the elevators. Going down, he did not speak. Once he glanced sidewise at Randolph and a look of slyness came into his dark, smoky eyes.

2

JACK, OR AT least the man who stood for that name and signed Jack to all his checks, was compactly built, with thick, barrel body, not too broad shoulders and solid legs. His head was more round than square, with thick grayish-white hair worn in close-cut pompadour. The nose was short and blunt above a wide, close-trimmed mustache. One ear was permanently thicker than the other.

Old timers would tell you that he had fought for several seasons and was a very creditable middleweight, and when you watched him you were reminded of ring habits, as if he had unconsciously retained his tricks of earlier days. He still weaved a little as he walked, although not so lithely as he might have done with less bulk.

When you faced him, his eyes did not meet yours directly, but concentrated somewhere about your midsection; you had the impression that not a flicker or expression of your eyes, a motion of your hand or foot escaped his observation. It was tricky, made you unconsciously watchful, discouraged any inclination toward too great familiarity.

Morrison greeted him, "Hiyah, Jack," received a toneless, " 'Morning."

Randolph, a little behind the lanky newspaperman, saw the white-haired man's glance flicker toward him, noted the slightly cauliflowered right ear, the manner in which his eyes observed him, and stiffened a little. He seemed subconsciously alert. As he followed Morrison, with a stride that was short for his leg length and kept his weight constantly poised, his own glance lanced around that of the white-haired man. Their eyes did not meet, yet in the moment's scrutiny each seemed to have noted every detail of the other.

Behind the counter a red-haired man with white apron, and white cap cocked sidewise, looked at the newspaperman without smiling, glanced past him with more interest at young Randolph. "Breakfast, Mr. Morrison?" he asked mechanically.

"Later, Sam," Morrison said flatly. "I'll take what Eddie can give me first."

He pushed open the right half of a pair of leather-covered swing doors, each with a small round light set at average height, and led the way into a still larger and at the moment much noisier room.

The rough wooden floor had been recently sprinkled, leaving an effect of heated moist air which was tossed about by ceiling fans with slow-moving, propeller-like blades. A dozen men were lined up at the bar, each with a foot on the rail, an elbow on the mahogany; some with straw hats on the backs of their heads; others in shirt sleeves, coatless or with coat slung over an arm. Fully a score more were seated at various tables in the big room. Their conversation racketed the place.

Morrison touched his arm, nodded toward a more aloof table near one of the corners. "I'll join you in a minute, kid, when I order mine. What'll you have?"

Randolph smiled. "Nothing, thanks." He walked over to the table, sat with long legs stretched before him.

Jack had stopped by a table at which two men sat, with tall beer glasses before them. He leaned over a little as he talked to them. The one facing Randolph was a well-dressed, gray-haired man. The other was a solid-bodied man of forty-odd. After a moment the latter turned and looked around the room, his glance sweeping Randolph in passing.

Randolph let his gaze stray toward the bar where Morrison was having a heads-together conference with two or three men, one of whom, a tall, sandy-haired fellow, Randolph remembered having seen in the newspaper office earlier that morning. There seemed to be considerable hilarity mixed with their talk. One after the other turned, glanced casually in Randolph's direction, then quickly back. Randolph, with his eyes fixed vacantly beyond them, gave no indication that he observed this.

Morrison spoke to one of the barmen, left his companions and started over. As he approached, Randolph met him with his disarming smile. He looked like an unsophisticated youngster, wondering what it was all about in unaccustomed surroundings and anxious to please any would-be friend.

Morrison had put a serious expression on his gloomy features. He shook his head slightly as he took a chair. His eyes, which he kept averted, were sly and bright under half closed lids.

"Trying to get some dope for you, kid. That's Scanlon of the office, that light-haired guy. He'll tell us plenty, if he ain't too plastered. Other two 're a couple o' guns. They know all about Burke's rackets. Didn't tell 'em you're goin' up for the paper. They got the idea you're out to get him and if we don't disabuse their minds they'll probably tell us something interesting."

He broke off, muttered, "Where th' hell?" turned and said, "Huh," satisfiedly as the barman appeared at his elbow bearing a tray with bottles and glasses.

The barman set a bottle of Seagram's on the table, placed a glass before each. Randolph, smiling, pushed his away.

"In trainin', eh?" the barman asked.

"I guess you don't drink much yourself, do you?"

"Can't in this business, 'd be finished in a month. Chaser, Mr. Morrison?"

"Not while you two 're trying to ruin my taste for liquor," Morrison growled. He uncorked the Seagram's. The bottle neck clinked several times against the glass rim as he poured a stiff measure which he swallowed neat. His thin lips curled a little as he replaced the glass on the table. His eyes grew brighter.

"Ginger ale, mister?"

"Nothing, thanks," Randolph told the barman.

"Want me to leave the bottle, Mr. Morrison?"

"Sure, Eddie; sure. Start Scanlon over here in 'bout five minutes, will you?"

The barman made swift estimate of the whiskey bottle's remaining quantity, said, "I'll send him," and turned away.

Morrison poured himself another drink, toyed with the glass with long, nervous fingers. His eyes were fixed moodily on the swirling liquor. Randolph watched him with open-faced candor.

"New to the news game, kid?"

"Yes. I've never been in it before. I have some things to do here in the East and thought I would like to see what it's like."

"Well, you better get out before you get in," Morrison said morosely. "Worst racket there is. Eventually 'll kill everything you got in you—ambition, brains, faith in humankind. Faith— hell!"

He finished half his glassful at a swallow, shivered a little. He sat silent a moment, holding his glass; then glanced sidewise at Randolph. When he spoke again his voice was slightly thick, as if his tongue was less nimble with the word sounds.

"Now 'bout this Burke. He's tough, kid. What I mean, tough. And slick. No one knew anything 'bout him till he won open an' shut case against th' D.A. Got a killer off. That was ten years ago. Then he had plenty clients. Crooks. Became damned smart criminal lawyer. Mostly big robbery cases; 'n' whether his men got off or went up, th' loot was damned hard to find. An' Ross Burke was in th' money.

"There was a lotta talk. Th' D.A. and Central office had men on him all th' time. Burke was too smart for 'em. Drew outa court work, called himself a consultant attorney. Hell. He quit loot splittin' and took up th' slickest blackmail racket this burg ever saw. Always claims he's just th' lawyer. They couldn't touch him. Can't put a finger on him today. Law can't, but I'm tellin' you he'll gyp jus' one too many fellers some day."

Morrison turned the rest of the drink into his mouth, took it at a swallow. He leaned forward and his manner became confidential.

"Burke's news. We all know it, but we can't get to him. He's got a big house in town, but his men 're all punks an' he ain't seein' anyone he don't want to see, an' he don't want to see newspapermen. Now you take his place up in th' country. Burke's rich, gettin' a little soft on women. He uses that Crossley Lake place for playin' an' for business an' he's got it plenty guarded for both. My gawd, feller, it makes me dry talkin'."

He reached for the bottle.

"I'm sorry to trouble you, Mr. Morrison. You're very kind."

Morrison poured another drink, shakily.

"Tha's aw right, kid." He frowned, repeated more carefully, "That's all right." He drank a little, hiccoughed, set his glass down. "You see ol' Scanlon over 't th' bar there? He knows somethin' 'bout Crossl' Lake."

"Shall I ask him to come over and sit with us?"

"Sit! Wow!" Morrison laughed unrestrainedly. "Tha's a good one. He can't sit. Won't for a week. He went up t' Crossl' Lake. Ol' Mac sent him; 'n' Slocum caught him with a coupla buck-shot goin' over th' garden wall. 'Over th' garden wall,'" he sang in lugubrious bass. "Y' know, kid? But don' sing it to ol' Scannie. He might lick you.... No; guess he wouldn't do that. You're too big."

"Who is Slocum, Mr. Morrison?"

"Slo—aheh—Slocum's Burke's watchdog. He's got lotsa dogs up there. But Sloc'm 's one th' killers Burke got off. 'f he kills you it'll be under th' law. Burke 'll make it under th' law."

Randolph laughed. "That assignment doesn't sound so hot."

"Tha's aw right, kid; aw right. We goin' fix you up so you won't get hurt—Scannie 'n' I. Forget jus' how we goin' fix you, but Scannie 'll tell me when he comes over. Now, wait a minute. Was tellin' you 'bout Burke—Ross Burke. Yeah. He's got 'nother business b'sides women 'n' blackmail, 'vestment bus'ness. Sssh! Nobody knows it. Got a partner runs it. Stan Fraser's nice, quiet feller. But he's Burke's partner. Burke had 'nother partner 'n law bus'ness. He—"

"What did you say his partner's name is?" Randolph's eyes had lost their lethargy and were suddenly alert.

"Huh? Fraser; Stan Fraser."

"What do they call their company?"

"Huh? Fraser 'nvestment Company, 'f course. Know 'em, kid?"

"I've heard of them. They send a lot of circulars out our way. They're up on Fifth Avenue, aren't they?"

"Fif' Avenue 'n' Forty—Forty-something Street. Only little way from here."

"And you say that's really Burke's company?"

"Y' got to keep it quiet, kid." Morrison made an effort to steady a severe look on Randolph. "'s a secret, 'm tellin' you. Ever'body says Burke's jus' lawyer for Fraser 'nvestment Company. But I know lotsa fellers lost their shirts with Stan Fraser 'n' Ross Burke got th' shirts. Get it? Sssh! Jack ov' there dropped some. Stan tried get it back for him 'n' Ross wouldn't let go. Know it for fact. But tha'sa secret, feller, b'tween newspap'rmen. You're newspap'rman now; you 'n' Scannie n' ol' Mac 'n' I. We're all newspap'rmen. We're damn' good fellers but jus' newspap'rmen."

Randolph consulted his watch, rose slowly to his feet.

"I'll have to start soon, Mr. Morrison. I'll run over and get—a car a friend of mine lets me have. It will take me about twenty minutes. Can you wait here, and tell me how to get there, what to do?"

"Sure 'll wait, kid. Mac tol' me to."

Randolph looked down at him with his wide smile. "Why don't you have lunch while I'm gone?"

"Br'kfas', kid; br'kfas'. Good idea. Order me some ham 'n'— hie—eggs, will you, kid? 'n' coffee. Lotsa coffee. Scannie 'n' I'll wait for you. We goin' take care you."

Randolph stopped at the serving counter to give Morrison's order. Observing a palatable looking cold roast he asked for a sandwich on rye and a glass of milk for himself. With his face turned slightly to his right, he saw the swing door open. Jack came through, weaving a little in his cat-like walk. His eyes were not lowered but his slightly bent head centered his glance on Randolph's chest. Randolph turned to the man behind the counter, with his amiable smile.

"No mustard. Thanks. And keep the pickle."

"Your first time here, isn't it?" a voice at his elbow said quietly.

Smiling, Randolph twisted around on his stool.

"Yes. Mr. Morrison brought me. You're Jack, aren't you?"

"Uh-huh." The white-haired man's glance ran quickly from the broad, compact shoulders to the flat stomach and narrow waist, back to the long arms and large, capable appearing hands. "Getting himself a bodyguard?"

Randolph laughed, as if embarrassed. "That's an idea."

Jack's glance flickered to his face for an instant.

"Done any fighting?"

"You couldn't call it that. A little college boxing."

"How'd you make out?"

"All right. But it didn't mean anything."

"You're wiser than most. These college fellers clean up in their circuit an' think they're good—till they turn pro and find out what it's all about."

"I hadn't thought of going in for that." Randolph munched his sandwich, drank his milk as he talked.

Jack shifted sidewise as if about to turn away, then swung back. "No?" He hesitated a moment. "I was talking with a coupla men in the bar. One's a fighters' manager. In the money—plenty. He thinks he saw you in a go in Reno, an' another in Frisco. K.O.'s, both in second round. He says you're good."

Randolph laughed. "I wish I was *that* good."

Jack's head came a little closer. "Who're you foolin', kid?"

"Not you," Randolph said, still smiling.

Jack turned to one side, frowned at the counter man who had edged close, waited until, with flushed face, he moved away.

"Lissen. If you change your mind, I can get you in a good stable with that manager. He's smart. And all the backing you need. He never yet picked a lug. Without tellin' you anything, he asked me to speak to you. Want to meet him?"

"I'll remember that, Jack, and thank you." He finished his milk; paid the check. "I can't just now. I've got a little business to do; and I'll have to see Morrison again."

"There's another thing," Jack said in lowered tone. He stood sidewise to Randolph and close beside him, letting his glance flicker over the room. "Those two newspaper fellers were talkin' too much at th'bar. They slipped the word that you're goin' out to call on Burke. They're havin' their fun, and you got a reason for lettin' 'em have it; an' they're too drunk to know it."

He waited until a couple of customers walked past, out through the swinging doors.

"You might say that ain't none o' my business. I got just enough interest to tell you whatever you do keep covered. An' if you get in a jam, try to head this way an' we'll see if we can do anything for you."

Randolph faced him, with his broad smile and a bright sparkle deep in his eyes. "That's white of you—and to a stranger too."

For the first time Jack's lips twisted into something like a faint grin. "You're no stranger, kid; not unless Tom—that guy in there—made a mistake. He said you had that same grin on your pan when you were knockin' 'em cold."

Randolph laughed with a lot of good-nature as he stood up from his stool. "Some day perhaps I'll meet the fellow who has given me such a good reputation."

Jack shrugged solid shoulders, clasped both hands in the fighter's salute as Randolph turned away.

3

RANDOLPH ENTERED A building on Fifth Avenue in the Forties. He consulted the wall directory, rode an elevator to the seventh floor and walked down the numbers to a door which bore the inscription: Fraser Investment Company.

He opened the door quietly, closed it softly behind him and heard a typewriter steadily clicking which his noiseless entrance had failed to interrupt. He stood in a small lobby partitioned off by opaque glass panels above dark stained wood. A small inquiry window with a shelf was at one side next to a closed door. Through the opening he saw a dark-haired girl bent over a machine not far from the window. Beyond her, in a corner, a beefy, red-haired, sour-faced man was reading a paper.

Randolph stepped to the closed door, swung it open and went inside. The girl looked around from her work, with her hands suspended above the keys. In the corner the newspaper was rustled violently, but Randolph did not glance in that direction. He looked at the girl with his artless smile. Her features were pretty, with good mouth and dark eyes that were hard. Her expression was cold and a little hostile.

"Is Mr. Fraser in?" he asked. "I'd like to see him."

She nodded her head toward the inquiry window. "Questions are usually asked through that." Her glance took in his height. "But perhaps you overlooked it."

His grin broadened. "I'm in now. It would be rather stupid to go back out and shout through the hole, wouldn't it? How about Mr. Fraser? Is he in?"

"No." She turned to her work. "He went out of town. Won't be back till next week."

"Is anyone in charge while he's away—or does the business just run itself?"

The red-haired man in the corner cleared his throat and shuffled his feet. The girl swung cold eyes back to Randolph.

"What do you want to see about?"

"Investment," Randolph said cheerfully.

She took up a telephone, slowly, spoke into the mouthpiece. "There is—a—gentleman asking about an investment.... Yes; I'll tell him." She replaced the instrument. "Mr. Webley will talk to you. He can spare you only five minutes." She indicated a door at the further side of the room, turned back to her typing.

Randolph opened the door on a youngish man seated at the end of a director's table. His black hair was slicked back over a high round head. He was carefully dressed, with a handkerchief showing in his breast pocket. His dark eyes were fixed on his visitor, and did not shift or change their disapproving expression as Randolph advanced.

Still with his innocuous smile, Randolph caught up a chair, set it close before the dark man and seated himself slowly.

"The name," he said, "is Randolph. This concern has fifty thousand dollars worth of securities in the name of Mrs. John A. Randolph. Together with it was a power of attorney in case an order to sell or to purchase other stock should be given. There was also a requirement that the stock should not be hypothecated meanwhile. What about it?"

Webley's eyes narrowed a little.

"Well—what about it?"

Randolph's smile did not fade, but his tanned cheeks grew slightly darker.

"We have written you three or four times since sending it, without reply, although we have the registered receipt."

Webley shrubbed his well-tailored shoulders.

"Really I can't tell you anything about it, Mr.—Randolph you said your name was?"

"You keep books, don't you?"

A slight sneer parted Webley's lips.

"What do you think?"

Randolph reached across the corner of the table. His hands caught the dark-haired Webley beneath his armpits, lifted him two feet in the air and slammed him back into the chair, hard. Webley gave a little squeal that was jarred into an explosive gasp as he landed. Color drained from his dark face.

Beyond the door there was the sound of heavy footfalls. The latch caught as the door came open heavily, shaking the partition. Randolph, turning in his chair, was facing the red-haired man who appeared and asked importantly, "You wish anything, Mr. Webley?"

Webley, with Randolph's back toward him, said, "Yes. Put him out. He—he grabbed me."

A pleased look took the place of the redhead's sour expression. "Now, now, young feller," he began as he came forward, "this ain't Oshkosh. You can act that way in the sticks but not in Noo York."

Randolph met the big man's approach with his meaningless, disarming smile. He started slowly to his feet as a beefy hand reached out to grasp his collar; then from his waist his left fist whipped upward, cracked solidly on the point of the round jaw. The red-haired man's eyes crossed. Completely out, he slumped face forward. Randolph caught him, lowered him easily to the rug, seated himself and faced Webley.

"I'll—I'll call the police," Webley gasped.

Randolph leaned one arm on the table.

"Go to it. And I'll have a bench warrant for arrest and search in thirty minutes after they get here."

"What do you want anyway?"

"Are you hard of hearing or just naturally dumb? I want to know where my stock is. Are you Fraser's assistant or office boy or what?"

"I am Mr. Fraser's chief clerk."

"Then you should know all about the business and where my stock is. Now that Fido is lying down, suppose you tell me."

Webley fidgeted. His eyes avoided Randolph's direct stare.

"Really, Mr. Randolph, I'd like to help you—"

"Mr. Webley," the girl spoke from the doorway, "why don't you make it plain to this man that if the stock he speaks of was right here in the office you couldn't give it to him without Mr. Fraser's approval?"

Randolph did not turn his head.

Webley looked relieved. "Yes, Miss Peel; that was what I started to tell him. Mr. Fraser is the only one who can release stock or pay out money."

"Quit kidding. You're not fooling me. Do you think a court order would have to wait on Fraser's approval?"

The girl came further into the room. Her right hand was hanging straight, behind a fold in her skirt. "Why do you want to do it that way? This is a perfectly respectable concern. We have regular business methods, with which you may not be familiar, but they are above question."

Randolph swung slowly around in his chair to face her.

"I am beginning to doubt that. And if this was regular, a chief clerk with an ounce of sense would tell a customer where his stock stands. If Fraser tries to play dumb like the rest of you he's liable to get his head bent before I call in the law."

The girl's eyes flashed. Her right hand came into view holding a small automatic. "We don't have to stand being threatened like that. If you can't act peacefully—"

Anger flamed suddenly in Randolph's eyes.

"Cut that out, sister," he rapped sharply, "or I'll wreck this place good and plenty. Get out of here and go back to your knitting." He turned back toward Webley.

"I'll wait until Fraser gets back but I won't wait any longer. If you see him before I do, Webley, you tell him to have that stock ready for me."

He stood up, oblivious of the girl who had retreated to the doorway and was standing there uncertainly, biting her lip. Resting a hand on the table corner, Randolph leaned over Webley who commenced to look very uncomfortable again.

"There's one thing you can tell me, Webley, without straining your business methods. Is Fraser the sole head of this outfit?"

"Why, yes; he's the president."

"Is everything that is done here on his sole responsibility?"

"I don't think I quite understand you."

"I'll make it plainer. I want to know whose hide to take it out of if there has been any monkeying with my stock. Perhaps you can understand this: What is Ross Burke's tie-up with the Fraser Investment Company?"

Webley glanced up quickly. His eyes were a little startled.

"Mr. Burke," he managed, "is Mr. Fraser's attorney."

"That's hooey. Does Burke own this outfit?"

"Pardon me, Mr. Webley," the girl said from the doorway, "I don't think we should answer these questions."

Randolph straightened slowly and turned around. "All right, sister; that gives me an idea of what I wanted to know." He stared at her thoughtfully for a moment; then shrugged and glanced down at the red-haired man who was beginning to show signs of returning consciousness. "You might sprinkle a little water on Fido's face, Webley. He'll wake up wiser." He raised his head and looked hard at the chief clerk. "There's an impression I want to leave with you, Webley, that you can pass along. You're not getting away with my money if I have to go to town with Burke, Fraser and the whole outfit. Tell Fraser to get wise."

He strode from the office, ignoring the girl who stepped back from his advance and glared at him with cold hatred, as he passed. He closed the outer door rather loudly, then holding the knob unlatched, reopened it a mere crack. He pressed his ear to the slot and waited.

He could hear indistinguishable voices, then the clock-clock of the girl's heels as she came into the main office. After a moment her words reached him clearly: "Long Distance... This is"—she gave the number—"I want Stanley Fraser at the home of Ross Burke, Crossley Lake, New York. Hurry it please."

Randolph eased the door shut and let the latch engage without sound. His eyes held a bright, satisfied look as he pushed the button for the elevator.

At the curb he caught a taxi and was driven to a parking place behind the newspaper office building. There he got into a Packard roadster, drove around the corner and drew up before Jack's. He glanced at his watch and observed that he had been absent from Morrison a trifle less than thirty minutes.

He went inside.

4

MORRISON WAS SEATED at the table where Randolph had left him. If he had had coffee it was cleared away with the other things that had borne what constituted the lanky newspaperman's breakfast. He was brooding over a half emptied brandy glass held between the fingers of both bony hands. He looked like a saturnine Quixote.

Randolph took the chair opposite him. "I got the car. Hope I didn't keep you waiting too long."

Morrison raised his head slowly. One eye was squinted almost shut; the other, lack-lustre, he fixed on Randolph with far-away, introspective look. "What matter?" he said bitterly. "I, who have prepared myself, have waited long for the opportunity of which when I was a mere kid like you I used to dream." His tone was slurred, but he spoke slowly as if careful of his choice of words.

"Dreams, ambition, aspirations—th' hell with them. They make only misery. Lissen, kid. I know the thoughts of men; I know philosophy. Spengler, Freud, Kant, Schopenhauer—I've read 'em all; studied 'em. I've thought beyond 'em, seeking th' truth that lies somewhere they couldn't reach. What has it got me? Nothing. Because in this cursed profession I've come to know men, human beings as they are, as rotten as they are. I can't think longer. Why? Because to think beyond our sphere you must have illusion. I've lost it. Can't regain it any more.

"Lissen, son. You're young, fresh. Get out of this business before it gets hold of you. In this work y'don't live your life; you live only th' lives other men 're livin'. You don't make anything of yourself. You jus' watch what other men 're makin' of themselves. Hell! Go back to th' office. Tell Mac you're through; don' want his assignment."

Randolph smiled. "I've started on this. I guess I'll go on through with it."

Morrison weaved a little in his chair as he regarded Randolph morosely. Then he lowered his glance, finished his brandy at a swallow. "Youth 'll never learn," he said, a little thickly. "Got to find it out for themselves 'n' pay th' price for it."

From the corner of his eye Randolph saw two men detach themselves from the group at the bar and start in his direction. The one in the lead carried a tall highball glass whose contents slopped a little in his uncertain walk. He was Scanlon of the newspaper office, a gangling, sandy-haired man with a large head that gave the curious impression of being loose on his neck.

The man who followed, with equal uncertainty, was shorter, a furtive dark-eyed fellow with sharp features.

Scanlon reached Morrison's chair, braced himself to a stop with a hand on the back. He leaned precariously forward, deposited his glass on the table, then straightened to a wobbling perpendicular and regarded Randolph owlishly. The short dark man, crouching a little as he advanced, placed a hand on an empty chair seat, slid into the seat. He looked at Morrison; then at Randolph and Scanlon. As each man spoke, he turned to look at him, soberly, with eyes that appeared to see only what was in their immediate focus.

Randolph stretched out a long arm, brought a fourth chair to the table and smiled up at Scanlon.

"Won't you sit down, Mr. Scanlon? Mr. Morrison said that you could give me some directions."

Scanlon waggled his big head mournfully.

"Can't si' down. Poor ol' Scannie 'll never si' down any more. Went up where you're goin', fella, 'n' nem'sis chased me. Was goin' faster 'n I could go an' caught up with me. It was *buck*-shot, 'n' I can't si' down. But's funny thing, Morrie. You lis'enin', Morrie? I can drink fas'er standin' up 'n sittin' down."

"Just how do you get there?" Randolph asked.

"Drivin'?"

"Yes."

"Go up Alb'ny Pos' Road. Ten miles b'yond Peekskill you turn off east." The sandy-haired man let go of his support to point eastward, but was obliged to relinquish his purpose and grab for the chair again. "Fifteen, twenty miles, railroad. Like Slinky's mind, here, single track, 'n' railroad station. Man there, bald-headed. That's Crossl' Lake station. Terr'ble coun-try. All—deserted. Five miles more 'n' there's where Ross Burke is an' Slocum an' *buck*-shot. Morrie, gimme my drink, 's good fella."

The dark man turned toward Randolph, leaned a little closer to him. "Lissen, big feller," he said in a hoarse, rasping voice. "You goin' up t' give Burke th' works, ain't you?"

Morrison, who had been watching with eyes that had grown brighter, and a tight grin, intervened. "Ssh, Slinky. Not s' loud. You don't have to spill it, do you?"

Slinky turned to Morrison.

"You guys ain't kiddin' me. Lookit this feller here; his size an' heft. I know what that ex-con Slocum did to Scanlon, an' I know you fellers got it in plenty for Ross. Mebbe you ain't plannin' he should bump him off, jus' give him a workin' over. What I mean, if he starts for Ross he's gotta shoot it out with Slocum an' no foolin'. I cased that place. Ne' mind what for. An' no one can get in. They got it wired an' a whole pack o' dogs, an' th' guy with a gun's Slocum."

He twisted around to face Randolph.

"Lissen, feller. I like your looks, an' I ain't got no love for Ross Burke an' not a damn' bit for that ex-con cowboy of his. Lissen. I got a gat here no one can trace. Numbers hammered off. Butt's checkered rubber an' won't hold prints. All you gotta do 's wipe off th' trigger an' keep your hands off th' barrel. You can have it, see?"

"That's damn' white of you, Slinky," Morrison growled. "Sure 't won't get you into trouble?"

"Nah. An' I'll take th' risk if he puts one of 'em out. He can heave th' gat in th' lake, an' they can't prove he done th' shootin'."

An annoyed look flashed across Randolph's face; then he was smiling again. "Thanks a lot, but I don't believe I'd better take it."

Slinky leered at him slyly. "Mebbe you got one 'f your own."

"No, I don't carry one. Against the law in New York State, without a permit, isn't it?"

"Sure it's 'gainst th' law. So 's shootin' a man. Better take it, or you'll come back worse off 'n Scanlon."

"Yeah, look at me an' weep," Scanlon crowed. He was weaving about his support like a Zeppelin at her mooring mast.

"Aw, th' kid thinks we're stringin' him," Slinky said disgustedly. "Then mebbe he thinks he can get by on his build. I al'ays says it don't buy you nothing to try 'n' help th' other feller. He gets you wrong an' you get hell. An' you fellers ain't kiddin' me neither. You're plannin' somethin' an' I don't want no part of it, see?"

Slinky slid out of his chair, took his disgruntled way between the tables and without a backward glance slunk through the doorway and was gone.

"Joke of it is," Morrison said, "we didn't tell him you were from th' paper. He thinks you're goin' after Burke." Morrison laughed immoderately; then sobered abruptly and put a serious look on his face. "But he wasn't foolin' any, kid. He knows what you're up against and he meant it 'bout th' gun." He winked at Scanlon. "But we goin' fix you 'nother way, eh, Scannie?"

Scanlon's head bobbed as if it was a marionette's on a string. "Sure, sure. Couldn't have *two* fellas standin' up 'round th' office. Ol' Mac wouldn't like it." He finished the last of his highball, lurched toward the table as far as his arm on the chair back would allow him and set the glass down. Morrison tossed off another brandy which a waiter had placed before him, and glanced at Randolph.

"You draw expense?"

"Yes."

A little clumsily, Morrison gathered up the slips that lay on the table. "Take 'em, will you, kid? That's what it's supposed to be for." He turned to the waiter. "Get th' count from Eddie."

The waiter produced another slip. "I have it here, Mr. Morrison."

"Then add 'em all up."

Randolph thrust a hand into his pocket, fiddled a single bill from his roll, which he brought out. He paid and stood up. He looked as if naively embarrassed.

Frowning seriously, Morrison led the way to the sidewalk.

Scanlon attempted jauntiness in following him. Both looked suspiciously at the sporty roadster to which Randolph guided them.

"How'm I goin' to ride, fellas?" Scanlon asked.

Randolph opened the rumble, shoved an over night bag to one side. "How about you getting in here, Mr. Morrison? Mr. Scanlon can kneel on the front seat, unless you want to hold him."

Morrison choked on a laugh, then glanced quickly at Randolph's guileless face. "I'll take th' rumble. Give me a hand, will you, kid? Didn't expect to do any climbin'."

Randolph stooped, placed an arm behind Morrison's knees and back, lifted him clear of the rumble and set him gently in the seat. A curious expression crept into the lanky newspaperman's foggy eyes. He waggled his head a little as he watched Scanlon being helped to a prayerful position facing him, then drew a hand hard down across his face, pinching mouth and chin. He made his brows frown and got a serious expression in his eye, but the sandy-haired man's broad face was wreathed in smiles. Randolph slid into the driver's seat and pressed the starter.

"Around the corner; up two blocks," Morrison directed.

As the car moved forward in gear, Scanlon collapsed against the seat back and slumped over it until his face was inches from Morrison's, in which position he said, "Bah!" suddenly.

"You got alcohol-hic-halitosis, Scannie," Morrison grumbled, and shoved him more upright.

Some people on the sidewalk laughed. Scanlon cocked an eye at them, waved an arm. "Hooray, folks!" he shouted. "We're off for a 'appy 'oliday!" then cursed luridly as the turn upset him into the corner with his back touching the door. Steering with one hand, Randolph helped him into more comfortable position.

Morrison called a halt before a haberdashery. Inside he singled out the proprietor.

"We want some cord'roy pants," he said very soberly. "The thickes' you've got."

The shopowner gaped in astonishment.

"But, mister, this is the summertime. It is a very hot day. You do not wear corduroy when it is hot. Mebbe you mean flannel. I have very fine flan—"

"I said cord'roy. I mean cord'roy."

"But three pairs of corduroy in the summer—"

"I didn't say anything 'bout three pairs." The lanky newspaperman indicated Randolph who was watching the proceedings with a peculiarly wry expression vying with the smile of awkward amiability which he was making effort to maintain. "One pair—for him. Thickes' you got."

Bewildered, the little round haberdasher fumbled out his tape, took Randolph's waist and leg measures, stepped back and eyed him doubtfully up and down. He shook his bald head.

"Don't do that," Morrison told him sharply. "It always makes me mad when a man shakes his head."

The bald-headed man put a finger to his pursed lips.

"You wait. Mebbe I got him in basement. Just a little moment." He trotted off.

"You think of everything," Randolph said. "But just why the corduroys? It's pretty hot, you know."

Morrison placed a hand on his arm. "Son, cord'roys best protection 'gainst dog bite I know." Frowning with great soberness he glanced at Scanlon who was facing the counter, leaning with both hands upon it and trying to follow events, with his head twisted over his shoulder. "Scannie, we gotta get something else. That takes care o' the dogs, but they won't stop what hit you."

Scanlon waggled his head loosely, looked front, then twisted around again. His face was very red but he spoke soberly. "Only thing's suit o' armor, Morrie."

Morrison snapped his fingers. "Got it. We'll fix him right."

The proprietor returned, a beaming smile on his round face, a pair of corduroys over one arm. He bustled up to Randolph, spread the pants wide and tried the waist measure.

"He do," he said triumphantly. "Mebbe not so long, but that doesn't make any matter. Four dollars, please."

Randolph thrust a hand into his pocket, reached for the trousers. Morrison intervened.

"Put 'em on now, kid. You'll need 'em when you get there, an' you won't have time to change."

The bald-headed man said, "You come with me," and led the way into a back room. Randolph followed meekly and pushed the door not quite shut. Morrison's voice floated in to him, in tones that were doubtless intended to be low: "It's a sure bet, Scannie, if there's shootin' up there, th' kid won't know a damn' thing about it, and I'll testify to that. My gawd, I didn't know there were any more left like him."

Randolph, grinning broadly, left the door, and quickly divested himself of his tweeds, disclosing long legs of unusual muscular development. The heavy corduroys fitted reasonably in the waist but left visible four inches of light stocking above his tan shoes. The shopman took one look at this discrepancy then bustled about Randolph, helping him run his belt through the loops.

Randolph sighed resignedly. He transferred money, watch, keys and handkerchief from the tweeds, paid the four dollars, then suddenly clamping his hands on the little proprietor's waist, lifted him high up and deposited him on a high shelf. Grabbing his trousers, he skipped to the doorway, stepped slowly through and closed the door on the squeals of protest that followed his departure.

The two newspapermen took one look at him then hastily glanced away.

"I guess I ought to hurry," Randolph said, frowning a little as he glanced at his watch. He started for the door. Morrison caught up with him and took his arm.

"Just one thing more, son; a coupla doors up here. We gotta tell Mac about it—that we made everything safe's poss'ble for you."

He led the way into a hardware store where, after some little difficulty in explaining, he obtained a rounded strip of light sheet iron a couple of feet long and a foot wide. This he and Scanlon insisted, with every protestation of seriousness, Randolph place around the small of his back, inside his shirt.

Back at the roadster, Randolph tucked his tweed trousers into his bag, closed the rumble and, a little stiffly, got into the driver's seat. About to press the starter, he turned toward the two men who were regarding him with most peculiar expressions not unmixed with awe.

"I am very grateful to you two fellows," he said steadily. "Now have you any idea how I can get into the place? What excuse would you suggest I give?"

Morrison choked a little before replying. "Son, I'd just walk right in and say nothing. You won't have to."

" 's all wrong," Scanlon protested. " 'f I was you, kid, I'd get a tel'photo an' climb a tree outside. But if you feel you gotta go in, don't forget to go in backwards."

Randolph smiled at them. "Thanks a lot." The starter whirred and the car slid into motion.

By twisting to one side, which he managed with a little difficulty, he had a parting glimpse of them in his rear-view mirror. Scanlon was seated on the curb, rocking to and fro. Morrison, beside his companion, was endeavoring to raise him to his feet.

Randolph grinned tightly to himself and stepped up the gas.

5

HE DROVE WITH easy familiarity with traffic and apparent knowledge of his route. The day was hot, the corduroys oppressive and the iron strip uncomfortable. He thought of stopping at the first convenient place to change; then decided that he could stand it until he should reach the little way station close to his destination. He was more concerned with the attempt to concoct some plausible plan by which he would gain entrance to Ross Burke's impregnable fortress.

Nothing reasonable occurred to him and he was forced to conclude that the matter must be left to wait upon chance. With the enviable confidence of youth in that fickle goddess, he drove serenely, blithely on.

Passing Peekskill he found the turn-off and twenty minutes later, on a road void of other vehicles, caught sight of a single track that swung in to parallel his course. In the distance was a low structure, obviously the station. As he drew close he read the sign, Crossley Lake, and then observed a feminine figure in light dress standing motionless beside the open door, steadily watching his approach.

As he came still nearer he saw that she was an attractive appearing young girl with dark hair beneath a tilted leghorn, and very dark eyes. Her figure was slender, notably well formed.

Randolph made this observation with sweeping, side-long glance while facing straight ahead. He slowed, turned into the station, braked before the door and looked up incuriously. The girl was regarding him with level eyes that while coldly impersonal were at the same time speculative. As their glances met, she frowned, then made a little grimace with mobile lips.

"Well," she said surprisingly, "you were long enough in getting here."

His eyes narrowed sharply. "Eh? Oh—sorry to be late; but I couldn't know you were waiting for me. Were you?"

"I'm not sure. Would you mind stepping out so I can see you better?"

Randolph hesitated a moment, suppressing a grin at this assurance. Then a little stiffly he got from his seat and walked around the roadster into fuller view.

Her eyes, looking him up and down, grew round. Suddenly laughter bubbled from lips in a face that was perfectly sober.

"Are you in disguise?"

Randolph grinned. "Yeah; something like that."

She raised a hand before her eyes. "Please go behind the car. I can't quite get you altogether. It is contradictory and a bit confusing."

He stepped to the further side of the roadster. She came to the car, placed a foot on the running-board. She continued to study him closely, obviously trying to make up her mind about him. It was all very strange to Randolph, but he met her scrutiny steadily, without expression. Altogether she appeared a young person quite assured and very much used to having her way. He waited, secretly amused, decidedly curious.

She flashed a glance down the empty road behind Randolph, then back to him. She drew her upper lip between her teeth, frowned again, then nodded slowly.

"I was just wondering," she said, "if you were the sort"—in

spite of her coolness, color rose slightly in her cheeks—"apt to jump to too hasty conclusions."

"Shall I tell you?" he asked tonelessly.

"No; I don't think it is necessary. It's a fad with me to judge people. I don't make many mistakes. Besides I've a faint idea that I've seen you before—at college games, or something. You're a college man, aren't you?"

He nodded.

"Well," she said slowly, "I suppose I can ask you. I'm really in a miserable fix."

He waited, saying nothing. Again her glance flicked down the road, to return to him. She drew a long breath.

"It's like this: I'm invited to a week-end at a place just beyond here. Mr. Ross Burke's. Do you know him?"

"Eh!" burst from Randolph in surprise. "Burke, did you say?" he added quickly. "No; I don't know him."

"That makes it better," she said firmly. "I'm to have a chaperon of course. She'll be along shortly. And a friend; her daughter. But—but I can't accomplish what I want to find out if I go alone—that is, without somebody with me. You understand that, of course?"

"Well, not altogether," Randolph said doubtfully.

"Hmm—but—oh, could I be invited to sit, and perhaps a cigarette?"

"Pardon."

He hastened to the nearer door but she anticipated him and was seated before he could reach over to open hers. He took an unbroken packet of cigarettes from the pocket beside the driver's seat and passed them to her. He found a paper of matches, struck one and held the light for her. She leaned toward him, momentarily resting a little finger on his bronzed hand. He was conscious of her dark eyes, half veiled under long lashes, as she drew flame into the tobacco. So close, she was distractingly pretty.

Randolph drew back and rested crossed arms on the door top. "Camels for composure, or something like that," he murmured. "I don't know what they really are. Keep them. I don't use them."

She looked at him a little doubtfully, glanced over her shoulder toward the open station door, then hunched around to face him more squarely.

"There's somebody inside—the station man. But I'm sure he's asleep in his chair by now. Well— Mr. Burke invited two of us; that is, the man to whom"—she glanced at her wrist-watch—"approximately thirty minutes ago I was engaged, and urged him to bring me along. So we started; engaged, friends and all that."

Her tone was light, purposefully so; and Randolph, aware of the effort, did not appear to watch her too closely. Yet when speaking, her mobile lips formed constantly changing, fascinating little curves which he observed without betraying his interest.

"On the way out," she continued, "he commenced to drop hints that Mr. Burke had asked him out for business reasons. I didn't catch it at first; only when finally he declared that he wasn't so keen about going on anyway. I asked what the business was, and he admitted that Mr. Burke, who is a lawyer, had told him that he wanted to talk over a claim a client had placed in his hands."

She paused to give a hard little laugh that held no impression of mirth, then drew on her almost forgotten cigarette.

"Naturally I pressed for details. When I cornered him he denied that there had ever been anything in his young life which would yield blackmail money. Mr. Burke, I believe, has something of a reputation of that sort. Girl-like, I suppose, the more strongly he denied, the more I suspected there might have been or still was.

"The upshot—when we reached this point, he had decided to go no further, and I had decided to go right along and discover the dark truth.

"We rowed over it a bit; and I am here and he—has gone back somewhere. Therefore, you. Now is everything clear, Mr.—?"

"Randolph. Richard is the first, with two in between that don't count. Dick for short."

Her brows puckered in reminiscent thought. "Dick Randolph," she murmured. "It seems to me—"

"No; it wouldn't be possible. So, I am to be 'he.' But doesn't this—er—Burke—"

"Mr. Burke has never seen him. He told me that. Their communication was by phone. The only people to be there I know of, who are slightly acquainted with him, are Mrs. Rodney St. Clair, our chaperon, and Barbara. You'll like Barbs. Do—do you think you can do it?"

"I think," he said slowly, "I can."

For the first time the semblance of a smile strayed across her lips and briefly lightened her eyes. "It's going to be fun and exciting. If we—you—are discovered they can only throw us out. They can't murder us. And I just have to know the truth. You see that?"

"Surely. Just two questions. Do you know a lanky, scrawny sort of fellow named Morrison?"

"No."

"Or a tall, big-headed, sandy-haired guy called Scanlon?"

"No-o," wonderingly.

"Then we're all set." He straightened, turning away from the door.

"What are you going to do?"

"Take off my disguise."

He stepped to the rumble, took out his bag. About to go toward the station, he turned and removed the ignition key from the dash, bent over and looked into her face.

"It isn't that I don't trust you," he said, "but I'm still convinced this is a dream. And I'm not going to wake up and find it so."

"I think," she said coolly, "someone must have been very unkind to you in your extreme youth."

"If they were it doesn't hurt any more." Half-way to the door he paused. "Say, didn't you have a bag or something?"

"Now that's a thoughtful young man," she said with the air of aged eighteen. "It's right inside the door." The curve of her mouth line changed, dipped a little in the corners. "He—he threw it out of the car after me. I— I had to pick it up out of the dust."

"Uh-huh. Well, I think 'was' engaged is correct."

"That's what we are going to find out," followed him into the station.

Randolph found a gray-haired, stout little man half asleep in a chair behind some grille work. A newspaper lay outspread before him on a ledge which held also a telegraphic instrument, blank forms and a partly filled spike file. He didn't even glance up as Randolph crossed the floor.

Randolph stepped into a small washroom, sighed with relief

as he removed the iron strip from his hot back. He quickly made his change of trousers and was out again in a few minutes.

Just inside the waiting-room door was an airplane night case and on top of that a soft purse. He took up the latter and frowned as his fingers felt the unmistakable outlines of a small automatic. He thrust the purse into a pocket, caught up the night case with his free hand and stepped outside. He looked very masculine and efficient in his well setting tweeds. His face was pleasant, although unsmiling. His gray-blue eyes concealed a certain wariness in a thoughtful expression.

The girl was facing him as he appeared and for the briefest moment her cool eyes lighted a little. Then she caught sight of the metal strip which he carried under the arm whose hand held his suit case.

"What," she demanded, "is that?"

"Well, you see," he said, stowing the things into the rumble, "that's a sort of—oven. I thought of camping out, you know."

He closed the rumble; suddenly snapped his fingers.

"I almost forgot." He stepped to her side of the car, took his stand six feet from it and pulled the candid camera from his pocket. "Would you be so kind? I mean—a little more in the clear?"

"Fiancé takes picture of his beloved," she murmured.

She opened the door and, still seated, swung her feet to the running-board. He held up a hand.

"Now, that's just fine... Light's right... Everything's right..." Between remarks he hastily snapped six pictures. "Thanks a lot. I'll just change this roll."

He strode into the station and hurriedly slipped the exposed film into one of the prepared containers. Sealing it, he tossed it onto the paper before the station agent. The stout little man jerked his head, as if suddenly awakened, and looked up over his shoulder. His eyes, which did not appear sleepy at all, were round and inquisitive. Randolph gave him a bill.

"Put that in the mail for me. And if any messages come for"—a momentary hesitation—"a guy named Randolph, hold 'em. I'll come back and get them for him."

"Hm. That th' feller was here a little while back?"

"Yeah. He was out there a short time ago."

"Must be that gal's brother. They fit like all git out."

"Uh-huh. Well, I'll be seeing you."

He hurried back to the car, slid into the seat beside the girl. Reaching for his keys, his fingers encountered the purse. He drew it from his pocket and handed it to her.

"This was on top of the case. Forgot I had it."

Her fingers pressed it as she received it from him. Her eyes narrowed slightly, searching his apparently for any significant expression; but he turned away to push the key into the ignition slot. She tucked the purse, with the little automatic, between her thigh and the side cushion.

Randolph pressed the starter and the car moved ahead. He kept the speed down to a sober twenty-five.

6

"DOESN'T IT EVER smile?" she asked when the little way station was a quarter mile behind them.

He turned his head and gave her a long, slow look. She puckered lips and brows at his scrutiny.

"Inwardly," he said, "it is riotous. On the surface it is meditating its new responsibilities. Say—you've forgotten to tell me who I am, and a lot of things."

"We were coming to that," she said brightly, "in all good time. We hesitated because we thought you might be regretting your hasty engagement."

His right hand left the wheel, and reached slowly toward her shoulder. She faced him coldly, frowned with a little shake of her head. His hand resumed its hold on the wheel.

"Yes," she said, "I understand perfectly. You're overjoyed, and I won't doubt you again." She spoke coolly although there was slightly more warmth in her cheeks. She looked snugly comfortable in her corner, with her slender, graceful legs stretched before her, an arm on the door top, showing rounded and firm under russet tan where the wind blew back her sleeve.

"So, back to business. You're the scion of a registered family, a bit snobbish, as it should be, bulwarked by wealth through several generations. We won't discuss you personally just now, for we expect to learn more about you through the kind offices of Mr. Ross Burke. We'll simply say that you are a very enviable person, and a proper catch."

"Of course," she said, with a little twist of her lips, "it's out of date to consider morals and flee from scandal; but this match was made not in heaven but in Newport, Rhode Island. And it just happens I'm a gal with oldfashioned ideas.

"But that's you anyway. And you move in a circle that is quite beyond Mr. Burke's powers even to approach. His only possible point of contact is where you may have strayed. With this exception you don't know anyone he knows; and you've been abroad so consistently the past few years that I hardly know you myself."

"Good Lord!" Randolph murmured. "With all that, no wonder I don't need a name."

She flashed him a quick glance that was a little puzzled.

"I thought I would break it to you easily," she said with exaggerated meekness. "Ready for it?"

"Ready."

"Want all of it at once?"

"One dose. Can take it better that way."

"John de Puyster Rittenhouse."

Randolph shook his head.

"Do I have to remember all that?"

She laughed. "You might remember it's Rittenhouse. R—i— well, Rittenhouse. I'll call you Jack, of course."

"And I'll call you—dear, darling—or—?"

She swung more to face him.

"Mm, *mm!* What a blow to my pride." Her brows puckered quizzically. "Don't you ever see the rotogravures?"

"Always turn to the sports pages."

"Don't you really know who I am?"

He turned from his regard of the road ahead to look at her. His face was sober, but there was laughter in his eyes.

"What but not who."

"I'll have to make one more try. Do you come from very far away?"

"I come from Park Avenue and Newport. My name is Ritten—"

"Stop it! Now it's secretive, and of course it has a right to be. Well, it's Beryl Rogers."

He glanced at her again. "I like that."

"You're teasing me."

"Nuh-uh. I'm scared pink."

"Of what? Mr. Burke?"

"Not exactly. I'm afraid I'll let you down. Here I'm in the social register, and I give you my word I don't know ten names in the book. I'm a swell and haven't the faintest idea how a swell acts."

Beryl laughed. "Just be yourself, and I'll take a chance."

"As Dick or—Jack?"

In her corner of the seat, she turned her head slowly, tilted it sidewise to regard him. Their glances met. The speedometer needle dropped steadily.

"Well, under the circumstances, with unknown peril before us, I think I shall say—"

From close behind them a horn honked loudly, once—twice.

Beryl turned all the way around, quickly. Then rose with one knee on the seat and waved her arm.

"Heigh-o!" she cried. "It's Barbs and her mother." She twisted lithely to glance ahead. "We're half-way there. I must explain you to them before we go in."

She turned toward the following car and gestured with both hands. "They're stopping. There's a man with them. Can't you have engine trouble or something? I'll send him up to help you. We're far enough ahead now."

"Sure, I'll take a look at the motor."

Randolph stopped the Packard. Beryl reached to open her door and he placed a hand on her arm. She glanced around at him.

"Which was it?" he asked.

She turned and unlatched the door. "Dick," she said, and hopped out.

Randolph did not move. Frowning vaguely, he watched, in the rear-view mirror, as Beryl approached a sedan which was a hundred or more feet behind. He saw a man step from the driver's door and stand waiting. Beryl came up to the other side, and one of the two ladies in the rear opened that door to greet her. Randolph saw the man introduced and after a moment start walking toward him. He then stepped leisurely out, and opened up the hood. The motor was still running and bending over he pressed the gas intake rod, turning his head sidewise as if listening. When the man was within twenty feet of him, he straightened, put down the hood and stepping back turned off the ignition.

The man who came up and stopped beside the running-board, as Randolph straightened and turned, was the *thé dasant* type; carefully dressed, a little elegant without particular class. His dark double-breasted tropical coat, looped at the narrow waist, gave his shoulders an appearance of greater breadth than they owned. His legs, encased in white flannels, were long and slender.

Black hair brushed smoothly back from a rather low, narrow forehead, topped a long face which a deep tan made unusually dark. A miniature mustache, like short black-penciled lines, accentuated a suggestion of hardness in the thin-lipped mouth.

He drew a gold cigarette case from his breast pocket, snapped it open and offered it to Randolph. A smile that lacked sincerity partially masked the curiosity in his quick-moving black eyes as he took in Randolph's appearance.

"A little engine trouble?"

"No, thanks. Carburetor choke. Seems all right now."

"I'm Gerald Wheatley. You're John Rittenhouse, I understand." Holding a lighter to his cigarette, he gave a slight nod over his shoulder. "Just met Miss Rogers. Believe you know the St. Clairs." Through the smoke he exhaled his eyes continued to study Randolph.

"Casually. I didn't know until a few moments ago they were coming out."

Wheatley glanced back down the road. He shrugged a little. "The girls seem to want to talk a bit. Beastly hot." Drawing a handkerchief from his pocket, he spread it on the running-board, carefully drawing up his creased trousers as he seated himself. His eyes shifted up to Randolph who was leaning back against the car, elbows on the door top, a heel hooked on the running-board. His expression was coolly indifferent.

"Fancy it's rather out of your line, isn't it," Wheatley said, "to put in a week-end with a chap like Burke?"

Randolph frowned. "It's not exactly pleasure," he said slowly. "More an opportunity to discuss a matter of business."

Wheatley laughed dryly. "Then we all have something in common. D'you know him well?"

Randolph turned his head to look down at the dark-haired man. "Never met him. Do you?"

"I know too much about him, and what I know I do not like. He's slick, smooth, unscrupulous as hell, with all the nerve in the world." He nodded his head sidewise toward the sedan. "Mrs. St. Clair had to come out on—er—business, as you call it. Barbara had to come along with her, and I'm here partly to look out for them and partly on my own. And I don't like either job too well. Say, if the going gets rough, why can't we hang together?"

Randolph, with his eyes on the countryside, smiled slightly. "I don't see why there should be any trouble. I understand he has quite a place here. I'm planning to have some fun out of it."

Wheatley's laugh grated. "You'll have fun, if that's what you're looking for. Ross Burke's parties are hot. Look, Mr. Rittenhouse; I'm in one hell of a lather. I guess you can take care of yourself and probably know what you are doing. I don't want to nose into your affairs, but your sort doesn't come out on an invitation from a man like Burke unless there's some damned good reason for it.

"That's your business and I don't want to butt in. But I know Burke. We're practically in his hands out here, and I've a hunch what he'll be up to, as far as our crowd is concerned. He'll make a play for Barbara, and I'm in a spot where I can't say much about it. See? If he goes too far I wouldn't say I won't stop him—someway; but that's what I don't want to have to do. Barbara and Miss Rogers 're pretty good friends. If it comes to a jam I'd like to stick close to you."

Randolph shrugged. "I don't believe you will have anything to worry about, Wheatley. Let's see how it stacks up."

The dark-haired man lit a second cigarette from the butt of the first. His eyes were fixed on Randolph's profile with a curiously intent scrutiny. "That's because you don't know Burke. All right; wait till you see him."

Randolph turned with apparent impatience.

"You know, you are the fourth person who has told me this man Burke is poison; that he gets a bunch inside his barbed wire, with an ex-convict bodyguard armed to the teeth, and buffaloes them. Another man says he is a very prominent lawyer, wealthy and a lavish entertainer. Either way it doesn't matter to me."

Wheatley flicked the ash from his cigarette with an angry gesture. "Yeah, that's all right for you, Mr. Rittenhouse. You stand for something, and beyond a certain point you don't have to take it." His tone lost its peevishness, became almost wheedling. "With me it's different. He can make it very disagreeable. If he wants to put the screws on he can make it worse. There's nothing to stop him—unless you said something to him."

He glanced up hopefully, but Randolph was looking off at the countryside with level gaze and said nothing.

"Say," Wheatley asked suddenly. "You haven't got a gun, have you, that you'd let me take?"

Randolph shook his head, smilingly. "I don't carry one. I shouldn't think of bringing one to a week-end party anyway."

"Damn it!" Wheatley growled morosely. "I wish to hell I hadn't come. I suppose I've got to go on with it now."

Randolph laughed. "You take it too seriously. We ought to have some fun out of it. There's the lake. We can get some swimming."

"Hell, I don't swim. I only dance, and now I'll have to dance to Ross Burke's tune."

"Oh—o—Jack!" floated up to them from the other car.

Randolph glanced at Wheatley, then turned with guilty abruptness. Beryl signaled to him, and he waved his arm.

"Guess they want us to come down there," he said.

"You go. It's too infernally hot to move, and they can pick me up here. Why don't they drive up anyway?"

Randolph strode off without answering.

The three ladies were standing beside the sedan as Randolph came to them.

Beryl said, "Mrs. St. Clair, I believe you have met my fiancé, Mr. Rittenhouse," and Randolph took the hand that was extended to him.

"Of course," Mrs. St. Clair said dryly, "and I must say you have greatly improved since I last saw you. But why do we have to pretend among ourselves?"

She was a faultlessly groomed woman, whose forty-five years were made to appear thirty; of a little more than average height and reasonably slender. At the moment her cheeks were flushed to a higher color than her makeup demanded; her look and manner were fretfully nervous.

"And Barbs—Miss St. Clair," Beryl said.

Randolph turned to a tall blond girl with hair like corn silk in August, very bright blue eyes and teeth that gleamed white and even in the slow, provocative smile she gave him. Her figure was straight, almost boyish in its suggestion of firm litheness. She held his hand in a strong clasp a little longer than seemed necessary.

"Beryl," she said, in a low, throaty drawl, "has all the luck. Why didn't I draw something like you in place of—well, my dear Gerald? How did you ever manage it, my dear?"

"Barbs," Beryl said tonelessly, "I will allow you to flirt with him discreetly, but remember, please, for the moment at least he is my betrothed."

"Flirt?" Barbara said, and in her tone was a hint of recklessness. "I warn you now I'm going to steal him."

A little hope grew in Mrs. St. Clair's worried eyes as she scanned Randolph's rangy build.

"So you are really going with us to beard the dreadful Mr. Burke in his den, Mr.—"

"Better call it Rittenhouse. I understand that complications might be dangerous."

"He is nice, Beryl," Barbara said.

Randolph turned to her with a little laugh. "Your friend, Mr. Wheatley, seems quite depressed. I should think on the contrary he'd be very happy."

"Poor Gerry is scared pink. In the ballroom I assure you he is a very gallant figure of a man, but among the rough, tough boys he dwindles. Besides he is probably suffering from an attack of what he thinks is conscience but which in reality is just plain funk. No, I'm afraid Gerry is not a brave defender. Now you—"

"You see, Di—Jack," Beryl said. "Just as I told you."

Barbara tilted her head sidewise as she gave Randolph a long, slow look. "I don't believe, my dear, you told him half enough." Her perfect teeth flashed in a smile; but behind the glint in her half-closed eyes there seemed a little hardness.

"Do be sensible, Barbs," Mrs. St. Clair said a little sharply. "Beryl, I do not know whether I should say anything, but I feel a great deal of confidence in this young man."

"It's unanimous," Barbara murmured.

"Well," Beryl said, "I took him on trust. Or rather, he has changed all his plans for the week-end to help me out. He isn't asking anything of us. It's the other way about." Her tone was just a shade nettled.

"Don't think of it that way," Randolph said. "I am beginning to feel I wouldn't miss this for a lot."

Beryl gave a heavy mock sigh. "There goes my romance. Well, I told you what Barbs would do to you."

Randolph looked at her steadily until she suddenly smiled.

"Mm-mm," Barbara murmured. "I'm afraid, my dear, you've started me with a longer handicap than I knew."

"Do let us be serious," Mrs. St. Clair said tartly. "God knows I, at least, have enough to worry about. You know it," she said turning to her daughter, "and I don't see why you can't be more considerate." She turned back to Randolph. She tried to make her air a little aloof and condescending but it wouldn't quite come off. Fear was too evident in her eyes and in the nervousness of her movements.

"I really think I should like to tell you something, Mr.—"

"Rittenhouse."

Barbara laughed outright. "Better concentrate on Jack, Moms. That's what I'm doing."

Petulant anger blazed in Mrs. St. Clair's very light blue eyes as she glared at her daughter. Her carmined lips parted; then she controlled herself.

"Of course. And we mustn't forget. You see—Mr. Rittenhouse, some years ago I was the innocent victim of a very unfortunate situation. Unfortunate in the way that if a wrong construction was put upon it"—she bit her lip—"it would cause me very much embarrassment. Mr. Burke advised me—"

"Just a moment, Mrs. St. Clair," Randolph interposed. "It isn't that I don't want to help if I can, but you should remember that even Miss Rogers doesn't know me from Adam's pet dog."

"Marvelous!" Barbara said in low tone. "He is also discreet."

Mrs. St. Clair flashed around upon her. "I could expect more sympathy in my trouble from a servant. I don't know why I ever brought you with me."

"But you must, Moms dear," Barbara said with icy sweetness, "for I haven't the faintest idea."

The older woman flushed deeply. "Well, you know very well that Mr. Burke was urgent that I should bring you with me."

"Yes," Barbara drawled, "I know that, but I still don't see why you did it."

Mrs. St. Clair's glance shifted from the blond girl's steady look. She turned to Randolph but for a moment avoided meeting his eyes.

"Of course I wasn't going to trouble you with details; only the general situation. May I tell you that?"

Randolph took swift note of Beryl's expression, then of Barbara's. "By all means."

"Then—he advised me that a client of his had come to him with knowledge of the—er—circumstance, and with the wrong interpretation. He—Mr. Burke—said that he had restrained his client who was on the point of going to my husband with it, and he suggested that I come out to his place here to talk the matter over."

She paused, pressed a handkerchief to her lips. Her eyes were a little wild and hunted.

"How did you think I could help?" Randolph asked. He turned a little, glancing at Wheatley's disconsolate figure sitting bent over on the running-board of the roadster, then back to Mrs. St. Clair.

"I-I don't quite know," she faltered. "You look so big and

strong. I thought if you could stand by me. A man can always browbeat a woman alone, and I've heard that Mr. Burke is very hard."

"If you can ignore it," he began.

"No-no. That is out of the question."

"Then you expect it is a question of settlement of some payment?"

"I—suppose so."

Her glance strayed, as if unconsciously, to her daughter, and Randolph following it saw the blond girl's lip curl slightly, her eyes, on her mother, grow hard and scornful.

"Did you want to tell him anything more?" Beryl asked quietly enough, although her tone had the effect of loudness in the sudden tension.

"N-no. Not now, I think."

"Then," Beryl said, "I believe we'd better be moving on."

7

BARBARA SAID TO Beryl and Randolph, "Let's walk to your car;" and to her mother, "I'll send Gerald back."

Half-way between the cars, out of earshot of both, she said: "It's only about two miles more. Let me ride with you two. Mother and Gerald give me the creeps."

Beryl in the middle, with her arm through Barbara's, glanced up at Randolph. "Isn't she the artful hussy? Something tells me I'm going to have trouble to hold my man."

Randolph, frowning soberly, looked over at both. Barbara tilted her head to glance past Beryl. Her teeth flashed in a wide smile; her eyes, half veiled, were mocking. Beryl glanced at her, murmured "Hm," then looked around at Randolph. Her lips, parted slightly, were unsmiling; her eyes were cool, but in their dark depths little lights were shining. Walking together the girls were of almost equal height; one with slightly more feminine lines that were all curves; the other of boyish slenderness from breast to ankles. He shook his head over them.

"I sure would hate to be caught offside between two such devastating forces. For the moment I feel safe. You see I've always been told that an engagement shouldn't be broken lightly."

"Ah!" Beryl breathed. "You don't know how that relieves me."

"Damn!" Barbara exploded. "If I didn't have more on my mind than you two, what fun we could have in this beastly place we're coming to with its bold bad wolf." Recklessness grew in her eyes. "And I think I'm going to anyway. So, Jack lad, look out. If they get me mad I'm hotcha and no holds barred." Her mood changed as quickly.

"Glimpse that magnificent specimen draped on your running-board," she said in low tone. "A wilted reed. And that's what stands between me and God knows what."

Beryl pressed her arm. "You forget we have Jack, my dear. I might spare a little of his attention now and then, to keep an eye on you."

"I'm strong for Jack," Barbara murmured, with her eyes on Wheatley whom they were closely approaching, "but, hell's bells, he can't mother our whole brood… Gerald," she called sweetly. "Be a dear and bring Moms along. I think she wants to talk with you. We'll drive slowly."

Wheatley got to his feet with a show of weariness. He carefully shook out the handkerchief on which he had been sitting, folded it exactly and stuffed it into a pocket. His eyes, sombre under dark brows, avoided Randolph.

"All right," he said, morosely, and started off.

The girls stepped in. Barbara said, "I mustn't come between you two quite so soon," and took the outside. The seat was not overly wide and when Randolph took his place to send the car ahead Beryl was obliged to move her knees for the shifting gears. Struck by a sudden thought she reached over Barbara and rescued her purse from the seat corner.

As her hand grasped it, she started slightly then looked slowly around to face Randolph. Her eyes, boring steadily into his, were filled with cold disdain. With an expressive little twist of her mobile lips, she turned away, letting the purse drop with careless disregard. It slipped from her knee and fell limply to the floorboards. With no change of expression, Randolph glanced down at it, stooped, picked it up, and thrust it into his pocket. There was no hard object in it now. The little pistol had disappeared.

He glanced in the rear-view mirror, saw that the sedan was coming close, then shifted the gear to neutral and braked the car to a stop in the middle of the narrow road. Opening his door he stepped out and strode into the path of the approaching sedan.

"Quitting us, Jack?" Barbara called.

He waved a hand without looking around. Wheatley stopped the car and Randolph stepped up beside him.

"Anything wrong?" Mrs. St. Clair asked nervously.

Randolph smiled, with his glance on Wheatley's shifting eyes. "Nothing at all," he said. "Mr. Wheatley neglected to return my cigarette case." He held his hand over the door top, palm up.

"What do you mean—cigarette case?" Wheatley blustered. "Why—you don't smoke. I haven't got it."

Randolph continued to smile. "Come on," he said, just above the hum of the motor, "or I'll drag you out of there and take it away from you. It won't make a pretty sight."

Wheatley's eyes blazed. He reached for the gear shift. Randolph caught his left wrist-joint between thumb and two fingers and pressed hard. Pulling Wheatley toward him, he reached out with his free hand and felt in the inside breast pocket. His fingers encountered what he sought. Concealing the little automatic in his broad palm, he stepped back, still smiling.

"Damn you!" Wheatley breathed. "I'll hand you something for that!"

The big car jerked as he shoved it ahead with grinding gears, careening on the shoulder of the road when he circled the roadster. Mrs. St. Clair gave a frightened cry. Her white face twisted back at them, but the sedan didn't pause.

Turned sidewise, Randolph worked the pistol back into the purse and strode back to the roadster. Barbara looked at him in wide-eyed curiosity as he slipped into his seat and started the Packard again. Beryl apparently was watching the sedan.

With the gear in high, Randolph took the purse from his pocket and put it into Beryl's hand. She took it, her fingers encountering his. Then he felt her shove it down between them. Her head turned toward him, slightly raised. Her eyes were very bright. Her lips formed, "Forgive me."

Barbara shot a quick glance ahead, then hitched around to face them more squarely. Her eyes were excited.

"Listen. I've only time to say a word. Something tells me that we're meeting up with Old Man Trouble. I thought it was only my own hard luck, but I didn't like the look Gerry handed us as he steamed by. Gerry's a nice boy to take around; he wants to marry me and promised he would provide the protection he said I'd need on this queer business up here. But he's up against it a little on his own. I know something about it and it's not so good. If he wants to take a runout to save himself he can make it damned unpleasant for the rest of us. I can't explain; but take my word for it. Heigh-o; it's in a lifetime."

Randolph laughed quietly. "Everything looks peaceful around here; but most people seem to think there's a guy up yonder who's going to bite us."

Barbara's eyes took on a peculiar glint. "Don't fool yourself, Jack boy; he can bite."

"Look, Barbs," Beryl said, "are you really worried about something—for yourself?"

"And plenty."

"Like to tell us?"

"You can't help, my dear." Barbara's tone was light; but it was also tight. "And I don't see why I should load it on Big Boy. Mother SOS'ed him and little Gerry was sure banking on the mighty name of Rittenhouse." She laughed dryly.

Randolph grinned across at her. "Shows what a goop I am. Here I was thinking you liked me."

She gave him a brief flashing smile. "Sure do." Then the smile was gone. She twisted around more squarely in her seat.

"Want to take a runout?" Beryl asked. "We don't *have* to go."

"Can't do. Have to stand by. She could never manage it alone. Besides—" She paused; bit her lip.

"Well?" Randolph asked.

Barbara gave an impatient shrug; then spoke with her eyes on the sedan ahead which had slowed its speed, apparently waiting.

"Mother was indiscreet, a few years ago. Letters. Evidently someone has turned up with them. Ross Burke's client. In my eye. She must have them—all of them. If they got to Dad— well, Reno, the well known smash of social prestige; matter of income which is *the* important thing."

"He'll want payment," Randolph said, repeating his comment made to Mrs. St. Clair.

"Of course. And *she* can't pay much; probably not enough."

The sedan had stopped now. Moving slowly, they were within fifty yards of it.

"So?" Randolph prompted.

The blond girl's eyes blazed suddenly. Her lip curled.

"To save a mother's honor?" She shrugged. "But I'll tell you, folks, I'd make damned tough lion's meat."

"She wouldn't!" Beryl flared.

"No? But I'm spoiling the party. Run me up alongside, Jack boy, and I'll join my crowd. It's been good to know you people."

Randolph laughed. "Here we're all getting jittery before we've even seen the big fellow."

"It isn't so much what he may be," Barbara said in lowered tone; they were almost upon the sedan. "It's what he can do that counts in this game. And if half what Gerald Wheatley tells me is correct, he can do plenty. Brr!… Hi, Gerry, I'm coming aboard. So—I'll be seeing you people later. Remember, Jack boy, if she throws you over, I'll be waitin' for you, honey."

Without bothering to open the door, she vaulted lightly over the side, skipped around the roadster and took the front seat of the sedan beside Wheatley. The latter had managed to force the frown from his face but it was still darkly glowering and the smile which he attempted was a sickly affair. He did not look at the occupants of the roadster and started the sedan off at once. Barbara thrust her head through the open door.

"Gerry says bad luck's just around the corner. Luck and cheerio."

They waved to her. Randolph was about to change gears when Beryl laid a hand on his arm.

"Let's give them a moment to get in. About the space of one of your cigarettes, if you'll be so kind. But I have them, of course."

Randolph turned off the ignition, struck a match and held it for her. Their eyes met through the smoke.

"So you like the blond gal?"

Randolph flipped out the match, folded both hands over the wheel. "Seems to me I must constantly remind you of the sanctity of my first choice."

"No. You've already reminded me twice. But is it only sanctity? Sometimes that makes a very frail bond."

"There's just one thing I don't understand in this whole affair."

"And what's that? If you must avoid my very direct and indiscreet question."

"It's a guy who calls himself Rittenhouse."

"Nicely done." Her fingers caught his arm, squeezed. "Lord, man, what a muscle! I almost think I should be afraid of you." She smiled up into his face. "Look; let's be serious. Really I'm beginning to get a little scared. This doesn't promise to be quite so—so mild as I supposed. They all seem to think such terrible things of this man Burke. Wheatley is scared pink. He was positively raving when you—took that back from him. And Mrs. St. Clair; and now what Barbs says. I thought I had nerve, but I'm telling you, I'm scared."

She leaned toward the side, looked around to him.

"It's strange too. Somehow it doesn't appear so vitally important that I should learn what I insisted on coming to find out. I wonder. I think, possibly, that meeting you had something to do with it. I didn't think you dared fall in with my plan. You surprised me so. Do you suppose that had anything to do with it?"

He regarded her soberly.

"Do you want to back out—not go on?" he asked.

"Why—what do you mean? How can we now?"

"Well, I'm beginning to get a little scared."

"You! Pouf!"

"Honest. I feel my courage ebbing away."

"Of all the absurdity. You—" She laughed, then said, with a dash of asperity, "Why couldn't you be John Rittenhouse really."

"Tell me," he said, "in your world does a fellow actually have to have a tag to be a man?"

"It helps," she said, "prodigiously. But tell me, you aren't worried, are you?"

"I could do with a bit of encouragement."

"Yes, I know. Well, there you are. But as I mentioned sometime previously on this very strange afternoon, I'm an oldfashioned gal. And now, if your courage has fully recovered—"

"It's considerably stronger," he said, and turned the ignition key.

Fifty yards further on they turned an abrupt corner around a clump of trees, and a gateway stood before them. Randolph brought the roadster to a stop with its nose a few inches away from the closed grille. The sedan was not in sight.

Heavy double gates were swung from massive granite posts. On one side was a narrower grille flanked by a smaller post of granite. On either side a ten-foot fence of thick wire with exceptionally small meshing ran until lost from sight. The gates themselves were of vertical steel rods set in a frame of flat steel bars.

Randolph peered through at a man several feet behind the gates, who was regarding them somberly. He was dressed in a blue suit that needed pressing, black unpolished shoes and a dark felt that shaded eyes that seemed black and were set too close together. His mouth was small, with tightly pressed thin lips. He was about five feet ten and appeared strongly built. A high powered rifle dangled carelessly under one arm. He looked as hard as the grille work behind which he stood motionless.

"Well?" he said. His tone was harsh.

"Miss Rogers and Mr. Rittenhouse," Randolph said pleasantly. A little of his apparently inane smile was on his lips. "I believe we are expected. Are you Mr. Burke?" Below the dash he felt Beryl clutch his arm.

The man set his rifle against the smaller post, stepped to the middle of the gates, unlocked them and swung them open.

"No," he said. "I'm only Slocum."

His glance ignored Beryl but bored into Randolph as they drove slowly in. Randolph stopped the roadster just beyond the gates and waited with an arm flung over the seat back and his head turned around. His fingers pressed Beryl's shoulder, once.

The gates swung closed with a dull clang. Slocum re-locked them, picked up his rifle and came alongside the car. His eyes flitted over Randolph's face but avoided Randolph's direct smiling look.

"You follow that road to the house," he said coldly. "Garage's back of it, but you're the last of 'em and you may not find room."

Randolph reached for the gear lever, then straightened.

"You the caretaker for Mr. Burke?"

"Yeah."

Randolph turned his head to look behind him.

"Might have to run back to that station tomorrow, for a stock report and to send a message. This the only way out?"

"Yeah. I'll let you out if he says so. Mostly they don't go out till they leave."

"Going up toward the house?"

"Uh-huh."

"Get in the rumble. We'll take you."

"I'll walk. Leave your key with my wife. I may have to move the cars."

Randolph sent the roadster ahead.

A turn in the winding road hid them from the man behind.

"Brr," Beryl shivered.

"Did you notice the wire leading to the fence and the rod above the gates?" Randolph asked.

"Lord, no! I didn't see anything but that man."

"Connections with the posts 're insulated. I don't believe they've got enough juice up here to do any hurt. Probably alarm system. This guy Burke is getting interesting."

Beryl's two hands clasped his arm. "If his man Friday's an indication I should say he could be too darned interesting. I feel as though I'd gone to jail. I don't know what I've let you in for, but I do know that I'm insisting on my engagement rights that you stick right close to me."

With an abrupt thought she released his arm, groped between them and recovered her purse.

A little further on they emerged from the trees. An end of a small lake stood before them, a clear body of water running away to their right, a half mile in its uniform width, perhaps three miles long. Close at hand its shore was rocky, rising to ledges of considerable height on the further side. At the nearer end a long boathouse was set half over the water. Seventy-five yards directly back of it, on slightly higher ground was a long two-storied, comfortable appearing structure with gabled roof and wide, screened porch.

While still a little distance away they saw Barbara and her mother talking with a man at the foot of the porch. He was dressed in a dark knickerbocker suit. A second man in flannels, stockily built, was standing a few steps above them. Wheatley was just coming around a corner of the house.

"Take me to the garage with you," Beryl said. "We'll meet this man Burke together."

8

BESIDES THE SEDAN there were three other cars in the wooden garage, taking all of its available space. Adjoining it, however, was a covered shed open at front and one side. Randolph ran the roadster under this protection, took out their two bags and relocked the rumble. As they turned toward the house two women appeared on the back porch and looked at them expectantly. One was very stout, gray-haired, aproned. The second was in her thirties, lean faced, with dark hair parted and drawn tightly back over her ears in a close bob. Her eyes were as full of knowledge and as enigmatic as the painted eyes of La Joconde, but they were cold and unsmiling. A white blouse showed rounded breasts on a slender, still pliant form; a rather short, dark skirt disclosed the silken clad legs of a dancer.

"Wait a moment," Randolph muttered, and strode the score of steps to the porch.

The stout woman said, "Mrs. Slocum and I'll take your bags up, mister. What's your name, and the young lady's?"

The younger woman had watched him approach with steady eyes and still regarded him with the same cool scrutiny.

"Miss Rogers—Mr. Rittenhouse," Randolph said. He swung the bags up over the half-dozen steps and set them lightly between the two women.

Mrs. Slocum gave him a faint, slow smile. "They might be heavy, but you wouldn't know it," she said. Her voice was low pitched and low in tone. "Will you let me have the key to your car?"

Randolph handed it over. "Why don't you just set those bags inside and I'll take 'em up when they show us our rooms."

The stout woman laughed heavily. "Sure, Dot," she said, "an' he takes us fer a coupla hothouse ladies."

"Thanks," Randolph said. The younger woman's eyes followed him as he turned away.

"My Gawd," Beryl complained, "I just get rid of the blond menace, temporarily, and here's a dark soubrette making eyes at you. I'll bet if Burke has any dogs they'll come right up and lick your hands, especially if they are she ones."

Randolph laughed outright.

"And now what was so funny?"

"You were speaking of dogs… I wonder if I understand our friend Slocum any better now. That is his wife. Still, I don't think so. That lad's carrying more than a jealous grouch around with him."

Beryl had slipped her hand through his arm. They were walking slowly along the side of the house.

"He looks to me," Beryl said, "exactly like a guard on a prison wall, ready to shoot the first convict that looks at him cross-eyed."

"I think he'd fit better inside looking out; and the gun fits that picture too."

They reached the corner. The little group at the foot of the porch steps appeared before them. Beryl tightened her clasp of his arm.

"That man in dark clothes," she murmured. "Suppose that's the famous Burke?"

"Not my idea of him," Randolph said in the same tone. "From the description you've all given me," he added. "This chap's profile looks more intelligent than shrewd, and that I should say is Burke's number."

"I'm getting scared again," Beryl whispered.

Randolph looked down at her. "I would be too—if we were still outside the gate."

Beryl gave his arm a little shake.

The dark clothed man turned toward them, then stepped forward. He was a well built, florid-faced man with the inscrutable blue eyes of some types of Englishmen, for English he undeniably was. His features were regular without any distinctive characteristic, with the possible exception of a lean hard jaw below a carefully trimmed blond mustache. He extended his hand to Beryl.

"I'm Fraser," he said. "Burke rather left me to do the honors. Out for a bit of a stroll. Lakeside I expect. You will be Miss Rogers? And Mr. Rittenhouse, I believe."

Randolph found the handshake without warmth.

"You are Mr. Burke's partner, I suppose?" he asked blandly.

Fraser gave him a quick, hard flash of a glance, then laughed easily. "Not so honored. A client rather… Er—I believe you know all these people but—ah, yes"—he turned to include the man in flannels who was watching them indifferently from the porch steps—"Mr. Robert Gordon, Miss Rogers—Mr. Rittenhouse."

Gordon nodded to both. "How do you do," he said coolly.

"And now how about a cocktail—all hands?" Fraser invited genially.

"I believe I should like one," Mrs. St. Clair said.

Fraser turned to Randolph. "And a spot of Scotch for you, no?" He started toward the steps.

"No, thanks," Randolph said, and his refusal seemed tacitly to include the girls. He was looking toward the lake and the boathouse whose shoreward door stood open. In the nearly level rays of the westering sun twin spots of light flashed momentarily in the doorway's dark rectangle.

"What say we have a look at the water?" he suggested.

"Let's," Barbara said eagerly.

Beryl turned with her and the three started off. Gerald Wheatley hesitated a moment, then followed Mrs. St. Clair and Fraser up the steps.

"Mind if I go look with you?" The tone was slightly sarcastic.

"Damn!" Barbara muttered.

Randolph turned. Gordon was coming down the steps.

"Come along," Randolph said.

Gordon was a youngish fellow, a half head shorter than Randolph but solidly built around shoulders and chest. His eyes were wide set and dark in a round muscled face. Neither dress nor appearance was significant of his station. He might have been a steel products' salesman or the right bower of a dealer in illicit liquor. His air was assured; his manner indifferent and coldly sarcastic.

Randolph walked between the two girls. Gordon strung along beside Beryl.

"You people hooked too?" Gordon asked. He glanced at Randolph.

"Not yet," Randolph said cheerfully.

"Huh. I've sized up these ladies. Ten gets you a hundred they're not here for fun."

Randolph laughed shortly. "I've an idea we're going to have quite a lot of fun. There must be things to do here."

"Play it dumb if you want to," Gordon said surlily. "It's not my business. At that, you'll probably have more fun out of it than the girls."

"I think we'll be well taken care of," Beryl said coolly.

"I guess you don't know this outfit very well," Gordon said. "Do you?" he asked Randolph.

"Never laid an eye on them before."

"Let's look in the boathouse," Barbara proposed. They were within a score of yards of it. "Perhaps there's a boat or something."

Randolph caught her arm; urged her a little off the path leading to it. "Let's look up the shore first," he said, in slightly lower tone. "I think there's a mouse in it now."

"You couldn't mean a rat, could you?" Gordon asked.

"Can't say till I see it."

Beryl glanced at Gordon, then back to Randolph. Her look was a little puzzled. Randolph took her arm and smiled down at her.

They strolled along the shore a short way, then stopped on a smooth ledge that ran at an abrupt angle into the water. Near the bank sunlight had left the surface. The water looked dark, coolly inviting. Further out a point of rock formed a small islet on which were sand, grass and one or two scrub trees. It seemed the only break in the smooth surface of the lake.

"Goes off steep," Randolph commented. "You'd have to take off on a run." He raised his glance, "About four hundred yards to that rock, Gordon?"

"All of that and a little more. Couple of loons out there. If they start hollering, it'll mean wind or a change."

"Where?" Barbara asked.

"To the left of that—"

His words were cut off by the sharp, whip-like crack of a high powered rifle. The birds disappeared, but immediately spray was kicked up seemingly at the very spot where they had gone down. Five more shots followed in rapid succession and from where they stood it looked as if a dozen feet would have covered the spray of the six shots. The reports rolled across the water, were thrown back in echoes from the high ledge that walled in the lake on its left shore.

"Slocum showing off," Gordon said disgustedly. "Wants us to know that he's good. This crowd makes me sore."

The marksman was standing on a rock near the shore line and about one hundred and fifty yards further along the lake. Behind him was a small cottage, evidently the caretaker's home.

"There goes your mouse," Gordon growled. "I knew damned well it was a rat."

Randolph and the two girls turned their heads.

A man was walking along the path leading from the boat-house to the main structure. His steps were short and rapid, and while he was not exactly slinking, with head silently bent he was moving as if not to attract attention and to get out of sight before doing so.

They could not make much of him, faced three-quarters away from them; an unimposing, rather plump figure of less than average height in baggy trousers and loose coat.

"Who is it?" Barbara drawled.

"Our esteemed host and the eminent attorney, Mr. Ross Burke," Gordon said. "And if ladies weren't present I'd add the proper embellishments."

"You don't seem particularly fond of him," Randolph said.

Gordon gave him a sour glance. "I don't know whether you're here just for scenery, are playing dumb or think I'm dumb. But there's no secret about my feelings for Ross Burke. I don't know anything I'd like more than to cut his heart to little pieces and feed them to the fishes. He's schemed for two years to get me in a jam. He's got me, and I've got to take it and like it—or else. Coming up here and being entertained for a week-end's a farce; but he's giving the orders and he likes to see 'em squirm."

"I expect you have plenty of reasons for your feelings, Mr. Gordon," Beryl said quietly.

"I have that, Miss Rogers." It was the first time that he had directly addressed either girl. "But I'm not goof enough to think I'm the only one who has troubles. Excuse me for letting go."

"Can't we go now and peek at the boathouse?" Barbara asked. "If there are no more mice inside."

"That's the only one you need worry about," Gordon said.

They found the single door at the end to be the sole entrance to the roomy boathouse except from the water side. Half the structure was set on the same ledge which appeared to form the bank for most of this end of the lake; the other half extended over the water. Smooth side walls followed close to the sloping rock and dipped under the water to the extreme outer end.

Crossing the stepped-up threshold they were on a broad platform which filled that end of the house for its full width. At either end of this, two other platforms ran along the walls to the outer end, and between these arms lay a twenty-six-foot motor boat, open except for a short decked over space forward.

"What are you looking for?" Beryl asked, watching Randolph, in the semi-obscurity, grope along the wall beside the door.

He came back into the better light of the open doorway holding a light leather binocular case with its strap, which he had taken from a hook on the wall. Opening it he removed the glasses and levelled them on the bottom steps of the house porch, of which he had an unobstructed view.

"About eight power," he commented. "Somebody's scuffed a splinter off that lower tread."

He returned them to the case, found the hook again and hung the strap over it.

"How did you know they were here?" Beryl asked as he stepped beside her.

"Probably caught a glint of the glasses," Gordon said. "Just like Burke to be looking you over and sizing you up. I told you he was a rat."

"Is that why you brought us here—to find out?" Beryl asked.

Randolph squeezed her arm.

"How's for a spin?" Barbara called from where she was standing beside the boat. The blond girl seemed to have lost some of her spirit and appeared restless and thoughtful.

"Let's," Beryl said quickly. "This place is giving me the creeps. Imagine that man watching us with high powered glasses, studying us, getting our expressions... Brr!"

"Might as well," Gordon said. "We'll pay for the gas anyway. Can you run the bus?" he asked Randolph.

"Let's have a look at her." Randolph stepped lightly over the side, knelt and examined the motor. He straightened and gave a hand to Beryl and then Barbara.

The boat was moored by two ropes forward and two aft, drawn taut enough to keep her from rubbing either platform. Randolph cast these off, then getting out on the opposite platform, with Gordon helping, pushed the boat stern foremost through the opening. They clambered aboard. Randolph started the motor whose stuttering roar reawakened the echoes.

He reversed with the rudder hard over; then shifted to speed ahead and straightened out toward the little islet a quarter of a mile away. They had covered half the distance, in practically a direct line from the boathouse, when suddenly something struck splinters from the base of one of the trees on the rock and simultaneously the sharp crack of Slocum's rifle sounded above the puttering of the motor.

Gordon swore luridly. Randolph glanced at the girls, then slowly turned his head. Slocum was plainly in sight on the shore, rifle levelled. As he watched, the caretaker shot again, but Randolph did not turn to see where the bullet struck. As yet they were not directly in the line of Slocum's fire on his target, although their present course would soon bring them into it.

"He's trying to run a shandy on us," Gordon said above the engine noise. "Damn him; let's call his bluff. That would be plain murder; not an accident, and, by God, I don't think he'd dare do it."

Randolph was seated in the stern, with his feet on the seat and the steering rope under one hand. He looked at Beryl. Her face was a little pale but her eyes were very bright. Barbara was watching him with reckless devils in her blue eyes.

He stood up, stepped ahead to the motor. "Get back in the stern," he told the girls, "and keep down low."

As they moved to obey, Slocum fired a third time.

Randolph shut off the motor, but with the headway she had the boat continued to forge ahead. Randolph swung the little wheel over, turning the boat sharply toward where Slocum was standing. A fourth bullet screamed close over their heads, the sound of its whistling passage lost immediately in the rifle's crack.

Randolph stooped, started the motor again and drove straight toward the shore. Slocum watched their coming, the rifle held carelessly in his hands. Within twenty yards, Randolph shifted the gear to neutral; then as they lost headway, shoved it into reverse and the boat came to a shuddering stop. Randolph threw the switch and straightened up, eying Slocum steadily. He was about to speak when Gordon pressed close beside him.

"What the hell do you think you're doing with that popgun?" he demanded.

"Who told you you could take that boat?" Slocum countered hoarsely. His cheeks were high with color; his black eyes pinpoints of light.

"Who said we couldn't?" Gordon retaliated. "That give you any right to shoot at us?"

Slocum laughed; a curious sound coming from his angry, unsmiling mouth. "If you think I wanted to shoot you, mister, go out and have a look at that tree."

Beryl had crept up close beside Randolph. "Careful, Jack," she whispered. "I think he's a little mad."

He pressed her arm.

"Are you all through your practice, Slocum?" he asked quietly.

Before the caretaker could answer, a woman's voice called to him from the direction of the main house. Without a word or a further glance, Slocum turned and stalked slowly toward his cabin. Randolph set the boat in motion again.

"The voice of his master," Gordon growled. "And that's something to remember. That guy is apt to act out of turn. And I'm telling you those bullets didn't miss us by such a very much." He grinned. "Excuse me, ladies, if I let go a few cuss words. I guess I was a little excited."

"We didn't hear you," Barbara said. "And anyway it was just what I was thinking."

"You know," Beryl said, "I don't think that man is quite sane. I never saw eyes with the look his had."

"He's sane enough," Gordon said. "He saw he couldn't scare us and it made him mad."

"He scared us all right," Barbara said. "If I hadn't been sitting down he would have heard my knees knocking together."

"But he didn't know it," said Gordon. "All he saw was that we wouldn't be bluffed; and we had to do it. I'll tell you something. This Slocum is a killer. He was up for a first degree and suspected of another. Burke got him off. Mixup in the evidence or something. I've heard it said that Burke has it fixed if anything happens to him, some papers on Slocum go into certain hands. Burke needs such a man, the game he's playing. Me—I'm peaceable; but a lot of fellows in my place would take a crack at him, if it weren't for Slocum."

They rounded the islet and Randolph headed the boat shoreward. The sun had set, leaving the afterglow. Beryl, sitting beside Randolph, glanced up into his face. "You're not saying anything. Thoughtful?"

"Not very. This is great, isn't it? How's for a swim in the morning?"

"You're on. Before breakfast, yes?"

"Right."

"You, Barbs?"

"Sure thing. That is, if I—" She came lithely erect, with a quick, impatient gesture. The wind of their passage wrapped her light dress closely about her slenderly rounded figure, blew her blond hair back from her forehead. In the fading light her eyes seemed dark. "You know, I'd like to sail around in this thing all night. But we've got to meet Mr. Gordon's rodent sometime; so, let's go."

Gordon looked around at Randolph, scowling. "Say, I like these girls. They're game. If Burke makes a pass at either one and you want to handle him, I'll hold off Slocum, if he leaves his big iron at home."

Randolph smiled. "We'll see if we can't persuade Mr. Burke to behave," he said quietly.

"Huh!" Gordon growled expressively.

Randolph shut off the motor. They glided slowly into the darkened boathouse, the dim rectangle of the open shoreward doorway their only guide. Randolph stepped overside, checked the boat's motion and felt for the mooring ropes, telling the girls to wait until he had all fast.

"I don't know much about these things," Gordon muttered. "I guess I'd only mess them." He got on to the platform and moved slowly toward the door.

With the last rope fastened to its cleat, Randolph reached out his arm in the near darkness until he touched Beryl, then lifted her lightly over.

Barbara was standing with one foot on the seat; the other on the gunwale. Randolph's groping hand encountered her knee. Immediately she let herself slump forward on him, her arms about his neck, her face close to his. "If I lose my nerve tonight," she breathed, "stand by." Her lips pressed warmly against his cheek. His arm about her tightened briefly; then he eased her to her feet.

Catching Beryl's arm, he led them along the platform, through the open doorway. Gordon had already started on.

Ahead of them and a little above them, lights glowed brightly in the lodge and in lesser brilliance on the porch. The sound of laughing voices came to them clearly. Barbara's arm in Randolph's clasp, trembled slightly; then stiffened. On his other side, her arm locked in his, Beryl pressed a little closer. The path was narrow for three; but not too narrow. Behind them from the darkening lake came the quavering, forlorn cry of a loon. Barbara shivered, then said, "Hot damn!"

9

THE THREE LINGERED a little at the end of the path until Gordon had gone on; then they mounted the steps slowly.

The house was set with one end toward the lake. A broad, screened porch covered this whole end and ran a short distance down the side at their right. Directly before them, as they entered the porch, were long, low windows showing portions of a large living-room. Tinted bulbs, strung at intervals, cast the porch in soft light, but the room beyond was brightly illuminated.

They rounded the corner and saw the open French windows that formed the entrance. Randolph stepped aside and Beryl entered first with Barbara close behind. All three wore rubber soled sports shoes and their appearance was not immediately observed. They paused automatically just inside.

The huge room, occupying the width of the lodge, was luxuriously furnished, partly on the order of a club lounge, partly that of a drawing-room. A brightly upholstered chaise-longue, a tête-à-tête, a love seat were set along one wall, with tabourets and nested tables between.

Across from the entrance stood a mahogany davenport table and backed to this was a massive leather couch facing an enormous fireplace, flanked by heavy, leather upholstered chairs. In a corner by the fireplace Wheatley was slumped in a deep chair, one hand, supported by the arm, holding a highball glass, the other a cigarette. His eyes were fixed on his shoe tips stretched out before him. To the right, Fraser was mixing drinks from a service wagon. Gordon, apparently just having stated his preference, was waiting beside him.

Mrs. St. Clair's head, without a hat, was visible above the couch back. Her voice was loud pitched, a little exhilarated. Close beside her, bent toward her, was a round head, sleek black and glistening on top, a trifle gray at the sides. The neck above the starched white collar was thick, a little reddened.

Barbara glanced up at Randolph, with a little, whimsical smile twisting one corner of her mouth. She gestured with one hand. "The estimable Mr. Burke," she murmured with heavy sarcasm.

Her tone could not have carried so far, above the noisy chatter, yet some sense seemed to warn the man of their presence. He twisted his head nervously half around; then his eyes caught their motionless figures. He appeared to bounce to his feet, and almost trotted around the corner of the couch.

In contrast to his brief appearance of the afternoon, he was carefully, almost foppishly groomed; a plump, over-indulged man of fifty-odd, with swarthy face, full cheeks, large, sensuous mouth. But the arresting feature about him was his eyes; bold, domineering, almost magnetic in their dark intensity. Without them and a very definite assurance of manner, his appearance would have been insignificant, with his soft body, small hands and feet.

He came toward them with both hands outstretched. His glance flashed briefly over Beryl and Randolph and centered upon the blond girl.

"Miss St. Clair—this is a pleasure I have been anticipating." He clasped her reluctantly extended hand with both his own. His voice, which had been low while speaking with Mrs. St. Clair, was full toned, of surprising volume.

"Your place is very charming," Barbara said tonelessly.

"I trust you will find it so." Smiling, he studied her closely a moment, then turned to the others.

"Miss Rogers—I am greatly honored; and Mr. Rittenhouse, you were kind to accept my invitation—and to bring Miss Rogers with you. I am delighted that you have so soon made yourself at home. The whole place is yours, I assure you."

Randolph held the plump hand for a brief moment, gripped it carelessly. Burke winced a little. His black eyes flashed up at Randolph probingly. But Randolph was grinning amiably.

"It seems very hospitable," he said. "Even your man gave us a warm reception."

"Indeed? I am very glad to hear it. But—allow me." He gestured gracefully toward the ruddy-faced Fraser and his competent appearing service wagon. "Let us have our cocktails."

They started to cross the room.

"The others did not wait," Burke said, with open-handed gesture. He turned his eyes glowingly on Barbara. "But I would not join them until all my guests were present."

Barbara avoided his glance, shrugged a little as she turned aside.

"At your service, ladies and Mr. Rittenhouse," Fraser said jovially. His florid face was more flushed now than earlier; his eyes bright.

Burke clasped his arm lightly. "Do your very best, Stanley. This is the start of a most auspicious occasion, and a proper start is important." He turned to Beryl and Randolph. "Fraser is most useful at this. I, as you see, am a very lonely and helpless bachelor. I trust that you will be kind enough to overlook the paucity of my service. In my town place it is quite different; but I come here to relax, to enjoy my friends, and too many servants annoy me. And here is the good Fraser."

"This," Fraser said, laughing, "is my real profession; as you will presently agree." He gestured toward the generous array of bottles. "Anything—anything you wish: White Lady, Sazarac, Major Bailey? Manhattan, Old Fashioned—no? Perhaps a plain Martini? But you are in doubt. Permit me then. One of my own. Yes?"

"I recommend it," Burke said.

"What is this marvelous concoction?" Beryl asked. She had been very quiet since entering the room, furtively studying both Burke and Fraser.

Fraser gestured elaborately. "With such encouragement, Miss Rogers, I shall be at my best."

He filled a shaker with ice, took up a measuring glass, paused. "Four, myself five." He cast a whimsical glance past them. "Ah, Mrs. St. Clair, can I tempt you again?"

Mrs. St. Clair turned toward them, pulling herself more erect with a hand on the couch back. Her face was flushed beyond the effect of her makeup. "You are very kind, Mr. Fraser"—she tittered—"but I've had, what—two already? And they seem to grow on one."

"It's a virtue they have," Fraser said. "How about you, Wheatley?"

"No, thank you," Wheatley said grumpily. He did not even look up.

"You, Gordon?" Burke asked.

"I'll have another, Burke." His tone was offensively hard.

Burke, with his lips still smiling, gave him a quick, cold look.

"Six," Fraser announced. "Now, Miss Rogers, for the big secret. Watch the professor. A portion of fresh orange juice—see? Then a teaspoon of confectioner's sugar. Many disagree with me, but to my mind lime and grenadine"—he stopped and took up a bottle from the lower shelf—"do not combine judiciously with the base which is fine Bacardi, besides disguising its flavor. So—Bacardi gets the major portion. Now for a third of dry vermouth and, the secret of the whole, a topper of gin. You wouldn't believe it? Wait."

He tapped the top on to the shaker and worked it vigorously, while Burke set out a row of six bar glasses. Fraser filled each close to the brim. He eyes sought Barbara's; shifted quickly to Beryl. "All set; let's go."

"But a toast," Burke proposed, and added, a little fatuously, "To the ladies! Our despair and our hope."

"That lets us out," Barbara said dryly, as Fraser and Burke drank. She turned to Beryl and Randolph. "So I'll add one: 'To the happy union.'" Her eyes smiled up at Randolph; then she partly closed one eye.

Randolph took his glass in his big hand, his fingers covering it to the top. He nodded at Barbara, raised it to his lips. He lowered his hand toward his side, away from Burke and Fraser.

"Oh, Rittenhouse," Wheatley called. His voice was slightly thick.

Randolph glanced over, and Wheatley beckoned him with a sidewise nod of his head. "Excuse me," he said to Beryl and Barbara, and started over. As he passed Mrs. St. Clair he saw that she was leaning back on the couch with her head on its back. Her eyes were almost closed; her lips were working. She looked as if she was about to cry.

Randolph observed at Wheatley's left a large porcelain jardiniere on its teakwood stand. He stepped to that side, turned so that he stood between it and the group at the cocktail wagon. Wheatley bent forward in his chair, threw the cigarette from his left hand into the fireplace. He turned somewhat bleary eyes up at Randolph, beckoned him to lean closer. Randolph stooped and at the same time let his cocktail drain slowly into the jardiniere.

"I want you to let me have that thing back," Wheatley grumbled.

Randolph straightened. "I'd advise you to forget it."

"I'm not forgetting it," Wheatley said in an ugly tone.

"You're talking out loud," Randolph told him.

"Well, what if I am?" he demanded, but his voice was lowered. "I tell you I'm not forgetting it and if you don't get it for me I'll tell Burke about it."

Randolph moved in front of him, leaned down. "You're half drunk, Wheatley, but try to get this. It's a promise. One peep out of you and you won't be pretty to look at for a week."

"Well, I ain't going to stand this," Wheatley whined. "I can't stand it. Look at him now. He'll be trying to paw her in a minute. He's already rigged something with Mrs. St. Clair. Take a look at her."

"What is Barbara St. Clair to you anyway?" Randolph asked.

"Huh? Haven't I asked her to marry me? He won't."

"I thought you had some trouble of your own that took first place."

Wheatley looked up at him quickly, sighed dejectedly and sunk his head. "That's the hell of it," he mumbled. "That's why I got to have it. Be a friend, Rittenhouse. You don't stack in with this crowd."

Randolph stood erect. "Keep your head down, Wheatley," he said quietly, "and lay off the drinks. You won't be in shape even to help yourself."

He turned and met Beryl's glance. She gave him a quick smile and turned to answer a remark of Fraser's. Gordon was standing a little back of the group, sipping his drink slowly. His eyes were sombre as they shifted from one to the other. His expression was one of cold disgust. Randolph strode over to them. He had the same look of harmless amiability as when he had talked with the two newspapermen. He appeared just a big, good-natured youngster.

He moved beside Beryl, pressed her arm lightly and smiled at Fraser who while talking to Beryl seemed to have difficulty in keeping his glance from wandering to Barbara. Randolph turned his head a little. Burke had pressed close to the blond girl. He had set down his glass and as he talked he kept reaching out with little gestures as if about to grasp one of her hands. His eyes were very bright.

"You know," he was saying, "while you were on the lake I was becoming acquainted with your mother, a most charming woman. We talked quite a bit. I think we understand each other. And I believe we shall get along famously."

Barbara raised her glass, which was still three-quarters full, and looked at him coolly over it. "It is possible," she drawled. "She makes acquaintances easily."

"But, my dear. It is of course you I mean—you and me," he said eagerly.

Barbara shrugged one shoulder, as if unaware of the gesture, turned toward Fraser and smiled as she met his glance. "This is awfully smooth. What d'you call it?"

"You may not believe it," Fraser said promptly, "but it's a fact, I assure you. I've been waiting for some particularly beautiful lady to christen it. Won't you—er—or Miss Rogers do me the honor?"

"Nerts," Gordon said. "It's sort of a modified swizzle."

Burke flashed him a hard look, but Fraser did not lose his good nature.

" 'Pon my honor," he said to Barbara, "it's a new one. Give me a good one, Miss St. Clair, and I'll start it off at the club. How 'bout a blond something or other?"

"Why not call it 'a promise'?" Burke suggested. "Of course it is very good, Stanley; but, you know, a promise of better things to come."

"Better call it a delusion," Gordon growled.

Barbara flashed him a smile, then turned back to Fraser.

"How is that, Mr. Fraser?"

Fraser glanced over where Wheatley was slumped morosely in his chair. He laughed. "We'd already had a couple or three. It might be appropriate, but I'm standing my ground very well, thank you. No; I don't like it. Think me up a better, Miss St. Clair."

Beryl pressed Randolph to turn a little aside. She held up her nearly full glass. "I've been waiting," she murmured, "that we should have ours together. That's appropriate, isn't it—Jack?"

Randolph smiled and showed her his empty glass. He bent his head close to her. "I don't drink," he said in a tone inaudible to the others. He nodded in the general direction of Wheatley and the jardiniere. She looked around.

"But he's already had too much."

"The man at his left. The one with the stony face."

"Oh! Then give him mine also."

Barbara came beside them.

"What are the lovers spooning about?" she said clearly, and under her breath, "Damnation!"

"What ho!" Fraser called.

Mrs. St. Clair sat up with a jerk, and even Wheatley glanced around.

"I neglected to advise you," Fraser said, laughingly, "that a plain gin cocktail is properly taken immediately following this what-d'you-call-it, Miss St. Clair."

"Not for mine," Barbara said. "I don't want to spoil the memory of this so soon, Mr. Fraser. Besides—the sun was hot on the lake. I should like to powder my nose."

Burke beamed on her. "You're altogether adorable as you are," he assured her, rubbing his small hands. "But—pardon."

With his short stride he stepped quickly to the portières which hid the entrance to what was presumably the dining-room beyond, and pulled a bell rope at one side. Almost immediately the portières parted and Slocum's wife stood between them.

She was in black which might have been demure had it not been for the close fitting dress moulded to her slenderly rounded form and the short skirt permitting generous view of her shapely legs. In neither face nor poise did she appear as a maid or a servant in any form; rather as an entertainer about to perform her act. The effect was heightened by the drapes which she pulled back of her, leaving enough space to admit light from the room behind that cast her in partial silhouette. Her face was set in its unsmiling immobility; her eyes, looking straight ahead, whether by chance or otherwise, were fixed steadily on Randolph.

"Humm!" Barbara murmured. "Isn't she the passionate thing!"

Burke frowned, as if to emphasize his disinterestedness in this undeniably attractive member of his menage.

"Martha," he said, "be so kind as to show the ladies to their rooms."

"And, Martha," Gordon said in careless boldness, "you can show me to mine also."

The woman did not so much as glance at Gordon. Her eyes left Randolph's face slowly; she turned and walked toward the broad, curving stairs which were set in a corner of the spacious room, at the left of the French windows. Her movements were professionally graceful.

"Er—Martha," Burke called. "Will dinner be served shortly?"

"Whenever you wish."

Mrs. St. Clair arose from the couch, with a hand on its back to steady herself. She stood uncertainly for a moment, frowning, her lips compressed.

"I say," Fraser called, "can I give you a hand, Mrs. St. Clair?" He started forward, the first time he had moved from his improvised cocktail bar, and stumbled slightly. He laughed loudly. "Can you fancy? Hoist on my own petard. But the effects are not bad, I assure you. Now just a little moment, Mrs. St. Clair, and I'll be alongside."

Mrs. St. Clair smiled stiffly. "I am quite all right, Mr. Fraser; thank you." She walked steadily enough toward the two girls who were waiting. The woman Martha had paused on a step above, glancing back over her shoulder. A look of faint, mocking amusement in her dark eyes was the only expression in her face. Gordon was watching her where she stood with one foot advanced to the higher tread; she did not appear to see him.

"You are going up, aren't you, Jack?" Beryl asked Randolph.

"I'd like to wash. We don't change, do we, Burke?"

"By no means, Mr. Rittenhouse. Please—I wish you all to be most informal. Wait; I'll go with you. I should like to show you my pride at Crossley Lodge."

"Sure; let's all go," Gordon said.

"But I'll stay and cheer up Wheatley," Fraser said. He was weaving slightly where he stood; but Randolph saw him flash Burke a quick, significant look and there was little befuddlement in the glance.

"Yeah; give him another one of those and let him pass out happy," Gordon said.

Fraser waved a hand and commenced to sing *Road to Mandalay* in a husky baritone as they filed up the curving stairway. The girls had started on. Randolph saw Burke take Mrs. St. Clair's arm, although she did not appear in any particular need of the support, and he took three treads at a time to catch up with Beryl and Barbara. Gordon was bringing up the rear.

"*... And a man can get a thirst,*" floated bravely up to them.

"Wonder what the caper is?" Beryl murmured. "He's not as drunk as that."

"Official pacemaker, if you ask me," Barbara said in the same tone. "And now, ladies and gentlemen, for an intimate view of the harem. My gawd, I felt as if a slug had crawled over my hand when he touched me."

They moved back on the landing and half turned, waiting for the others to come up. Martha had walked down the corridor a few steps and stood with her back toward them. Barbara pressed close to Randolph. "Come into Beryl's room, wherever it is," she whispered, "before we go down." She pressed his arm, then let her hand slide down his arm to his fingers and squeezed them. He nodded. She turned her face upward, looked searchingly into his eyes.

Beryl slipped close to them.

"Do you feel that drink, Barbs?" she whispered.

"Sure do; but it won't get me. Why—do I act like it?"

Beryl bit her lip. "I didn't mean it that way," she murmured.

Burke and Mrs. St. Clair appeared above the landing. He was fussily solicitous, an attention with which she apparently wished to dispense but was uncertain how to avoid.

"I really am quite all right, Mr. Burke," she said coldly; then unexpectedly laughed in a peculiar, unnatural key. "I was a bit heady at first, I'll admit," she said in a forced tone of lightness. "But it has altogether worn off. Mr. Fraser is very clever."

Burke turned to a door at his left which closed that end of the corridor. He paused with his hand on the knob and looked around at his guests. His expression at first was that of a pampered child who is about to exhibit some unusual toy to bring envy to his playmates. Then his glance fell upon Randolph and Beryl and faltered a little. It shifted to Barbara, and a different light grew in his eyes.

"Please, Miss St. Clair," he said, "you are—er—the only unattached lady present this evening, and I am what you might call a bit superstitious. Be the first to cross the threshold, I beg you."

"What you got there, Burke," Gordon asked in his mockingly surly tone, "Haile Selassie's crown room?"

"Nothing so elaborate as that, *Mr.* Gordon. Ah, thank you," as Barbara, with a little, whimsical frown, came forward, followed closely by Beryl.

Burke threw the door open, reached a hand inside and pressed some buttons. Dim light glowed beyond the doorway. One after the other, the two girls stepped inside. Burke, looking after them, gestured for Mrs. St. Clair, placed his hand on her arm and led her through. Gordon followed.

Randolph, furthest from the door, moved slowly toward it. He heard Beryl say coolly, "It is very lovely, Mr. Burke;" then he paused and glanced down the corridor. The woman Martha was watching him. Immediately she pressed a finger to her lips, gestured toward a door slightly beyond and back of her. There was nothing coquettish either in the gesture or in her expression; rather an imperative summons. He nodded slowly; then turned, frowning slightly, and entered Burke's room.

10

CLAIMING THE FULL width of the building, the master's room at Crossley occupied an area nearly equal to that of the living-room immediately beneath it; yet the amount and arrangement of the furnishings did not at first give an impression of spaciousness.

The front corner of the end at the left, as Randolph entered, was fitted as a barrister's study complete with a library of legal volumes, a huge mahogany flat-topped desk, a secretary's equipment and filing cabinets. The same scheme was carried a little further into the room, in the way of other bookcases, with their diamond-shaped, leaded panes, deeply uphol-stered reading chairs, a davenport table piled with maga-zines, other smaller tables of teakwood and mahogany, and smoking stands.

From this point on, the character of the place changed first to a resting room by day and finally to full sleeping accommo-dations whose tone, in both decoration and equipment, was almost effeminate and certainly most unbachelor-like.

Rugs with extraordinarily deep piling covered the floor. Against one wall was a Turkish couch set in a nook formed between two wardrobes. Opposite stood a huge fourposter, with silken canopy, faintly lighted by colored bulbs. Before the porcelain-faced fireplace two lounging chairs were set in intimate proximity; at one side was a love seat.

The master of all this bizarre extravagance moved from one place to another with an air of almost childish delight, calling attention, quite unnecessarily, to the different pieces, as the group moved from one end of the big room to the other. Mostly he endeavored to capture the interest of Barbara, but the blond girl eluded him from time to time, only to be caught up again as he stepped quickly after her.

Below stairs, Ross Burke had maintained a little of polite dignity, as he construed it, and at times his resonant voice, the magnetism of his eyes when cold, suggested a certain power that must have marked him as a figure to be reckoned with in his unprincipled fight among men.

Here, and especially amidst the sensuous furnishings of the far end, there was no suggestion of power in the man; rather he appeared softened by the gratification which his money had brought him, an eager prey to lecherous desire, repulsive in his feigned apology for such luxury.

Resignedly the two girls, trailed by Mrs. St. Clair and the others, had followed Burke's guidance from point to point. As he started to manipulate the soft, colored lights in the canopy, they turned away with arched eyebrows and moved toward the further end. Randolph, who had lingered in the rear, joined them. Barbara impulsively took his arm.

"But wait a moment," Burke called. "I have a surprise, even for you, Mr. Rittenhouse, in a country lodge. It is my bath. I put ten thousand dollars in it and I can assure you that you haven't seen many its equal."

"My God, Burke," Gordon said. "You don't mean to tell us there's only one bath in the whole place!"

Burke swung around upon him, his face dark with anger.

"Thank you so much, Mr. Burke," Beryl said, unable to keep laughter entirely from her voice, "we are already quite overwhelmed. And I think we should hurry if we are not to keep dinner waiting."

"And am I hungry!" Barbara added, pressing Randolph onward. "That cocktail of Mr. Fraser's sure did its stuff."

Burke pattered after them. "Ah, Miss St. Clair, I think we shall satisfy you. And now let me see that you are comfortable in your rooms."

They reached the doorway. The girls crowded through, it seemed almost precipitately, and Randolph's big form moved slowly behind them.

"Thanks," Beryl said coolly. "It won't be necessary. Martha has been kind enough to wait."

"Very well," Burke spoke from the doorway as Gordon pushed past him. "But I feel very selfish. If you are not satisfied, I will gladly exchange with either one of you."

"I might call you on that," Gordon threw over his shoulder.

Burke forced himself to laugh. "But of course I meant the ladies, although you wouldn't know that, Gordon. Let us say, then, in fifteen or twenty minutes?"

Randolph said, "Right," and Burke slowly closed his door.

The wide corridor, with its warm red runner, ran from the master's room the length of the building, with rooms at either side. Martha pushed open the first door at the left and stood at one side. "This is yours, Miss St. Clair," she said tonelessly.

Barbara cast a glance back over her shoulder. "Brr! Can't you make it the end of the hall?"

"I can only show you, Miss," Martha said. "I did not arrange. But you will find that your bath connects with Miss Rogers' room which is just beyond."

Barbara stepped inside and Beryl, following, paused on the threshold. "Where do you go, Jack?"

Martha indicated a door beyond the stairway at the right. "It is directly opposite yours, Miss Rogers."

"And where do I check in, Martha?" Gordon asked.

"The one next to Mr. Rittenhouse," she answered without looking at him.

Gordon moved on.

"Please," Mrs. St. Clair broke in. Her voice sounded very weary and strained. "Will you show me to my room now? I wish to take some aspirin at once."

"Certainly, madame. If you will follow me. It is the third door on the left."

Mrs. St. Clair looked past Beryl into the room. "Barbara," she said, "I wish you would come to me in about five minutes." Without waiting for an answer, she walked, a little unsteadily, along the corridor.

Beryl looked up at Randolph and smiled wryly. "Isn't he detestable?" she whispered. "Come into my room after Barbs comes back. She wants to see you—and so do I. That room there gave me the shivers. Oh—did you bring the cigarettes?"

"No. They must be in the pocket of the car. I'll get them."

"If you don't mind. I'd dislike asking our host. He might suggest that I come into the harem for them." She smiled with that curious little twist of her lips. "And bring them with you?"

He nodded, smiling.

"Don't you drink at all?" she asked.

He shook his head. "I like to keep in shape."

"How will you get by? They're sure to have plenty at dinner and afterward."

"I'll duck the first two, somehow. After that they won't notice."

"I can't so easily. Will you watch out—if they give me too many?"

"Of course."

"You've been swell. I'm pretty good at taking care of myself, but I certainly would be leery of this crowd if"—she lowered her tone to a whisper—"if someone else were here." She held out her hand to him, with her beautifully rounded arm straight. He caught her fingertips, was bending over them when her fingers tightened on his, drew him toward her. He kissed her lightly on the lips.

Barbara came to them in the open doorway. "My dear, did you observe the look the dark, silent woman gave our protector?"

"Our?"

"Well, Gerald is distinctly out of the picture; and I told you before if this is a free for all I'm in it." She tried to make tone and air gaily reckless, but a certain tenseness about her mouth and in her eyes showed that she was nervous.

Beryl said, "You'll have to hurry—Jack."

"Wise woman," Barbara said. "But I'll have my inning yet, before I yield him entirely to the black peril."

The door closed behind them.

Randolph started along the corridor and saw the woman Martha emerge from the room to which she had shown Mrs. St. Clair and turn to meet him. He kept on and stopped beside her.

"Isn't there a back stairway?" he asked, in quiet tone. "I want to get something from my car."

She gave him a slow smile. "Yes, sir; at the end of the corridor," and added in a whisper, "You're not slow. The porch is dark. Don't make a light outside."

She walked beside him to the stairhead, then paused to let him go down. In the dimly lighted lower hallway Randolph heard kitchen noises behind a closed door at his right. Without especial care, yet making little sound, he let himself through the unlatched screen door, crossed the porch on rubber soled shoes, found the treads and stepped from the lowest on to grass. He couldn't see the open shed, but remembered its location and started in that direction.

The night was starlit, without a moon. It was sluggishly warm, with little air stirring. The loon was still calling from the lake. He turned once to glance over his shoulder. The nearer end of the lodge was in darkness. Faint window lights showed on the second floor and brighter illumination streamed from the living-room at the far end.

Randolph came to the car, and with a hand on it to guide him, moved forward to the right side door. He felt in the pocket without result, then, stooping over, groped along the seat close to the back. His fingers encountered the missing packet, and at the same time a hand rested lightly on his shoulder.

He thrust the cigarettes into a pocket, straightened and turned. The woman slipped past, then faced him, standing close. Her hand caught his arm; the pressure urged him to bend nearer. He noted curiously the slight scent of delicate perfume.

"Maybe I'm a sap," she whispered—so close was she that her breath was soft on his face—"but I don't want to see them trip you, Big Boy. You don't know this crowd, but perhaps you will before morning."

She paused, and her other hand came up to hold his other arm.

"Burke won't stop for anything, and I guess you know what he wants. Fraser won't want to but he'll side him. He's got to. You could handle a dozen of them, but they've an ace if they want to use it. Don't let them catch you offside or somebody might slip you a dose of lead."

Her mouth was almost against his cheek now.

"Keep Gordon friendly if you can. Don't cross him. He seems all right with you now, but you can't tell what he'll do next. He doesn't know me, but I know where that lad comes from and what he was. Gordon! The nearest he comes to being a Highlander is a bottle of Scotch. But the man you want to watch is Steve. That's Slocum: my husband, damn him. I'm tied to him but he's no husband to me.

"Usually I can control him. I've a way with me." One hand squeezed his arm. "But don't make any mistake about him. Staying up here in the woods has got him. He killed a man once and he's kill crazy now. If Burke lifts his little finger, Slocum will shoot you like a dog. And Burke will fix it for the courts. You can't beat that slimy crook."

She had spoken swiftly, and paused for breath. Randolph raised his right hand, disengaging her clasp, caught her arm and pressed it.

"You're a trump, Martha," he whispered. "You don't belong here. Why don't you beat it out of here?"

"Can't. Burke has something on me, like he has on Slocum. Not too bad; enough to hold me. But he can't have me. No man, not even Slocum, can have me that I don't want, and"— she barely breathed—"it's a long while since I've seen a man I could really want."

Suddenly her arms were about his body; her body pressed close. One leg entwined about his, and he could feel the hard muscles of her calf forced against his.

And at that particular moment, at no great distance a dry twig snapped.

"My God," she whispered frantically, "that's Slocum. He'll kill us both!"

"Get in the car," he told her quickly. "Crouch down. I'll handle this."

He waited a moment, taking the cigarettes from his pocket into his hand. He heard the faint rustle of movement at his side; then moved along the car, whistling quietly. As he came out from under the shed there came the swift patter of rushing feet. A dim form sped toward him, hurtled against his thigh.

"So, boy," he said softly, and let his hand hang loosely. A cold muzzle sniffed at it. His fingers stroked it gently. Otherwise he stood perfectly still. Then the nose pressed against him.

"That you, Slocum?" he called quietly.

A heavy step came nearer.

"Yeah. What the hell you doin' here?"

"Miss Rogers forgot her cigarettes. I came out to get them. I have them now. Quiet night. Those loons mean weather, don't they?" He moved a step away from the shed.

"To hell with the loons. You took a chance, mister, 'nother second and I'd let you have it."

Randolph continued to move slowly along.

"How's that?" he said a little sharply.

"Burke's orders," Slocum growled. "He don't 'low any prowlin' round after dark."

The dog kept pace with Randolph, and his fingers continued their gentle rubbing. Slocum walked at his other side. Randolph laughed, shortly.

"You ought to post that in the Lodge. How would a fellow know? I might have taken it in my mind to stroll by the lake."

"We don't have to post nothing," Slocum said surlily. "Burke knows his business and he tells me mine. And mine is to cut down any guy I catch sneakin' in the dark."

They had reached the porch steps. Randolph patted the dog's head, turned to Slocum. "Cigarette?"

"Yeah, I'll take one."

In the match's flare, Randolph saw Slocum's beady eyes looking at him darkly from under lowered brows; saw the sagging pocket where a heavy pistol bulged.

"You ain't seen my wife, have you?" Slocum asked unexpectedly.

"Which one is she? The maid, I suppose. A short while before I came down I saw her go into Mrs. St. Clair's room. If I see her do you want me to tell her to come out?"

"Naw. Leave her alone."

The caretaker turned abruptly away, moving slowly in the direction of the lake. Randolph started up the steps. The big police dog hesitated a moment then went silent-footed after his master. Over his shoulder Randolph watched Slocum's progress by the spasmodic glowing of the cigarette. He reached the screen door, opened it, closed it with an audible bang, then stepped back a pace on the porch.

He caught another glimpse of the faint radiance, like a firefly's momentary glow, and made his way cautiously to the steps. He had gone a half dozen paces from them when a form came to him out of the darkness.

"For God's sake," Martha breathed, "let me get inside quick!"

Without sound they reached the entrance. She closed the screen door softly, then the inner one. She motioned him up the back stairs and followed him a little way. In the dim reflected light from the upper corridor her face looked white; by contrast, her eyes dark, and large.

"He would have killed us," she whispered. "He doesn't bother me, but he told me he would kill me if he ever caught me with a man, and I know he would. Here—feel my heart beat." She caught his hand, pressed it flat against her breast. Before he withdrew it he could feel the rapid pulse. Randolph did not say anything.

"You're good, Big Boy, and you have nerve. You came back to get me. Listen: I must go now." She stepped lithely to the tread beside him, readied up and pulled his head down until her lips were close to his ear. "Watch your drinks later on," she barely breathed. "I'd give you your coffee myself; but everything else." She turned his face, pressed her lips hard against his cheek, then went swiftly down.

Randolph took the remaining treads three at a time and strode along the corridor with his light, easy step. As he passed Mrs. St. Clair's door he could faintly hear voices inside. One seemed excited; the other had the sound of crying in its tone.

In his room he washed face and hands and changed into fresh shirt and tie. He did not set things out from his bag, but instead replaced his discarded linen and snapped the lock. He grinned once, while brushing his hair; otherwise his expression was grim and a little angry.

A survey of the room showed a door near the outer wall and toward the rear of the building. He opened it, into the room, and saw a long bath with another door at the further end. He saw no key in either door, and closing his own, he set a chair at a slant beneath the knob. Of the two windows one, he found, overlooked the front porch roof. Both were opened and he satisfied himself that the fastenings were secure.

The room door, he perceived, had neither lock, bolt nor inner knob; merely a flat metal strip like that inside a closet. He opened the door a crack and listened.

In a very few moments, steps came hurriedly along the corridor from the direction of Mrs. St. Clair's room, stopped at the door opposite. The door was opened and closed. He waited a short while longer, then stepped across and tapped lightly.

11

BERYL OPENED THE door a crack, then swung it wide, stepping back with it. Randolph walked in and she closed it softly after him. His face had lost its hard expression, and he was smiling.

The blond Barbara stood by one of the windows, heedless of his entrance. Her head was bent a little; her right hand clasped her chin and the tip of her forefinger was caught between her white teeth. Very obviously she was struggling for control against some emotion.

As Randolph paused, Beryl caught his arm, pressed it lightly and gestured toward the silent girl. "This is sweet!" she said disgustedly, then turned to Barbara. "Barbs, why don't you tell him about it? I think you'll have to. There's nothing else you can do."

"Here're the cigarettes," he said casually. "Suppose you both light up. We have still five minutes or more."

He held a match for Beryl, then stepped over to Barbara. Her hand trembled slightly as she took one from the packet. Her lips trembled more as she bent her head forward to the flame, so that the cigarette end bobbed curiously and she was forced to grasp his hand with both her own and bring the light to it. Her fingertips were cold.

She drew deeply on the tobacco, then exhaled slowly. "Thanks," she said and gave him a swift, faint smile. But immediately it was erased and mortification, anger and perplexity took its place. Then resentment became dominant and she faced him with a little gesture of defiance. Her softly moulded mouth took harder lines; her blue eyes were like dark bits of glittering ice. With her light blond hair and her straight, lithe figure she was strikingly attractive.

"My mother," she said, in a cold, hard tone, "is bordering on hysterics. Whether it is synthetic or real, the sound is the same." She shrugged. "Why I ever came to this damnable place, I haven't the faintest idea. It must be my easy going nature not to have enough strength of character to refuse them both when they begged me. And I pay for it."

Randolph made no comment. As he listened, he was frowning slightly, but it seemed more from thoughtfulness than concern. Beryl moved nearer them and seated herself on the bed. She watched Randolph more than Barbara.

Barbara glanced once at her, drew deeply on her cigarette then looked back at Randolph.

"I don't know why I tell you this. God knows I'm ashamed to. I was idiot enough to fool about it back along. Perhaps you can tell me what a girl is supposed to do in a case like this—if it ever occurred before. Want it?"

Randolph nodded silently.

Barbara shrugged again, but a little scarlet was creeping into her cheeks.

"Well, in plain-spoken English, here it is. Mother says she is ruined and, believe it or not, passes the buck to her beloved daughter."

Randolph shook his head. "That may be plain English but it doesn't give the details."

Barbara looked at him, and her eyes grew reckless. She nodded her head sidewise, in the direction of Burke's room.

"He doesn't mince matters. He told her he has her letters—all of them, in a safe in his room. He said that his instructions were to deliver them only for a sum of money that is out of the question. There is no possibility of her getting it. She told him so. He said that he sympathized with her—yes, that's what he said; that if the letters were lost while in his care nothing could be done about it except that he would run great risk with his client. He—he suggested that he wouldn't run such risk unless—that is, he suggested I might redeem them."

"Humm." Randolph let his glance wander away from Barbara. "In still plainer English, he will give your mother the letters if you promise to leave your room unlocked."

"Leaving it unlocked is a mere figure of speech. There isn't a lock or a key in my room or Beryl's. Yes; that's about it."

Beryl stood up, facing Randolph. Her face was hot.

"The man is a fatuous fool. He must know he never could do a thing like that with you in the house."

Randolph started to grin; then made his expression serious. "I suspect he figures I won't count."

"You mean"—she lowered her voice to a whisper—"as John Rittenhouse? We'll tell him the truth before it gets that far. I don't care any more anyway."

"Either as that," Randolph said as softly, "or as Dick Randolph." He ignored her sudden look of perplexity and turned to Barbara. "Your room connects with this, through the bath?"

"Yes."

"Mind if I have a look at it?"

"Come. I'll show you."

"Better wait here. We wouldn't want to speak in there anyway."

He found the room a replica of Beryl's, even to the same lavish furnishings. He stood for a few moments on the threshold of the bathroom door, carefully noting the location of each article of furniture; then, stepping lightly, walked around the bed and closely examined the wall forming the opposite partition. In less than a minute he was back in the other room, closing the door without sound behind him.

"It might be dangerous, and it certainly would be disagreeable," he said to Barbara, "if you want to play it. It all depends on how badly you want those letters for your mother."

"Not too badly," she said, and her tone was hard. "I still have my life to live, I suppose. It means Reno and wreck for her, and of course it wouldn't be so nice for me either. I'd take some risk for them, if that is what you mean."

He nodded. "It would mean," he said slowly, "that he would have to believe it."

"And then shoot him with he comes to collect," Barbara said just as slowly. "I'd do it too, in a wink, only I haven't a pistol."

Beryl started to say something, but Randolph silenced her with a gesture. "Then if you are game, suppose you tell your mother to ask for the letters; and to destroy them the instant she gets them. He probably wouldn't make delivery until late and would be guided by your attitude this evening. That's the hard part of it."

"Look," Beryl said. "Won't it mean an unholy row?"

Randolph said, "It might, but if we get a break he's apt to think he bungled it."

Barbara was regarding him keenly; her eyes held a quizzical expression but her lips were hard set.

"I'm putting a lot on you, mister," she murmured. "If you muff it, it's the lake for me."

Randolph's look at her was unworried. "Better hurry along," he said. "Beryl and I are going to check up with him now. Wish you would come along the corridor and send your mother in when we come out. By the way," he added, "my bag is packed and locked. You both 'd better leave yours that way."

They parted in the corridor, Barbara hastening toward her mother's room. Beryl took Randolph's arm and leaned close to him. "Are we going to make a break for it?"

He shook his head. "I don't think so; not tonight anyway."

"Why are we seeing him now?"

"To make sure what is on his mind in respect to me."

She gave his arm a little shake. "Can't you tell me?"

"Later. We haven't time now."

He knocked at Burke's door. It was opened almost immediately. Burke's first expression was one of slight surprise. His glance went beyond them, then he gave them his oily smile. He stepped back. "Won't you come in?"

Randolph pressed Beryl across the threshold and closed the door. He shook his head as Burke motioned them further in. "We'll take only a moment. I understand of course that you asked me out to discuss a business matter. Would you like to take it up this evening?"

Burke spread both hands in a deprecatory gesture. "Oh, no, no. Business is a harsh word. It shouldn't intrude on social pleasure. Let us enjoy ourselves this evening, Mr. Rittenhouse—and Miss Rogers, and become better acquainted. In the morning, perhaps; or at your convenience. But this evening I do not wish to see my guests annoyed."

Randolph nodded soberly. "An excellent sentiment. Tomorrow then."

He opened the door and let Beryl precede him. Burke was a little at one side. Randolph saw Barbara and Mrs. St. Clair approaching and closed the door quickly. They met at the stairhead. Mrs. St. Clair avoided looking at them, and Randolph caught Barbara's hand. The three started down together while Mrs. St. Clair continued to Burke's door. Her color was very high; but the poise of her head, the set of her parted lips, the look in her wide open eyes were all implacably hard.

Randolph turned from his swift glance at her. *"Sauve qu'il peut,"* he murmured, and Barbara pressed his hand.

They heard her admitted and the door closed softly behind her. Randolph checked them on the landing. "If anything happens to me tonight," he whispered, "you two manage to stick by."

Beryl pressed around in front of him. "Tell it," she demanded in a tense whisper. "What do you mean?"

He smiled down at her. "Wait," his lips formed.

Barbara glanced back over her shoulder. "The die is cast now," she murmured through stiff lips. "I still can't believe it."

"Forget it now," Randolph breathed in her ear. "Afterward, play it your way."

He turned and placed both hands on Beryl's shoulders.

"Come on now; not a care in the world. It's her best chance."

The look she gave him was a little questioning, not wholly trusting. He gave her shoulders a playful shake, smiled at her broadly. "You're cold to me, sweetheart," he whispered. Light grew in her dark cool eyes as she continued to look at him. He shook his head. "I know all you're thinking, and it's all wrong."

Barbara grasped an arm of each. "There's one thing you've got to promise," she said in low tone to Randolph. "I've trusted you this far and will have to go the limit. You keep your door unlocked for the both of us if we stampede."

"That also is a figure of speech. Come; let's go. Beryl, if you don't smile at me I'll be desolated."

She glanced at him quickly, then away; her look was still dissatisfied. He commenced to mark time on the landing. They linked arms in his and the three descended.

As they turned from the stairway, at first no one was visible in the big living-room; only smoke arising from the further side of the couch told of some presence there. Then a gong *bonged* softly three times in the room beyond, its sound traveling in vibrating waves that seemed to lose no volume with distance.

Fraser stood up by the couch, pipe in mouth, stretching. Evidently he had not heard the three advancing slowly over the rug covered floor. He turned to knock the ashes from his pipe into a tray on a nearby tabouret, and they came within his range of vision.

" 'Pon my word," he said, "I'd given you all up. I'm fair perished with hunger. Was about to turn cannibal, really. Only thing deterred me was that Wheatley over there, my lone prospect, did not appeal to me as a tempting morsel. I say, old thing, mess will be served directly. Cheerio, m' lad; the ladies!"

They now saw Wheatley, still in his chair by the fireplace, legs outstretched before him, his chin sunk on his chest. He looked haggard and drooping. He swiveled a glance toward them from under lowered brows. Slowly gathering his legs under him he stood up. One hand beckoned Barbara. "Come here a minute, will you, Barbs," he said a little hoarsely. "I want to speak with you."

Barbara kept her hold of Randolph's arm and urged him forward. Fraser stepped a little before Beryl. "Now don't tell me you're not famished, Miss Rogers. You're altogether too healthy looking not to admit it."

"I suppose so," she said in a tone she made light. "I really hadn't thought of it."

"Splendid! At least I'm not alone in my misery. And now for cocktails. It's Stanley this, and Stanley that, and Stanley make the cocktails." His glance wandered after Barbara and his blond eyebrows arched; then he turned back to Beryl. "Want to advise?"

"Simple and dry is the thing, isn't it?"

"Righto! And there're eight of us, no?"

A door closed on the upper landing; there was the soft thud of footfalls.

"Yes, Gerry," Barbara said coolly. "What did you want?"

Wheatley scowled up at Randolph; then shrugged.

"Has"—his head nodded upward—"bothered you yet?" he asked in a low, grumbling tone.

"Not in the least," Barbara said clearly. "Why do you ask?"

"I got something of what he said to your mother—before he talked to me. It didn't listen so hot."

"I think you must have misunderstood, Gerry. Why do you look so miserable?"

Wheatley made a wry grimace, then turned his scowling glance on Randolph. Randolph smiled down at him. "It doesn't taste so good, does it, Wheatley?" he said and laughed.

Wheatley shot a quick glance at Fraser, who was already busy with bottles and shaker, and then to the stairway beyond, where Mrs. St. Clair and Burke were just appearing. He clutched Randolph's sleeve.

"He's got me in a jam," he whispered hoarsely, "and I'm worried about Barbs. By God, Randolph, you've got to give me that—that thing back. I can't stand by and—"

The blond girl's hand rested lightly on his arm and interrupted him. "Don't be dramatic, Gerry," she said swiftly in a tone under the shaker's rattling. "You won't do anything, and I'm not worried. Buck up. Get another drink or something and be more lifelike. You look licked before you start."

Wheatley stared at her. Then a little wildness grew in his smouldering eyes, and the limpness went out of his posture.

"By God, I will. I'll make a night of it, if it's my last, and remorse be damned." He strode over to Fraser and clapped him on the shoulder. "Shake 'em up, old top. I've a fire to quench."

Fraser's strong hands were operating the shaker with a vigor that caused his sturdy shoulders to shake. He cocked an eye toward Wheatley, but his glance slid past him to Barbara's sleek blond head. "Come to life, eh, what? Glad to see it. You were pretty boring company the past half hour, y'know. Now, Miss Rogers, a couple more shakes and we'll be ready. If one must drink cocktails, let's have them cold."

Randolph stole a glance at Burke and Mrs. St. Clair as they approached. She appeared perfectly self-possessed. At some remark of Burke's she smiled slightly; but she had the same faraway, detached look of hard purposefulness which Randolph had observed when on the upper landing.

Burke fixed his eyes on the little group by the cocktail wagon. He came up to it, rubbing his hands and fairly glowing. "Ah,

Stanley, my good fellow: we're just in time." He smiled expansively at Wheatley, Beryl and Mrs. St. Clair. "It is good of you all to honor my modest little place. We shall have a very happy evening I am sure."

He stepped back a pace, as Fraser commenced to fill the eight glasses arrayed before him, peered around and pretended to discover Barbara. His eyes sparkled; he bowed a little. "But, my dear, you are positively lovely this evening. Join us, please; and—ah—Mr. Rittenhouse. Of course you will wish to clink glasses with the charming Miss Rogers. I fear we have been a little remiss in our felicitations, and we shall drink to your happiness now."

Randolph turned to let Barbara precede him, saw that she was smiling, with her eyes fixed nowhere in particular. He looked up to meet Beryl's level gaze. She continued for a moment to look at him expressionlessly, then averted her glance. He moved slowly toward her, while Barbara stepped between Burke and Fraser.

Burke began fussily to pass each a glass, took up his own and found one still remaining. "But we are not all here," he cried. "Oh, yes—Gordon. We shall have to arouse him, I expect. But we need not wait."

Wheatley drank his cocktail at a swallow. He reached for the odd glass. "Let me have it. It's his own hard luck."

"Oh, yeah?" The portières parted and Gordon came through. "Thought that gong meant dinner, Burke. I came the shortest way."

"But of course; in a moment," Burke said. "And now—I propose, happiness to us all, my very dear friends, and the speedy fulfillment of the wish nearest each one's heart."

Gordon laughed roughly. "Better take it back, Burke. That'd mean off the short end for you."

Burke spluttered a little over his cocktail. His plump face grew red and his black eyes flashed venomously. Then he recovered and forced a laugh. "I shall not allow even you, Mr. Gordon, to spoil a perfect evening for me."

Randolph touched his glass lightly to Beryl's. "Smile" his lips formed. She gave him a little wry grimace, with a provocative curl of her lips. Then light grew in her dark eyes as she looked steadily up at him. "And thus we renew our vows, Jack, dear," she said, and hid her smile behind her glass.

The portières were opened bruskly by Martha, disclosing the white-clothed table beyond. As the others involuntarily looked that way, Randolph emptied his glass in the cocktail shaker that stood conveniently near his hand. Beryl soberly shook her head at him. "No pledge?" she said mockingly.

"All bonded and sealed," he told her. "But I'll mark this for another proof on better occasion," he added below the sound of general movement.

She glanced up at him under arched eyebrows, with the characteristic sidewise tilt of her lovely head. "Now that really sounds like old times," she said, and unconsciously sighed.

Burke minced over beside Mrs. St. Clair and extended his crooked arm. "Do me the honor, my dear Mrs. St. Clair. Come, gentlemen."

Fraser turned to Barbara with almost suspicious promptness. "My pleasure," he murmured.

Gordon grinned with his hard mouth. "Permit me, my dear Miss Wheatley."

"Go to hell," Wheatley advised him. "Let's see if Fraser left anything in the shaker. By Jove, he did," he added jubilantly as he filled his glass.

Beryl's hand sought Randolph's arm. Her head was close to his shoulder. "How can we ever keep up this ghastly farce!" she murmured. "I thought I had no nerves, but I want to scream and run out in the open, anywhere."

"Better not. Slocum's out there, with a dog and a gun."

"You saw him?"

"Uh—huh. Gave him one of your cigarettes."

"You didn't tell me."

"Didn't have time."

They crossed the threshold. Burke had seated Mrs. St. Clair at the further end of the long table and was obviously waiting. Barbara and Fraser stood at one side. He was laughing heartily at some remark between them.

"Don't forget—swim in the morning," Randolph said, in confidential tone. "I'll get you up."

"I wish it was morning," she murmured with little movement of her lips.

Gordon and Wheatley came in behind them.

Burke advanced along the table, dispensing a smirk of humble beneficence from side to side, but refraining to look directly at Barbara. He paused with his hands on the back of the end chair.

"The host's privilege," he said in the manner of a toastmaster's address. He wore carefully pressed, spotless white flannel trousers and blue worsted coat which, open and without vest, showed a pleated shirt studded with overly large diamonds beneath a bat wing bow tie. There was about him the odor of lavender water and scented talcum. His jowls were freshly shaven and powdered, with flakes still visible in the attempt to ameliorate the dark welts that were pouches below his eyes. "Beauty at both sides of me—and of course, Mrs. St. Clair"— with a little bow—"opposite me as well. Miss St. Clair, if you please, at my right; and, Miss Rogers, if you will be so kind, here at my left. Thank you.

"Mr. Rittenhouse, beside Miss St. Clair, if you please. Stanley, you rogue, you would dispute my claim to Miss Rogers' attention; and Mr. Wheatley and Mr. Gordon—yes, of course; you will keep Mrs. St. Clair amused I trust.

"So here we are." He beamed to right and left. "A very rough thorn between two lovely roses, my dears."

"You got that quote wrong, Burke," Gordon said. "It's a dicky bird with a coupla wrens."

Barbara laughed outright; then checked it with a little gasp at the end. "What did you put in that one, Mr. Fraser, besides gin?"

Fraser chuckled. "A bit of all right, eh? But you'll have to blame Miss Rogers if it was a trifle steep. I *might* have been looking at her when I poured and she's quite distracting, y' know."

"Yes, I know," Barbara said a little mechanically, as she selected from the *hors d'œuvres* which Martha offered her.

Burke leaned toward her solicitously. "But surely you'll try the caviar. Such a little mite, and you so strong."

Barbara managed a smile, without looking at him directly. "Thanks. This is only the beginning and I'm sure there is much to come."

"And I am so anxious that you should like it," he said, in a slightly lowered tone. "A confession: You see I had you in mind when I ordered from the caterer's in the city. I did not know your taste but I speculated with what I thought might please you."

He twisted to his right as Martha returned to serve Randolph. "The Berncastler Doktor, Martha, as soon as possible. Is the champagne well iced?"

Abruptly, without turning her body, Barbara moved her knees until the nearer one touched Randolph. He felt its slight trembling.

12

MRS. ST. CLAIR said: "Oh, no, no; no more champagne, please, Martha. Mr. Burke, I can't see you very well, you're such a long distance away. Please tell Martha, no more." She laughed, and it grew upon her. "It's so funny. Mr. Gordon has been telling me such a funny story. And he speaks so queerly. I don't know when I have laughed so much." She touched her eyes with a small lace handkerchief. "Oh, dear."

"That's nothing," Gordon assured her. "I know a lots worse 'n that. Hey, Marty. Don't pass me up like that. Some more of my wine."

Wheatley shook his head; rubbed a hand across his brow. "Your wine, Gordon? How y' get that way. Tha's our host— down there. Rosh Burke."

"Huh! I'm payin' for it, ain't I?"

Burke cleared his throat. His eyes were a little watery; perspiration beaded his forehead and made small globules of moisture on his reddened face.

"I shall tell you a little story of my profession," he said a bit pompously. His voice was steady and resonant. "You reminded me of it, my dear Mrs. St. Clair."

"Oh, good. I know it'll be funny. Ha, ha, ha! Oh, why do I laugh so!"

"Bite your lip," Gordon told her.

"Really? Will that help?"

"Uh-huh."

"This happened in Kentucky," Burke resumed. "A circuit

judge and a prominent attorney were to appear in a case some distance from Louisville where they resided. The evening of their departure they were wined and dined. In the compartment of their train they discovered several magnums of champagne awaiting them. Calling in one or two friends they passed the night in poker and the consumption of the wine.

"On their arrival at their destination in the morning both were exceedingly worse for their sleepless night of imbibing. The attorney turned to the judge and said, 'Yuh surely aren't goin' to hold coht this mornin', suh?'

" 'Jus' same as ushual; jus' same as ushual.' 'Well,' answered the attorney, 'if yuh can hold coht, I reckon I can 'pear.'

"Court was convened and the judge, weaving as he stood, rapped sharply for order, then slumped into his chair, resting his elbow on the bench and holding his head fairly steady in his hand. The attorney had many legal volumes spread before him, opened one or two at random and commenced his address.

"Almost immediately the judge's gavel pounded. The judge gazed in the general direction of the attorney. 'Mr. So-and-so,' he said, 'I must ask yuh to speak louder. The coht can't hear you.' 'Hah,' called the attorney. 'Your Honor's got nothing on me. I can't *see* yuh.'"

"Excellent!" said Barbara and clapped her hands.

Burke beamed upon her. "You liked it, my dear?"

Barbara smiled warmly across at Fraser; then, with her lips still parted, turned squarely around to Randolph. Her eyes, behind half closed lids, were cool and questioning.

"Make you a bet, Burke," Gordon called from his end of the table.

"On what?" Burke said a little sharply.

"That was the cleanest story you ever told."

Burke winced a little. "It seems, Mr. Gordon," he said slowly, "I must constantly remind you of the ladies present."

"But not me," Fraser said heartily. His florid face was very flushed. He smiled at Beryl beside him, then turned his glance to Barbara and his eyes grew bright. "These American beauties." He sighed. "I like my England, but I shall greatly miss them."

"Going abroad soon, Fraser?" Randolph asked. He was sitting very erect but his head appeared unsteady. The strong fingers of one hand toyed with the stem of his wine glass.

"Righto. Sailin' next week."

"What's that?" Burke asked quickly.

"But you knew it, Ross."

"Not at all. You can't leave now." His tone was sharp and he was frowning angrily.

Fraser tossed off the rest of his champagne, pushed his glass out and nodded to Martha. His glance returned to Burke.

"Goin' just the same, old chap. Booked for Wednesday."

Burke leaned a hand on the table, bent a little toward him. "You have matters to settle with me first you know."

Fraser looked at him steadily, a little insolently, perhaps, and with an expression of complete assurance.

"You'll find things quite in order. Webley will take over."

"Oh, no." Burke seemed momentarily to have forgotten the others. He had drunk considerable but now his eyes were bright and hard. "You can't get away with it, Fraser. Don't think for a moment you are going to walk out on me with a cool half million. If you're ready to assign that over to me you can get out."

A peculiar gleam grew in Fraser's pale blue eyes, destroying every vestige of easy good-nature. "There's nothing to talk about, Burke. You haven't any legitimate claim to that, any more than you have to the stuff of the chap that Webley phoned about."

Burke laughed harshly. His face, mottled with anger, was most unpleasant. "Don't fool yourself. I'll take it, and leave you as broke as when you landed, an English gentleman on the bum and on the make. You're forgetting certain things, Fraser, if you think for a moment you can skip out on me and take the swag with you."

"Swag may apply to you, Burke," Fraser said hotly, "but it's not the name for what I've put aside these past few years. I'll tell you something if you don't know it. What is mine I jolly well take and you can bring on your whole flotilla of punks."

"Oh, Mr. Burke," Mrs. St. Clair called. She laughed a little giddily. "I never did understand business, and if the gentlemen are going to talk business I think the ladies should leave them to their cordials, no?"

Burke recovered himself with a start and a little display of confusion as he turned to Barbara. He forced a laugh. "Your pardon, my dear... Confound you, Stanley, you know how excitable I am these days over business discussions. Ah, me; I had hoped I had left them all behind me. But surely, Mrs. St. Clair, you are not leaving us so early."

"But it is not early, Mr. Burke. The dinner has been marvelous. I don't see how you managed it so far from the city. If you will excuse me I believe I shall retire now. My head, you know." She came to her feet, and hesitated uncertainly.

The others rose. As Randolph stood up he stumbled a little

against his chair and swayed perceptibly. He was smiling, without looking at anyone in particular. Barbara glanced at him with a little dismay. From across the table Beryl regarded him coldly from under lowering brows. As his glance swept toward her she looked away and her lip curved slightly with an expression of disdain.

Mrs. St. Clair laughed. "Gerald," she said to Wheatley, "be a good boy and give me your arm. I feel quite giddy. Isn't it silly?"

Gordon watched Wheatley's attempt at least to make a show of support. "Gerald," he said, trying to make his husky voice sweet, "don't you want me to take your other arm?"

Wheatley half turned, knocked a chair aside and gave up the effort. "You steer, Mrs. St. Clair," he mumbled, "and I'll push."

Mrs. St. Clair paused as she reached the end of the table and Wheatley perforce stopped with her. "Barbs," she said, without looking at her daughter, "why don't you and Beryl sit out in the living-room and wait for the gentlemen? Oh, Mr. Burke," she said, not waiting for the reply Barbara showed no intention of making, "you promised me a fascinating book with which to read myself to sleep. Have you forgotten it, and is it handy?"

Burke turned to Barbara. He spoke lightly, but the look he bent upon her was significant. "And what do you think, Miss St. Clair—do you approve that I should give her this?"

Barbara was facing partly toward Randolph. Her eyes raised swiftly to his, a little frightened, appealing. The fixed smile on his face did not change. Her glance swept Beryl whose attention at the moment was distracted. Barbara stood with eyes downcast to the table, under their long, curved lashes, her cheeks flushed. "I suppose so," she said, a little tremulously. "Why, yes, of course."

"Thank you, my dear," he breathed. "It will be no trouble at all, Mrs. St. Clair. I'll go up with you."

"You are very kind," she said. "Ah, good-night, Mr.—er—Rittenhouse. Oh, don't tell me you have been taking too much of Mr. Burke's champagne. Or is it that I just seem to see you wobbling? Anyway it makes me, a poor weak woman, feel better. Mr. Burke is so hospitable. It is rare that one finds such freedom from restraint in such well ordered surroundings. There, that's quite a speech. Come, Gerald."

A moment after the three had gone, Beryl and Barbara passed into the living-room, walked slowly to the fireplace and paused there, conversing in tones that did not reach the three men. From where Randolph stood, they were in his view. He looked at them uncertainly, as if undecided whether he should join them; then moved up his chair and reseated himself at the table, with one arm resting heavily on it.

Fraser had already resumed his seat and was busily stuffing his pipe, his frowning eyes fixed on his occupation. Gordon brought his refilled champagne glass and took a chair beside Fraser. Except for a deeper red in his cheeks, he showed not the slightest indication that he had taken his full share of the copious services of liquor and wine that had been a distinguishing phase of Burke's long dinner. He studied Randolph closely a few moments, with a partly puzzled, half amused expression, then turned to Fraser.

"The Big Fellow's caught you stepping outa turn, huh?"

Fraser moved his head slowly around, looked at Gordon coldly while he drew flame into his tobacco. "I expect you wouldn't understand it, old chap, so why speak of it?"

"You're wrong there, Fraser," said Gordon. "Ross Burke don't pitch any curves I don't know. Say, listen. He's fed me a fast one and I ain't got an out by myself." He glanced quickly toward the open doorway and slightly lowered his tone. "How 'bout you and me seein' if we can make a deal together?"

"Not int'rested, really." Fraser puffed steadily on his pipe and his eyes narrowed, got a little ugly. "I never mix in Burke's business, Gordon. Have my own, y'know, and that's well enough for me."

Gordon said roughly: "Who you foolin'? Everybody knows you're only frontin' for Burke. That adds up you're runnin' one end of his business for him."

Fraser's eyes blazed, then he shrugged.

"You're mixing things a bit, old fellow. I said I have nothing to do with his affairs. If he happens to be the attorney for my company that's something else, see?"

Randolph raised his head from his cupped hand. "I'm interested in investments." His voice was a little thick and he spoke slowly. "Tell me something, Fraser. If I should send you some stock, say in place of cash, with an idea of buying other securities, who would be responsible for the account—you or Burke?"

Fraser looked at him closely with sudden suspicion; but Randolph's expression was wholly casual. "I'll answer that, Mr. Rittenhouse, in this way: A short while ago I was the sole head. Lately I have been making changes in the organization with the idea of withdrawing and returning to England. These haven't been entirely affected yet. At the moment my first assistant, a capable chap by the name of Webley, is the nominal head, although Burke has been talking of buying in for the control, which naturally is agreeable to me."

"I guess I don't understand very clearly," Randolph said

and smiled. "Would I look to you or this fellow—what's his name—or Burke?"

Fraser laughed. "It's quite the same. I'll be altogether out of it first of the week; but if you wish to open an account it will be taken care of in the regular way."

"Now let me tell you something," Gordon said. "If you put anything in where Burke can get his hands on it, you'd better kiss it good-by."

"Oh, I say, old chap," Fraser said quickly, "you're putting it on rather thick, no?"

Gordon laughed nastily. "Some of us may be drunk, Fraser, but we're not all deaf. We heard Burke clearly enough. What 're the odds you get yours?"

A vein stood out on Fraser's forehead. Like Gordon, he was compactly built with solid chest and shoulders. He took the pipe from his mouth with slow deliberation and swung around to face Gordon. "I'll advise you to keep your damn' nose out of my business, Gordon."

Gordon started to make an angry reply, but Randolph broke in as if he was not aware of the sudden tension. "Well, s'pose I had stuff already in, Fraser—just for example—and changed my mind and wanted to take it out. Who'd I go to then?"

Fraser turned to face him, his anger forgotten. "Is this something actual, Mr. Rittenhouse, or just a hypothetical question?"

"Wouldn't make any difference, would it? Answer 'd be the same."

Fraser lowered frowning eyes to the table, tracing an idle pattern on the cloth with his pipe stem. Abruptly he glanced toward the doorway in an attitude of listening, then looked back at Randolph. "I'll tell you frankly, Mr. Rittenhouse," he said in low tone, "I'm really out of it now. That is, I have signed all papers and they're in Burke's hands awaiting his acceptance. He's your man, if your case is not hypothetical."

"Like I said," Gordon growled, "kiss 'em good-by. You couldn't pry anything loose from him short of blasting."

Randolph smiled at him blandly, and turned his gaze slowly back to Fraser. "But until he accepts, it would be you, no?"

Fraser shook his head and a puzzled look grew in his eyes. "I still don't understand this, but I expect you're right. Anything specific on your mind? I can't recall your name on our books. Perhaps you have something in under another name, eh?" He leaned back in his chair and his glance wandered interestedly over Randolph's broad shoulders and one big, loosely-knotted fist resting on the table. "I say, Rittenhouse, you weren't by any chance in our office today?"

"Who—me?" Randolph said a little stupidly. "Why you know Miss Rogers and I motored up from the country today."

Fraser's eyes fell to his half-filled champagne glass. He took it up and drank it slowly. He looked toward the further end of the table where Martha was just finishing clearing the last of the glasses and cups. "Er—Martha; is there any wine left in that cooler? Be a good girl and let us have it, no? Thanks. And then skidoo—I think you say it—before there are any more orders. You've done splendidly and enough."

Martha took the dripping bottle from the melted ice in the cooler, wrapped a napkin about it and brought it to Fraser. As she passed behind the two men she looked hard at Randolph. If he was aware of it, he did not raise his sleepy eyes. She went around the end of the table, taking up the coffee service. She paused by Randolph, bending a little over him. Her elbow pressed his shoulder. "Can I bring you more coffee, Mr. Rittenhouse?" she asked.

Randolph turned his head, smiled up at her. "Thank you," he said thickly. "Guess I've taken all of everything I should."

Fraser said, "That's all, Martha. If we want anything more I'll get it."

Her elbow again nudged Randolph before she straightened and walked out. Gordon watched her going with interested eyes; then shook his head, finished his glass and passed it toward Fraser. "Come on. I'm payin' for this tomorrow."

A step sounded lightly in the adjoining room. Randolph slowly turned his head. Burke crossed the opening with his quick, mincing step, and went on to the fireplace where the two girls were still standing, idly smoking. What he said was too low for the men at the table to catch. He bowed, stepped backward a pace then came quickly to the doorway, turned, waved a hand and drew the portières together.

He came to the table with a jaunty air, rubbing his hands in his characteristic gesture, his plump face wreathed in smiles. The effect of his liberal potions was observable less in his manner of the moment than in his wide, staring eyes, the hectic flush in his cheeks and a certain looseness of his sensuous lips. He appeared, too, emotionally excited, whereas Fraser gave the impression of having lost much of his surface urbanity with glimpses of a hard, somewhat sullen nature beneath.

Burke leaned both hands on the table and bent forward a little on their support as if it was a habitual pose. He turned his smile upon Randolph. "My dear Mr. Rittenhouse, I trust you have found our modest dinner satisfactory? But, my dear fellow, your glass is empty."

"Had enough. Thanks."

"You are quite sure? A cigar—no? Oh, I remember, you do not smoke. But we shall have our cordial shortly; then we can rejoin the ladies." He shook his head with mock seriousness at Fraser. "Ah, Stan, you should not have baited me to our little spat. It was not nice before our guests." He sighed and seated himself. "Sorry if I was hasty. We'll have no trouble settling all those matters, but at the proper time."

Gordon laughed gratingly. " 'Old settle 'em Burke.' "

Burke ignored him. "Isn't it strange," he said, "how dull we men become without our charming companions! You know, I was planning that Martha should entertain us a bit. She dances superbly."

Fraser said a little gruffly, "I think she's done enough. We've been at it a couple or three hours."

"Yes, our delightful dinner was prolonged more than ordinarily; and I think our friend Mr. Rittenhouse is becoming a little sleepy—no?"

Randolph started, with a slight jerk of his nodding head. He smiled a little sheepishly.

Burke frowned sympathetically. "Stanley, won't you choose our cordial? Shall I ring for Martha?"

Fraser aroused himself from the meditative silence into which he had lapsed, knocked the ashes from his pipe and stood up. His eyes, fixed steadily on Burke, seemed to question him. "Not at all. I know where everything is. The poor gal must be fagged. Er—Burke, we could talk a bit over them, no? Mr. Rittenhouse has raised an int'resting question."

"Mr. Rittenhouse? Why, yes; of course."

"And that other matter—my own affairs; do you want to

push that further, or do you consider it settled, according to the books, of course?"

Burke smiled. "My dear fellow, whatever you can prove is your own, I naturally would not question. But let's get on."

Randolph had been looking from one to the other owlishly, as if the talk confused him. He watched, without interest, as Fraser walked the length of the room and went out the service exit. He acted as if the drinks which had been offered him so liberally were proving too much for his resistance.

Burke smiled with great good-nature. "Trouble with these pleasant dinners, we all take more than we realize. I am ordinarily abstemious but tonight is an occasion and I feel, as they say, as if I had a skinful. Just a nightcap, and then—sweet dreams."

Gordon grinned across at Randolph. "Guess you can't take it, Big Fellow. Like everything else, you gotta go in trainin' for it. Burke and me now, we been in hard trainin' for some time."

Randolph said, speaking as if he was having trouble with his tongue, " 's fact, I'm not much used to this." He made an effort and sat with his shoulders more erect, but his head swayed slightly from side to side. Gordon winked at Burke who did not seem to see it.

The service door opened and Martha stepped in, holding it to let Fraser through. He came down the table with a half-dozen glasses in one hand, a squat bottle of Benedictine in the other. He set the bottle before his place on the cloth; then with his free hand took the glasses one by one from the other, arranged them in a row, and commenced to fill them.

Martha was still standing beside the door. Burke glanced at her interrogatively. "Steve is here," she said tonelessly. "Do you want to see him?"

"Ah—yes. Send him in, please."

She pushed the door away from her and without going out, nodded. Slocum came past her and strode toward Burke. He had his hat on. His face was dark and surly. A cartridge belt was strapped around his waist beneath his opened coat. The butt of a heavy pistol showed in its holster, worn over his right thigh.

Martha caught up a small tray, came down the opposite side of the table and stopped behind Fraser. From under down-drawn brows her eyes were fixed steadily on Randolph. Fraser looked around at her, and she lowered her gaze to him. "Do you wish me to serve them?"

"Take these to the young ladies, there's a good girl."

He took up the two glasses at the left of the line and passed them to her. She waited with tray extended. He looked up at her again, with raised eyebrows.

"For Mr. Rittenhouse."

Fraser cocked one eye at her, but her face was impassive.

"Don't bother," he said. "I'll just hand it across. Don't mind, old fellow, do you?"

With his right hand he took what had been the third glass from the left and reached across to set it before Randolph. Randolph said, "Thanks," and closed his big hand around it. Martha flashed him a quick look, then went through the portières.

Slocum came around to stand behind Burke's chair, and Burke fidgeted, finally turned his chair half around. He said a little querulously, "Don't ever get behind me, Slocum. You ought to know I can't bear it."

Gordon, watching him, grinned sarcastically, and Slocum, catching it, gave him a hard look. Gordon laughed.

"Getting nerves, Burke? 'bout time, I guess."

Burke frowned and twisted his head to glance up at Slocum.

"Everything's quiet, Boss," Slocum said in his deep, rough voice. "Want anything special?"

"Got the dogs out?"

"Of course."

Burke smiled. "Fine, Steve. I was just asking. That will be all, then. And, Steve," as Slocum, with another dark look at Gordon, started to leave, "you won't have to come to the house again tonight—unless, of course, I ring for you."

"All right," Slocum said surlily. "How 'bout Marty? She through yet?"

"I believe they're clearing up. Got to have everything out of the way for morning. If she's late, she can bunk in with Mary, I guess. But don't wait. Night."

Without replying Slocum left the room.

"Why all the artillery," Gordon growled, "or is it just a show?"
Burke said nothing.

Fraser passed two of the remaining three glasses to Gordon and Burke and took up his own. Martha came from the other room, paused expectantly and her eyes, now bright and hard, again sought Randolph's glance. Burke waved a pudgy hand at her. "We'll manage now, Martha. Nothing more tonight. It's late. I told Steve you could stay with Mary if you want to."

"I'm not tired, if you want anything more," she persisted.

"Nothing," Burke said a little sharply. "Thank you," he added.

Fraser watched her going, curiously, then, with the same expression, turned to glance at Burke.

Burke squared his chair to the table, took up his glass and

smiled at Randolph.

Fraser said: "Mr. Rittenhouse was asking me—ah, yes; your health, gentlemen."

As Randolph raised his glass, both Burke and Fraser were watching him, but when he tilted back his head and his glance seem to meet theirs, they looked away. He swallowed, lowered his hand wearily and, still holding the glass, let his elbow rest on his chair arm. With his left hand he fumbled for his napkin and wiped his lips. He shivered slightly. "Fine stuff, Fraser," he said thickly, "but pretty strong."

Gordon glanced quickly at Fraser and Burke, then looked curiously at Randolph. His eyes were sharp and wary.

Fraser said: "I was going to tell you something, Ross." He laughed. "Funny. Just what was it, Mr. Rittenhouse?"

Randolph looked at him dazedly. He raised his right hand slowly and set the glass on the table. It was three-quarters empty. He shook his head, passed the knuckles of one hand hard across his brow. "I can't—seem to remember," he mumbled in a barely audible tone.

Burke said, "Oh, well, let's not trouble now, Stan. We can talk about it in the morning."

Randolph gripped the table edge with both big hands, pushed his chair away from it. His eyes, through nearly closed lids, held a dazed, puzzled look. He shook his head again, hard. "What's matter with me!" he said gutturally. "Can't seem to see you fellows't all."

Suddenly he raised a fist and pounded on the table, so that the glasses jumped. His eyes came a little more open, looked wild and angry.

"By God, Fraser, you put something in that!"

"What's that?" Fraser said sharply. "What are you saying, Rittenhouse?"

Randolph struggled to unsteady legs. Still gripping the table edge, he turned his body and lurched ahead. Burke got hastily from his chair and moved backward beyond Fraser.

Sliding his hand along for support, Randolph came to the table end, tried to pass beyond it and stood swaying, his eyes staring straight before him. He looked punch drunk, shifting on his feet, his arms weakly raising a little, out but trying valiantly to keep up.

The portières parted, showing two blanched, dismayed faces; but Randolph seemed unable to see even that far. Fraser got up from his chair and stepped toward him. "Here let me have your arm, old fellow. You'll be all right. That last one was a bit too much, I expect."

"Damn you, Fraser," Randolph mouthed. "You fixed me. Get outa my way."

His right arm swept suddenly in a looping swing. It caught Fraser in the chest, sent him backward, crashing over his chair to the floor. He scrambled up with an oath. Gordon caught his arm. "Hold it!" he said sharply. "He'll drop in a minute."

"Won't drop," Randolph muttered. "Can't put me out. Nob'dy ever did."

He stood facing Fraser briefly, his chin sunk to his slightly raised left shoulder, left hand before him, his right held loosely across his body, in weak semblance of a fighter's posture. Then, turning slowly, he staggered to the portières, grasped one to save himself from falling and tore it from its fastening.

Lurching sidewise, he struck against the door-frame where he clung while he seemed to measure the distance to the stairway, with eyes that looked fixed and glassy.

The two girls, their faces white and strained, stood hesitantly, midway between him and the stairs. After one look at his face, Barbara moved slowly toward the foot, glancing backward over her shoulder. Beryl advanced toward him uncertainly, and Randolph, apparently discerning some figure before him, gave a weak gesture with his right hand.

"Don't touch me," he muttered, barely intelligibly. "Don't anyone touch me… gotta make… my corner."

He set his gaze on his goal, pushed away from his support and walking with feet far apart, staggered slowly across the floor. There was something magnificent and pathetic in his supreme effort to force his splendid muscles to obey the brain that now seemed numbing fast. Heart and will power, the fighter's persistence long after sensible volition, appeared all that still kept him on his feet.

Barbara mounted the stairs, glancing backward, while Beryl waited on the first step. The doorway, with its dismantled portière behind Randolph, framed Burke, Fraser and Gordon. Burke's face was frowning in mock concern. Fraser's expression was angry and sneering, while Gordon's eyes told nothing. Beryl's cheeks were flushed now with an angry red; her eyes blazing.

Randolph reached the newel post, caught it with one hand and pulled himself desperately up the first tread. His hand slid to the banister and drew him slowly onward and upward. Beryl slipped beside him, grasped his right arm and drew it around her young shoulders, holding to his waist.

"Come on!" she called clearly. "Keep going. Damn those hounds! We'll beat them yet. Up we go!"

With the help of his one hand and Beryl's support, Randolph dragged one leaden foot after the other from tread to tread. They reached the first landing, turned and passed slowly from the sight of the men who had not advanced beyond the doorway.

Steadily, with slight pauses between, Randolph's heavy footfalls groped upward, thumped irregularly in the corridor. Suddenly there was a crash as a door burst inward, followed almost immediately by a second loud thump as it was slammed heavily shut. A moment later another door closed with hardly less violence. There was no further sound.

Burke's face lost its look of fake concern. His eyes, avoiding Gordon, were crafty and leering as he glanced at Fraser.

13

SILENCE REIGNED THROUGHOUT the big lodge.

Near one end a shaded light showed Mrs. St. Clair sitting motionless in a deep chair beside her bed. Her windows were opened wide but a faint odor of burned paper still clung in the room. Her wide, staring eyes, fixed without focus on the opposite wall, were hard, a little triumphant. They held no worry. She sighed deeply, even as a slight smile curled her lips.

Rising, she sniffed the air; then extinguishing the light, retired.

At the opposite end of the lodge, a night lamp burned in the study part of Burke's enormous room. He came from the further end, noiselessly on slippered feet, in silken pajamas and robe. The faint scent of lavender and an expensive perfume accompanied his advance.

He walked to the corner of the study and turned the shade of the lamp so that all but a portion of the book shelves was in shadow. Then he stepped softly to the door, opened it a little, without sound, and put an ear to the crack. After a moment of listening, he closed it, returned to the night lamp and switched it off. He waited until his eyes should become accustomed to the dim illumination that filtered through the unshaded windows, then started slowly toward the opposite end, reaching a hand out carefully before him to avoid colliding with the numerous pieces of furniture.

Outside the night seemed hushed. A light cloud scum, that had arisen from the east, covered the sky, obscuring the outline of the three-quarter moon until its light was only a dim, diffused glow.

The monotonous, dry cheeping of crickets, the full-throated, guttural frog chorus when the moonlight was clear, had almost ceased. At times a light, vagrant breeze rustled the leaves and barely stirred the dark surface of the lake where the loons had long since fallen silent....

In Barbara's room a section of wall partitioning it from the huge chamber, opened on a crack that slowly widened to a rectangle. The room itself, with its closely drawn shades, was in comparatively greater darkness than the chamber beyond, so that a robed form was faintly visible in the frame of the opened secret doorway. It advanced a step, and the rectangle was again blanked.

Burke came slowly, cautiously forward, making his furtive way toward the bed that stood in the center of the room. He paused midway. Then a long, faint sigh, as of one partially awakened from slumber, broke upon his ears.

At once he commenced to speak in a low whisper, his tone slightly tremulous although evidently, as well as his words, calculated to be soothing.

"There, there; don't be alarmed. It's only Rossie. He wants to talk with you, to tell you how beautiful you are." As he spoke, he continued his careful advance until he reached the side of the bed. "Wait, my little rose petal. I'll just turn on this little light, so I can see your wonderful eyes, your glorious hair, your—"

The light switch clicked and a dim, colored glow rescued the room from its utter darkness.

"Good God!" burst hoarsely from Burke's lips.

He started back in disbelieving horror, his eyes wide, panic stricken.

Slowly from the bed rose Randolph's great shoulders, until he sat upright. One big hand drew across his eyes, then hard over his mouth, hiding his grin and checking the laugh that rose in his throat. His eyes, apparently dazed, gazed curiously at the intruder.

"What is this? What do you want?" he mumbled in peculiar tone.

"Damn!" broke uncontrollably from Burke. "What are you doing in this room, Rittenhouse? How *d'you* get here?"

"What's that—what's that?" Randolph muttered, still a little stupidly. He shook his head, glanced around him; then his gaze returned to Burke. He appeared to come more awake. "What am I doing here? Sleeping, of course, until you woke me up. Why shouldn't I be here? What do you mean anyway?" His eyes, frowning, began to study Burke closely, as if with slowly dawning comprehension.

"Why—why," Burke stuttered. "This isn't the room assigned to you. I—I—er—" His eyes wavered from Randolph's steady stare, commenced to dart about him as if he sought a way to retreat and the words to make it plausible.

One of Randolph's hands shot out and clamped on Burke's wrist. "I'm beginning to get a little of this now, Burke." His tone grew hard. "It's beginning to come back to me. That damnable cur of yours, Fraser, fed me dope downstairs. Yeah; I remember it now, although it is like a dream. You thought you could put me out; but you didn't—not down there. I remember coming up here, climbing those stairs. I fell through a door. That partly waked me." Still holding Burke in spite of his futile struggle to pull away, he glanced over at the room door, then nodded.

"Look at it. That's where I fell through. See—the door is

splintered by the lock. If this isn't my room, it's your fault, or Fraser's, I'm here. That crash brought me to enough to get to the bed. Later I came out of it, found my bag here and got into my pajamas. If this isn't my room, whose is it?"

"All—all right, Mr. Rittenhouse. I'm sorry if I disturbed you. But no one put dope into your drink. You're wrong there. You drank too much and probably aren't used to it. Let me go now."

Randolph's grip was as unbreakable as that of a vise, He swung his feet from the bed until he was sitting on it.

"You're lying, Burke. You know damned well I was doped. But we'll let that go now." His hand twisted a little, and Burke commenced to writhe. His face grew red with anger and mortification, while fear commenced to dawn in his eyes.

"Let me go; let me go, damn it. You've no right to hold me like that."

"Just a moment, Burke." Randolph's voice was ugly. "Just whose room did you think this was, and what did you mean by coming into it? Come on; speak up. Damn you. If you believed Miss Rogers was here, by God, I'll wring your filthy neck."

"No, no—please, Mr. Rittenhouse. You're hurting my wrist. I swear I didn't think she was here. I—I wanted to speak with Fraser. Something I forgot to tell him. Yes; that was it. Now let me go."

"You're lying by the clock," Randolph told him fiercely. "Wherever Fraser's room is, I know this isn't it. It can't be. Fraser was near the end of the hall. I didn't go that far from the stairs. If it isn't mine, it must be near mine. One of the girls'—Burke, you damned dirty cur!"

With a sudden motion, he drew Burke to him, twisted him until he lay flat across his knees. His big right hand rose, came down hard, with open palm and a resounding thwack. Again and again, it rose and fell; then his fingers closed and the knuckles beat, until Burke, squirming and struggling, cried for mercy.

Rising suddenly, Randolph lifted Burke with him, set him on his feet, then grasping his shoulder, whirled him around and bent his head close to Burke's.

"I don't know why I don't kill you," he whispered tensely. He glared at him a moment, then pushed Burke from him so that he staggered backward.

Burke stepped further away, limping toward the wall.

"You'll pay for this," he croaked. "I've got something on you that'll make you pay plenty. You can't treat me—me, Ross Burke, like this, damn you. I'll get Slocum over." His hand groped behind him, pressing on the wall. "He'll shoot the—"

Randolph crossed the intervening space in a swift stride. His hand closed hard on Burke's shoulder.

"Get this into your head, you beast," he hissed. "I'm not afraid of Slocum and all his guns. I'm wide awake now, no thanks to you. If I hear anyone coming into this place tonight, I'll get into your room first and I'll kill you with my bare hands. Now—do you call Slocum or don't you?"

"No, no. I won't; I swear I won't. We're both—a little excited. Let's—let's forget all about—this—tonight."

"It's up to you, Burke," Randolph said grimly. He withdrew his hand, stepped back a pace. "You say you have something on me. All right. You can spill it tomorrow. And I have something for you to think of too. I'll tell you about it tomorrow. You can go as far as you like on your end, but if I get the idea you won't play square with me on mine, well, it will be just too bad for you, Mr. Ross Burke, and you can take that to your slimy bed and chew over it."

Burke's fingers found the catch and the concealed door opened sufficiently for him to pull it wide. His eyes on Randolph were still fearful and a little puzzled.

"We'll talk matters over tomorrow, Mr. Rittenhouse. I—I think we were both a little wrong tonight. You were mistaken—about that other thing, and I don't blame you if you really thought you were right. Let's not say anything about it. Our party is too pleasant to break up on a misunderstanding. Good night, Mr. Rittenhouse." He spoke more calmly, and even attempted a smile, but his eyes, as he stepped slowly backward through the doorway, were venomous.

Randolph waited, without replying, until the door was closed, then returned to his bed. For several minutes he sat on the edge, at times grinning broadly; then frowning in deep thought.

After a time, he switched off the light and turned in.

Some hours later he awakened to broad daylight. He rose immediately, consulted his watch and found that it lacked a few minutes of seven. From his bag he dug out a swim suit. Discarding his pajamas, he drew on the one-piece bathing suit over his hard muscled body. He found a light robe and put that on.

He stood easily, erect, clear-eyed; he looked to be in the pink of condition. His face, with its good forehead, straight nose, firm, generous mouth and strong chin, would have been rugged if it were not for its fine modeling which gave to the whole an impression of refined strength. It was not a handsome face, as types go, but it was distinctly wholesome.

Randolph eased the broken door open and stepped into the corridor. A glance in either direction showed that it was otherwise deserted. No sound of movement in any of the rooms came to his ears. Crossing the hall obliquely he tapped lightly at the door to which the woman Martha had first directed him.

Almost immediately a voice called softly, "Is that you—Jack?"

Randolph put his mouth close to the door edge. "Time for the swim," he said in low tone. "How soon?"

"In two jiffies," Beryl's voice answered close to the door. "Will you wait?"

"Right here."

He heard the creak of springs, the murmur of Barbara's voice and crossed the corridor to lean, with folded arms, against the door-frame. His glance sought Burke's closed door and he grinned; then, as he continued to regard it, his eyes grew hard and relentless.

In a surprisingly few moments he heard the latch click in the opposite door, and as he turned his head the steely glint went from his eyes; a smile grew in its place and twisted his lips. The door opened and Beryl appeared, rosy and radiant in her dark beauty. Barbara, following close behind, sent a quick, almost frightened glance toward the door at the end of the corridor. Both girls, in their tightly drawn silken robes, looked slender and small beside Randolph's big frame. Each took one of his arms and side by side they went softly along the corridor and descended the stairs.

At the foot, a sound at their right attracted them. They looked in that direction. Martha, on a chair, was engaged in hooking up the rent portière. As her glance met theirs, her eyes were inscrutable, but a little irrepressible smile tugged at her lips.

She beckoned to Randolph, and the three went over. Martha stepped from her chair, glanced once behind her.

"Did you beat him up!" she asked Randolph in low tone. "I heard the ruckus in the night. I hope you gave him plenty."

"Just a little first aid treatment," Randolph drawled grinning.

"You should've broken his damn' neck," she said in a fierce whisper. "He's had it coming to him a long while. But watch your step today and tonight, mister. He hasn't seen Steve yet, and I don't know what he'll tell him; but I do know he isn't easy to lick."

She turned and pointed where Randolph's chair had been pushed back from the table. "I've been scrubbing an hour to get that liquor stain out of the rug. The Benedictine sticks like hell."

Her eyes sought Randolph's with a look of admiration. "I'll hand it to you. I was peeking through the door and you had me plumb fooled. I tried to warn you off that dope but you wouldn't see me. It was only when I found that mess this morning I knew you'd ditched it." She shrugged rounded shoulders. "It was a hell of a job, but it's worth it."

Her glance turned to the two girls with open frankness.

"You, and him," with a nod at Randolph, "are the only decent people who've been here for months." Her glance went once more behind her, toward the closed kitchen door. "I wish to God," she said in a whisper, "you could get me out of this mess. I can take care of myself but I want to get clear here."

Beryl tugged at Randolph's arm.

"You're square as a brick, Martha," he said. "Wait and see what comes off tonight. Things might be different then."

She looked at him keenly; then nodded.

"What do you wish for breakfast?" she asked coolly, in normal tone. "I'll serve it on the porch when you are ready."

"Anything," Randolph said, "that sounds like grapefruit or a melon, bacon and eggs, toast and coffee." He turned to Beryl and Barbara. "Right?"

"As rain," Beryl answered. "I'm starved already. Come on."

An odor of stale smoke and liquor still hung about the big living-room. They went out into the clear fresh air, down the steps and along the path toward the boat-house. The girls wore bathing slippers; Randolph was barefooted and kept to the grass.

Away from the house Barbara glanced half backward over one shoulder. "My Gawd, what a nightmare last night!" She looked up at Randolph with a light deep in her violet eyes. "I could beat you for the scare you gave me. Why couldn't you have told us?"

Randolph grinned. "Sorry, but it might have spoiled everything. You two had to act natural or it would have been no go. But get the taste out of your mouth now—Barbs. Isn't this a honey of a morning!"

They turned and stepped out on the ledge, at one side of the boathouse, that sloped abruptly to the water.

"What I'd like to know," Beryl drawled, with a little twist to her lips, "is how that very attractive female has become so friendly with you and so suddenly."

"Judas Priest!" Randolph exclaimed. "Would you believe it!" He turned suddenly, rested his hands on Beryl's shoulders and kissed her swiftly. "Engaged and already its privileges overlooked."

"Let's go in," Beryl said meekly. Rich color rose in her cheeks. "Do we take off from here—Jack?"

"It looks deep enough, but a pretty tough leap. I'll try it. You better get down to the edge." He slipped off his robe as he spoke, eying the contour of the ledge and the water.

"Whew!" Barbara whistled. "What have we here, anyway—a Pharnese Hercules?"

"Nuh-uh," Beryl murmured. "Cleaner built. Mercury. Say"—she turned, with her robe half off one shoulder—"what are you anyway, a professional something or other?"

Randolph turned from his survey of the water to glance at her soberly. "A professional nitwit, I'd say, from the way I've forgotten things this morning." He grinned suddenly. "But I assure you it won't happen again."

"I think," she said, "you'd better take your suicide leap. But for heaven's sake be careful. Something tells me we still need you."

He stepped back a couple of paces, and with a swift run sprang outward in a jacknife. Then arms and legs whipped upward and he cut the water cleanly. He swam under water for a score of yards, then shot suddenly upward, twisting as he rose. A dark and a blond head were almost upon him, coming up fast with an easy crawl.

He waited, then matched his strokes to theirs, with one on either side of him. At a hundred yards out, he called, "Turn!" and almost with one accord the three twisted in the water like sleek otters and headed back.

"Better take the boathouse," he advised. "That rock will be slippery."

Beryl turned her face toward him, for her breath. Her dark eyes were gleaming. "Race you!" she challenged.

He nodded, and both girls went into faster stroke.

Randolph lagged behind until the distance was three-quarters covered. Then he shot into his speed, swept up beside them and the three touched the platform together.

Randolph pulled himself up, got to his feet; then reached down, grasped Beryl's hands and lifted her lightly to the planking. He drew Barbara up, and the two girls sat there, panting a little, idly paddling the water.

"Gee!" Barbara exclaimed. "That was gorgeous. What a place, if it wasn't for that filthy old toad that owns it."

Randolph was looking intently into the water. "Curious," he said, "how deep it is here. Wait; I want to try it."

He sprang off the platform, feet first, body straight. He sank rapidly, turned and paddled downward. He was up in a moment, resting one hand on the platform edge. "Must be all of twenty feet." He drew himself up to sit beside them. "How's the old appetite now?"

"Starved!" Barbara said.

"Mind getting our robes?" Beryl asked. "Those binoculars may be up at the house now, and I don't feel like parading for his benefit."

Randolph raised himself on his hands, got easily to his feet. He shadow-boxed a little as he skipped lightly up the platform. His skin was glowing; his eyes bright.

He picked the three robes from the ledge and balled them together in one hand, but in place of returning by the ledge he slipped cautiously to the water's edge, let himself in easily, holding the robes high as he swam with one arm.

As he rounded the corner and appeared at the open end, Barbara started slightly; then laughed. "Why did you ever come that way?" she asked.

Randolph tossed up the robes, drew himself after them.

"Was curious to see how abruptly that ledge dips. You can't wade out five feet."

He shook out the robes, held out Beryl's yellow one. She smiled up at him, turned and extended her arms for the sleeves. He performed the same service for Barbara. Both were perfect specimens of healthy young womanhood; Barbara almost boyish, with her straight legs, square shoulders and flat chest; Beryl slightly more developed, a symphony of curves from her full throat to her daintily rounded ankles. Randolph slipped into his own robe, and they started on.

Barbara sighed. "Oh, if it was only the three of us, this would be great. I'm fair starved, but I hate going back up there."

"We've got by so far," Randolph reminded her. "I think we'll manage it the rest of the way. Today should be all clean fun. So keep that bad taste out of your mouth, Barbs."

"Righto, Jack." Her eyes danced, then got sober. Her hand rested lightly on his arm. "But don't ever imagine I'll forget what you did for me last night."

"Come on, come on. We're not thinking of that any more."

"But do we have to see the rest of them?" Beryl asked. "Why can't we get away by ourselves—up the lake somewhere?"

"Sure; but it seems to me I have a little business matter to discuss first."

"Oh, that." Beryl frowned. "I don't believe that is so very important."

Randolph turned his head to look at her. She met his glance steadily. "You sure about that?" he asked.

"I am almost sure," she murmured.

They came to the porch, and Randolph suggested they go around and enter by the rear. At the back steps, Barbara paused.

"Tell your girl friend to set our table for just three," she said in low tone. "I don't want to see my mother this morning. I don't want ever to see her again, but I suppose I must."

"Attagirl," Randolph said. "Chin up all the way now. I'm supposed to be mad, disgraced, chagrined or something; but when I look at you two I just can't be. You're swell medicine."

Beryl laughed. "On to breakfast. I'm just disgracefully hungry." She skipped lightly up the steps.

At her door she left Barbara go in first, then turned her head to look at Randolph over her shoulder. "When you're ready, tap," she whispered. "We'll hurry. And—last night—you fooled me too, for a little while. I'm sorry for what I thought then. Forgive me? You didn't deserve it."

He leaned closer; her head raised a little but did not turn away. Their lips met.

Her face was sober as she looked at him; her eyes as well, except for a light in their dark depths. "I am very nearly certain now," she whispered, and slipped behind the door.

14

THEIRS WAS THE only table set on the porch. They were just finishing their coffee, and the girls had lighted cigarettes when the screen door to the living-room was opened and Gordon and Fraser appeared.

"Morning, folks," Gordon said tonelessly. "You beat us to it." His manner was strained.

Fraser looked at the girls, his glance resting longer on Barbara. He tried to put a smile on his face, but it was plain that his mood was sober. And it was equally obvious that he was making an attempt to disguise some embarrassment. He greeted both girls formally, Randolph coolly. All three responded indifferently.

Martha appeared in the doorway and said coldly, "Your breakfast is served in the dining-room," turned and disappeared.

Gordon rubbed his hands together. "Ah," he said without much gusto, "lead me to it." He went inside.

Fraser hesitated, seemed about to say something but uncertain how to put it into words.

Beryl was looking at Randolph. "You were telling us about that boat race—Jack."

"Yes," Barbara chimed in. "But tell us first—were you stroke?"

"Number seven," Randolph said promptly.

Fraser turned toward the door, paused and came back a pace. "Mind if I sit in with you here?" he asked. "From what I've seen of 'em they're rotten company inside."

Barbara turned a little in her chair, without glancing at him. "Of course you can have the table. We've just finished."

"Oh, I say, Miss St. Clair—"

The screen door opened again, swiftly. Mrs. St. Clair stepped out. "Good morning, my dears, and Mr. Rittenhouse," she said, a little too effusively. "I do hope you are all feeling brighter than I." She stooped to kiss Barbara. The blond girl turned her face away, stood up slowly.

"Let's take our cigarettes to that ledge by the lake, Beryl. Jack can finish his story there."

Beryl and Randolph got to their feet, and Barbara came around the table and joined them. Wheatley pushed open the door, stood there, saying nothing. His face was white; his eyes dull. Mrs. St. Clair turned to Fraser. Red showed in her face above the rouge. "If they are finished, let's you and I eat here, Mr. Fraser. I do love the fresh air"—she laughed, a little unnaturally—"and I do feel the need of it this morning. Oh, dear, I can hardly remember last night at all."

"I'll tell Martha," Fraser said; then turned toward Randolph who was about to follow the two girls. "Wonder if I can have a word with you later, Rittenhouse?"

Randolph swung slowly around to face him. His eyes were hard, frowning. "It might be possible," he said quietly, "if you have anything worth while to say, Fraser."

Fraser's florid face went an angry red. He took a quick step forward. "I don't s'pose you know much about it," he said, sneeringly, a little hoarsely, "but you accused me of a rotten trick last night and struck me. I'm not the chap to pass either, y'know."

Fraser was inches shorter than Randolph, but powerfully built, with heavy shoulders and thick wrists and arms.

A smile twisted Randolph's lips as he looked at him.

"You're wrong about one thing, Fraser," he said slowly. "If I'd hit you, I'd know it and possibly you would too. Sort of a kid trick, isn't it?"

Fraser stepped in swiftly, swung his right fist. Without shifting, Randolph's left shot out, open-handed, caught Fraser squarely in the face, sending him staggering backward.

Mrs. St. Clair gave a little scream. "Oh, Mr. Fraser, please. Please do be quiet. I'm sure Mr.—ah—Mr. Rittenhouse didn't mean anything. And I'm so—so jittery this morning. Do run along, girls—and take Mr. Rittenhouse with you. Come, Mr. Fraser; we'll have our cozy little breakfast here. And tell the maid, please, lots of coffee for me."

Fraser stood uncertainly. Then he bowed stiffly to Barbara and Beryl who were watching, bright-eyed. "I'm sorry. Er—excuse, Rittenhouse. Always, before breakfast, I've a jolly bad temper." He laughed, forcedly, turned and entered the house.

"Why didn't you take him?" Beryl whispered when they were down the steps. "I knew you could and I'd have liked to see it. He's just the kind of Britisher I don't care for. He could be decent; he has the front for it, but he just isn't."

"Yeh-o," Barbara added. "I'm aching to see you smash somebody around here. It would make me a feel a whole lot better and cleaner."

Randolph laughed. "'s funny. It used to be bad manners to scrap before ladies; but with fights and kids growing up so fast, I guess it isn't any more."

The girls seated themselves on the ledge facing the water, renewed their cigarettes and were about to light up when the sound of a step on the gravel of the path caused them to glance around. Wheatley had followed them out.

He had a worried, sick look which seemed more deep-rooted than the after effects of his evening's reckless dissipation. No one greeted him. He gave Barbara a swift sidewise glance then looked more directly at Beryl and finally at Randolph.

"I've an awful nerve coming to you, Mr. Rittenhouse," he said very meekly, "but I haven't a single other out."

Randolph seated himself cross-legged between the two girls and looked Wheatley over with mild curiosity. "What's on your mind?" he asked carelessly.

"I want you to let me have five thousand for a couple of months or so," Wheatley blurted out all in one breath.

Barbara turned to him with blazing eyes. "Look here," she said sharply. "I thought nothing could possibly make me more disgusted with you than I already am. I was mistaken. You forget that you were supposed to be in my party. When you come out with a cheap thing like that, it sort of involves me too and I won't stand for it."

"I guess you can't afford to be so damned fussy yourself," Wheatley said angrily, "after last night?"

"What do you mean," Beryl said coolly, "after last night?"

"Oh, everyone knows what the deal was. That might have gone askew, but we saw you coming out of Rittenhouse's room this morning."

"'We?'" Barbara blazed. "I suppose that means you and my sainted mother—huh?"

"Did you happen to see me come out of the same room with her?" Beryl asked coldly. "Not that I give a damn for your opinion, but Barbs and I spent the night there."

"Wait a minute," Randolph said with a little, dry laugh. "Before I yield to the impulse to drop you into the lake, Wheatley, suppose you tell me what you are so hot and bothered over."

"Oh, hell!" Wheatley said morosely. "Burke is calling me for five thousand. He's got me dead to rights on it. I haven't got it, you wouldn't miss it, and if I don't ante up by tomorrow I'm through. It isn't only being broke, but he's dug up something that he can twist around so it'll look like I'm lucky if I get off with ten years."

"And I still don't see," Barbara said nastily, "why you should have the nerve to ask Mr. Rittenhouse for it?"

"All right; then I'll tell you something you don't know. I'm sorry for Miss Rogers, but you three're playing together and high hatting everyone else, so she's in it anyway. Burke's got a live one on you, Rittenhouse. You'll shake down plenty or leave the country, or both. It's that kind. If you don't already know about it," he added with a sneer, "he'll tell you this morning. He's telling everyone this morning, then we're to have a good time until tomorrow when we settle up or jump off. I thought if Rittenhouse would help me, I'd try to get Burke to ease up on him. That's fair enough, seems to me."

"Wheatley," Randolph said very softly, "you run along and get your breakfast. You need it. We'll see how things shape up later. Go on"—when Wheatley hesitated—"you're spoiling the air around here."

When Wheatley was out of hearing, Beryl laughed. "I suppose it does seem silly—high hatting the rest, as he says. It isn't that. It's not wanting them to think we're blind or just stupid, that they can get away with anything and we'll take it."

"It isn't so damned silly," Barbara said hotly. "All of my life, as far as I can remember, I've played on mother's side, and look what it's got me. Dad's business is in the West and it keeps him pretty close. She wanted to live East because she thought it was smart. He's a poor sap, I guess, for he puts up for it. Anyway I hardly know him at all; but I'm starting right now to get acquainted with him. You'll let me ride out with you two, won't you? And I start packing the moment I get home."

"I think what Beryl meant," Randolph said carefully, "is that it might be wise if we watched our step and were a bit more diplomatic, even if they should think us stupid."

"What makes you say that?" Beryl asked quickly.

"Well, you see, the party isn't over yet; won't be till tomorrow morning."

"I don't see why we can't call it off when we want to; tell 'em who you are, take Barbs and roll our hoop."

Randolph shook his head. "Things aren't finished yet. Burke hasn't yet shown his claws." He laughed lightly. "Judging from Wheatley, he's just beginning to sharpen 'em."

He saw that Beryl was watching him closely and that Barbara's gaze was fixed on the water, and nodded his head toward the blond girl.

Beryl frowned. "You think—there's more to come?"

Barbara looked around quickly, her eyes growing wide with sudden apprehension.

"I've a hunch," Randolph said, "there'll be a showdown, some time today or this evening, and that we ought to stick around. It should be interesting—Gordon, Wheatley; and Fraser too has some unfinished business," he added lightly.

Beryl's dark eyes were troubled. Unconsciously she glanced back toward the lodge. She faced the other way quickly. "Ah," she said in low tone, "here comes your girl friend. Perhaps she has a message."

"And that," Randolph said, "entitles me to another reminder. I'll collect on the first suitable occasion."

"You're too darned quick on the take-up," Beryl drawled. "I'll be good. Matter of fact, I really don't think you'd step out of your class. See the trusting gal I am?"

Martha stopped at the foot of the ledge. "Mr. Rittenhouse," she said tonelessly, "Burke wants to know if you and Miss Rogers will come up to his study."

Randolph got to his feet and smiled down at Beryl. "Want to come?"

"You bet I do." Randolph grasped her hand and she leaped lightly to her feet. "How about you, Barbs?"

Barbara stood up on crossed feet, with little effort. "I think I'll get our suits out to dry. We must have another swim."

Martha said, "They all hang their suits on a line beside the lodge. Let me have them, Miss."

"Just tell me where it is," Barbara said. "I want something to do. Let's go the back way; can we?"

"Martha," Randolph said, "would you mind hanging mine out? I left it on the tub—in the room across the hall."

"It's already out."

Randolph said, "Thanks," and grinned down when Beryl looked up at him sidewise.

They passed Mrs. St. Clair and Fraser breakfasting on the porch, with a casual nod exchanged. As they were climbing the stairs, Beryl murmured, "What are you thinking of? You look so serious."

"Don't make me laugh now. I'm trying to make my face look

like Wheatley's."

She pinched his arm. "Do you really think he'll bother Barbs any more?" she whispered. They were rounding the top of the stairs.

"He's tricky," Randolph growled. "That's all I know."

She shivered. "I'm getting cold feet."

"Fine. That'll make it easier for me."

She glanced up at him, with her sidelong tilt of the head. He bent over, kissed her lightly on the hair, and rapped on Burke's door.

There was the sound of quick footsteps, then the door was opened and Burke bowed them in.

This was a different Burke; unsmiling, brusk, very business-like. He closed the door, waved them toward chairs beside his desk, with a gesture that made a little gleam of light from the single large solitaire on one plump finger.

As they seated themselves, he skipped around the desk, took the leather upholstered swivel-chair behind it, leaned back and pressed the tips of his fingers together above a flowered silk waistcoat. He glanced first at Beryl, then fixed cold eyes on Randolph.

"The business of being an attorney," he began, in a courtroom tone, "is not always a pleasant one. Clients come to one with affairs of a nature with which one does not want to be identified, but we have no choice." He shrugged fat shoulders, let his chair swing a little forward. "In some instances, however, such as this one perhaps, I have the consolation that by making myself the court, the arbiter, I am in position to save very disagreeable and harmful publicity." He paused, reached out and took up an ivory letter opener and commenced to toy with it.

"Suppose," Randolph said surlily, "you skip the prologue and tell me what you have on your books against me."

Burke shot him a hard glance. He dropped the letter opener, with a little clatter, jerked himself more upright.

"As you please, Mr. Rittenhouse," he began sneeringly, when the faint tinkling of a bell interrupted him.

He swung around in his chair, took a small Continental phone from a hook and clapped the receiver to an ear.

"Yes... Wait."

He lowered the phone, held it with his elbow on the arm of his chair. After a moment he swung back and looked at Beryl. "Your brother is at the gate, Miss Rogers," he said suavely. "He says it is important that he should see you. If you wish, ask him here, or present him my compliments and invite him to lunch."

"My brother!" Beryl exclaimed, perplexed.

"What is odd about that?" Randolph said matter of factly. "Dick knew you were to be here and was probably motoring past. I can't guess what the important part is."

"Why—yes, of course. That's just like—Dick," she added dryly and with a little hesitation before the name. "But I think we should both go out and speak with him—at the gate. Come with me. I'm sure Mr. Burke will excuse us for a moment."

"By all means," Burke said with suspicious heartiness. "And, Miss Rogers"—with a sarcastic glance at Randolph—"it is very much my wish that you ask him to return here with you and Mr. Rittenhouse."

In spite of himself, Randolph could not repress a grin which he tried to make as sour as possible. "It will add to the smash, eh, Burke?"

"Precisely." Burke lifted the phone. "All right, Slocum. Have him wait outside until Miss Rogers comes. I want him to return with her. If he does, have him leave his car outside."

They heard the last of this as they crossed the study to the door.

Beryl did not speak until they were away from the house; then she turned a puzzled glance on Randolph. "What did you mean by 'Dick'? I haven't any brother—at least old enough to drive a car; and his name is Arnold. Who can it be anyway?"

"Unless you know—and you didn't act as if you did—it's got to be just he who I am not."

"What? Oh—you think it is John Rittenhouse?" she whispered, although it was obvious there were no listening ears in the immediate vicinity.

"Bound to be. Thought he'd turn up before this."

"Huh? I guess you don't know that lad."

They were walking rapidly along the graveled road that wound between the trees.

"Sure. But I know you."

"But what would he want—now?"

"That's easy. You," he said grumpily.

She flashed him a quick smile. "Oh, how I'm hoping you will turn out to—and I don't know that it matters greatly now." She frowned suddenly. "What a mess this is going to be."

"Maybe not. Could have been worse if he'd said, 'This is Mr. Rittenhouse. I want Miss Rogers.' What gets me is how he happened to cook up the brother act."

"You won't know any better from seeing him. He—he doesn't look that bright. Look. That's his scarlet roadster, and himself in person under the Panama, glaring haughtily at Slocum and puffing impatiently at his cigarette."

They passed behind thick young growth, and it was evident that the occupant of the roadster had not yet seen them. Randolph caught Beryl's arm.

"Want him in, or are you going to send him away?"

Beryl laughed a little grimly. "I am going to bring him right up there and let him hear the works—if he'll come as brother Dick."

"Want me to hang back a bit?"

"Not too far—not more than ten feet. I want you with me. Besides, when he sees you, it might arouse his—curiosity. Come on."

Slocum turned a sour face toward them as they approached. He waited stolidly. Randolph saw a tall, rather slender man get out of the roadster, throw away his cigarette and advance to the gate. He was, fortunately for the situation, as dark as Beryl. There any resemblance ended.

"All right, Slocum," Beryl said. "You can let him in." She stopped a few feet from the gate, while Randolph stood a little way behind her.

Slocum unfastened the lock of a smaller gate which he swung open. Rittenhouse paused in the opening and turned a scowling glance from Randolph back to Beryl. He was a rather good-looking young fellow of not particularly strong type, and showed class in appearance and dress.

"Come on, Beryl," he said crossly, "I've come to take you home."

She shook her head. "I'm not going yet. Come in. I want to talk to you."

"What's the good of my coming in if you're not going?"

"Perhaps you'll let me tell you; but I'm not going to shout it through a gate. Besides there's my bag."

"Can't this fellow fetch it?"

"I don't fetch bags, mister," Slocum said roughly.

"Oh, don't be a bear," Beryl said a little sharply. "Come on in. No one's going to bite you."

Rittenhouse walked slowly in, his gaze as much on Randolph as on the dark girl. Slocum turned to close the gate and Beryl whispered, "I don't want him to hear us talking. Wait till we get away from him."

The three paced along in silence, Beryl between the two men. After they had covered fifty yards, Rittenhouse stopped. "How about this fellow here"—with a nod toward Randolph—"Is he going to hear us talking?"

"He most certainly is," Beryl said emphatically. "If it weren't for him I'd be sunk. A fine mess you let me in for."

"That's good. I let you in for. You had to be stubborn and went into it yourself. Well, is it a secret, or who is he anyway?"

Randolph laughed good-naturedly. "For the moment," he said, "I'm John de Puyster Rittenhouse."

"You're—who?" Rittenhouse said disgustedly.

"I told you I was going through with it," Beryl broke in. "Mr. Randolph was kind enough to interrupt his own plans to help me out. It was the only thing to do. I gave him your name, and the way he has acted should make you proud of it."

"Oh, say; I'm not going to stand for this, not by a damned sight." His face flushed angrily; he made a downward gesture with both clenched hands. "If you want to queer yourself, Beryl, with a whole lot of strange people, run yourself out of your own set, let's call the whole thing off and be done with it. I don't want any part of this."

"You don't quite get it," Randolph said, before Beryl could

reply. "The point is this: We were closeted with Burke. Your coming interrupted him when he was just going to tell me, as Rittenhouse of course, all the things he has charged against me and the amount I should pay to squelch them. The question is, do you want to listen in or don't you? If you don't, I'd agree with you that you'd better get out fast."

Rittenhouse seemed about to make an angry retort. He opened his mouth to speak, then something, perhaps Randolph's half amused, half ironic look, held him speechless.

"There's another way of looking at it," Randolph said. "If it's very bad, I might be inclined to promise more than you would care to pay."

Beryl's face had darkened with indignation. Now as she caught the scathing undertone of Randolph's quietly spoken words, she seemed quite satisfied to leave the guidance of the matter to him. The flush subsided in her cheeks; scorn gave place to faint amusement in her eyes which were at the same time unforgiving and pitiless.

"Oh, hell!" Rittenhouse said suddenly. "I don't need anyone meddling in my affairs. Where is this fellow? I'll go talk to him alone. You two can do as you damned please—if that's where you stand, Beryl."

He turned and started ahead on the road. Randolph's hand on his shoulder brought him to an abrupt halt. Rittenhouse squirmed, but the grip still held. He raised his arm to twist Randolph's grasp loose. Randolph's hand slid from shoulder to upper arm and squeezed hard. When Rittenhouse ceased to struggle, Randolph took his hand away.

"No," he said. "You play it our way, or out you go."

"Why the hell should I do as you say?"

"There are several reasons. The most important is that Miss Rogers wants it that way. Another thing—you've let us in for a fine mess. I'm not the least interested in your personal history, but I've got to see it through. I'm on a spot with a half senile lawyer and a guy with a high powered rifle. If they get on to this shenanagin, they'll start popping. And if you spill the works, Rittenhouse, I'll break your neck in two pieces before they begin on me. Now, do you want to go on with it, or don't you? If you've nothing to be ashamed of, I don't see what's holding you back. But, come on; make up your mind."

Rittenhouse stole a glance at Beryl, but received no help from that quarter. She wasn't even looking at him.

"All right," he grumbled. "Let's get it over with."

They started on.

"You going back with me, Beryl?" Rittenhouse asked.

"We will see first how this comes out," she said coolly. "Probably not. Certainly not if it would make trouble for Mr. Randolph."

Rittenhouse scowled at this; then another thought caught his attention. "What d'you say his name is? Randolph?" He fumbled in a pocket. "Then I guess this is for you." He handed over a telegraph envelope. Randolph put it in his pocket unopened, avoiding Beryl's look of curiosity.

"There's one thing about it in your favor, Rittenhouse," he said lightly. "If it's as bad as your expression indicates, it will be easier listening as a brother. I'll be the goat, as far as Burke will know."

Rittenhouse murmured something under his breath that sounded considerably like an oath.

"By the way," Beryl said, "by what miracle did you send in your name as my brother?"

"It was that bald-headed goat at the little dinky station where I asked questions about what had become of you. He insisted I was your brother, and that you'd gone on with a lover, or something."

"I thought it must have been like that," Beryl murmured, but the sarcasm was entirely lost on young Rittenhouse.

They came out from the trees, in sight of the lodge. Rittenhouse paused. "What's my name supposed to be?"

"Dick Rogers," Beryl told him. "And don't forget it whatever happens."

He turned toward Randolph. "See here; if I give you the high sign, call it off, will you? Agree to anything and shut him up."

"I'll be as easy as I can," Randolph said. "You can't easily fool a guy like Burke. He's so rotten himself he'll smell anything off color, so we've got to play it straight goods. I had my face all set for the part when you busted in."

Rittenhouse groaned.

Randolph stole a sidewise glance at Beryl. She was looking at him. The lid fluttered down over one sparkling eye.

15

BURKE AGAIN OPENED his door. His glance lit on the third visitor and he rubbed his hands. "It was nice of you to persuade your brother to come in, Miss Rogers. I am, of course, Mr. Burke. I am very glad to make your acquaintance, Mr. Rogers. I shall be happy if you will lunch with us."

"How are you?" Rittenhouse said gruffly, ignored the outstretched hand and followed the others to the chairs before the desk. He seated himself and eyed the legal aspects of the place with visible perturbation.

Burke, having closed the door, bustled around to his swivel-chair. He beamed at Beryl, then fixed a cold look on Randolph. "You were asking me to come directly to the point, Mr. Rittenhouse," he began bruskly.

"Hey?" Rittenhouse said.

Randolph coughed. "Of course," he said quickly, "I do not admit that I have the slightest suspicion of the reason for this discussion, and assume that you have come upon some misleading information. However, I am naturally embarrassed in the presence of Miss Rogers, and now in that of her brother, Dick, as well. So I will request you to state your matter briefly and as circumspectly as possible."

Beryl found a tiny lace handkerchief and pressed it against her lips. Her long lashes shaded her eyes and rendered their expression inscrutable.

"Ahem," Burke said, and Rittenhouse started slightly. Beneath his tan, his face had become a dull red. "I should like," Burke went on, "to spare Miss Rogers; but after all it is wise that she should be here. It will come to her first hand and confidentially, which, you will agree, is better than having her read it in the tabloids. No doubt she will advise you the proper course to pursue so that such an—ah—unfortunate contingency may not eventuate."

He paused; cleared his throat again. "But as to the matter itself—I can only state the case as presented by my client, and it is of such a nature that it doesn't admit of the mincing of words. Miss Rogers will of course bear that in mind."

He tilted forward in his swivel-chair, moved some papers on his desk, selected one or two and leaned back in his chair, scrutinizing them. Rittenhouse was staring around at the different objects. He even turned his head so far that the door came within his glance. He looked at it a moment with evident longing.

Randolph was leaning forward, his big hands knotted on his knees. His brows were bent in a deep frown; the muscles in his face were working. Beryl caught a side-wise glance of him and made a little choking sound in her handkerchief.

Burke glanced over his spectacles at her. "There, there, Miss Rogers. In this world of today, one has to meet such things. I will be as brief as possible."

Beryl bent her head low. Something that wasn't exactly a sob escaped her. When she looked up there were tears in her eyes. She kept the handkerchief pressed to her lips. Rittenhouse looked at her with a curious, half puzzled expression. Randolph did not risk a glance at either.

"You have been abroad considerably, Mr. Rittenhouse?" Burke asked abruptly.

"Why, yes; of course," Randolph said hastily.

"But you have been in this country"—Burke consulted his papers—"continually from July of last year?"

"Yes; I believe so," Randolph muttered.

"You, or your family, have a large estate near Roslyn, Long Island, where you have been staying for the majority of the time since your return from Europe? I ask this as a matter of form; for I have had the facts verified, of course."

Randolph stole a quick glance at Beryl, looked back as quickly and nodded.

Burke turned the papers over, tossed them, face downward, on the desk. "My communication—and complaint," he said slowly, "are from the mother of two little girls; one, Bertha, aged fourteen; the other, Isobel, a year or so younger; that is to say, well under the legal age of consent. They reside, or, to be exact, did reside last August, in a small cottage on the outskirts of Roslyn, on a road leading directly past your estate, Mr. Rittenhouse.

"Ahem... This communication speaks of an automobile ride to which they were persuaded at first against their better judgment and wish. It relates that the ride continued, or at least they did not return from the ride, until early evening, when they left the automobile at a spot which required them to walk a half-mile or more to their home. That, however, is beside the point except in so far as it establishes the details. More interesting is the fact that immediately following that ride both young girls were subjected to medical treatment." He rustled the papers again. "I have the report here—let me see..."

"I don't want to hear any more of this," burst suddenly from Rittenhouse. "Of course it is a bunch of damnable lies, but you can't tell about these things. Once they get in the papers—"

"That's white of you to say that, Rogers," Randolph broke in quickly. As he turned from Rittenhouse, his glance swept Beryl. There was no tears in her eyes now. They, as well as her cheeks, were flaming. She was sitting very erect and seemed almost on the point of taking a part in the conversation. Randolph faced Burke. "All right. What is the proposition?"

Burke extended both plump hands in a deprecatory gesture; then formed another short steeple with his fingertips. He appeared smugly at ease; his lips pursed; his shoe-button eyes bright beneath their judicial frown. He took swift note of Beryl's attitude and expression, gauging, no doubt, the value of her indignation; and turned to Randolph.

"My dear Mr. Rittenhouse, it is impossible to treat a matter of this weight so bluntly. There are considerations to be borne in mind; on one side the irreparable damage to two little girls and the outrage done them and their family; on the other, a penal offense, social damage, the havoc to be wrought an old and established family by publicity of a matter of this sort. No, my dear Mr. Rittenhouse, one can hardly set a price on such a situation as on a piece of merchandise."

Randolph lifted his lowered head. "It's a matter of money, isn't it?"

"It is true," Burke said suavely, "money can do much to assuage; it cannot restore." He raised a hand to forestall interruption. "My instructions, or recommendation if you prefer, are to institute suit forthwith. Personally I dislike to do that in many cases. There is a prolongation of distress to both parties; the labor of preparation; the uncertainty of court and jury ruling—although in this particular case there can be no question of doubt as to the liberality of the verdict."

He sighed.

"I expect I have become fatigued from my long experience in forensic practice. I appear now only when absolutely necessary. Moreover, this experience has made me a capable arbiter, far more expert, let us say, than the average jury. Decidedly, Mr. Rittenhouse, if you will make it reasonable to do so, I shall in this case recommend arbitration out of court."

"Very well," Randolph said dolefully. "Then what figure do you suggest?"

Burke knit his brows. "To be frank, until now I had not given thought to an exact amount. Hummm." He looked at Beryl; then turned his glance slowly back to Randolph. "Of course I do not know that anything can be accomplished; but offhand, since you press me, I should not advise an offer of anything less than fifty thousand dollars."

"Why that—" Randolph began.

"See here," Rittenhouse broke in, facing Burke. Beryl swung quickly part way toward him, without, however, looking at him, and Rittenhouse paused, then turned toward Randolph. "Er—seems to me I remember you spoke to me of something like this. As I recall it, it was to the effect that you had paid ten thousand dollars to certain people who—er—you said were making a false claim against you, for complete relinquishment of the affair."

Burke leaned forward. His eyes were very sharp.

"Yes, of course," Randolph muttered. "And I had reason, have reason to consider the matter closed."

"But you see," Burke said, spreading his hands apart, "it has come up again; and in very virile form, I assure you."

"Well," Randolph said, making his voice low and so hoarse that it cracked a little, "I think your figure is preposterous,

Burke. I was going to suggest"—he broke off, turned to Ritten-house—"what do you think, Dick? The amount I had in mind was half what Burke names."

"That's enough," Rittenhouse growled.

"So," Randolph continued, "with the ten already paid, and for a release, mind you, Burke, that makes thirty-five which more than splits the difference between our ideas."

Burke shrugged. "I can only put it up to my client. But my recommendation to you"—he glanced meaningly at Beryl—"for your own sake alone, if you have no consideration for the other parties, is to be more liberal."

"That," Randolph said more decisively, "is enough. You have my phone number," he added. "You will let me know?"

"The first of the week," Burke said musingly.

"Say," Rittenhouse said to Randolph, "you want to make absolutely certain it sticks this time."

"My cases are always complete," Burke said coldly, "when I have finally passed upon them. If this offer is accepted, I shall prepare binding papers."

Randolph stood up. "Then it isn't necessary to carry this on any longer."

Burke sprang up with alacrity. His face was wreathed in smiles. "Now let us, for the rest of your stay, dear Miss Rogers and Mr. Rittenhouse, forget all about this unpleasantness. I dislike its intrusion on our happy party, but of course you understand its necessity. And, Mr. Rogers, you will stay for lunch with us and enjoy the afternoon here, no?"

"I can't do it," Rittenhouse said gruffly. "I've got to get back to town." He led the way to the door; Beryl followed and Randolph, with downcast head, came behind her.

Once with the door closed behind them, Beryl whirled and grasped Randolph's arm, linking her own through it. Rittenhouse kept in the lead, and no word was spoken as they descended the stairs and sought the roadway leading to the gate.

In the concealment of the trees, Beryl withdrew her arm, opened the wrist-purse she was carrying and fumbled in it. Then quickening her pace, she slipped a small object into Rittenhouse's pocket. He turned to look at her with sullen eyes.

"You don't believe all that rot, do you?" he demanded.

"If I had had any doubt," she said coldly, "the ten thousand paid was quite enough to convince me."

He gave an impatient gesture. "It still could be a frame, couldn't it?"

"For thirty-five thousand?"

Rittenhouse did not reply to this. After a few more paces he said, "Well, are you going back with me?"

"Not now or ever," Beryl said tonelessly.

He shrugged. "Of course our affair, such as it was, is off. That was settled yesterday when you took the bit in your teeth."

"Then why did you return?" Beryl asked.

"Er—I thought I might still get you home without too much damage to your reputation. I see, however, that I was too—"

Randolph laid a forefinger on his shoulder, turned him partly around. "If I were you," he said softly, "I should keep my own counsel."

Rittenhouse shrugged away and strode on. Randolph fell back with Beryl. "By Jingo!" he exclaimed suddenly. "I clean forget my telegram."

He pulled the envelope from his pocket, ripped it open and read, to himself:

"I admit the legs are beautiful and six views of them most generous stop Of course you couldn't send face or name with them stop
After exhaustive search of our files staff agrees they belong either
to disappearing Hollywood star or noted Newport heiress stop In
either case at Burke's it is news too important for you to handle stop
Morrison and Scanlon will relieve you stop Watch for them turn over
everything to them and get out stop Don't come back here.

"MacArthur."

"Oh, hum," Randolph said, carefully refolded the day
message and returned it to his pocket.

"Anything serious?" Beryl asked, her eyes bright as she
glanced up at him.

"Only something to prove that I am really the professional
nitwit. Say," he asked abruptly, "didn't I point that darned thing
high enough—at your face?" he explained hurriedly.

"Why—why—"

"Oh, nothing serious at all." He laughed hesitantly. "But
didn't I?"

"Why," she said demurely, "I thought you kept it pretty low.
I've had so many of those darned things shot at me."

Ahead of them Rittenhouse growled something unintelli-
gible to them and strode on.

Slocum was waiting close by the gate, his inevitable rifle
cradled under one arm, and peering through the bars.

"All right, Slocum," Randolph called. "Mr. Rogers can't stay
with us."

"Yeah, I know," Slocum growled, without looking around,
and began to unfasten the bolt. Still peering ahead, he swung
the small gate open, and without a word Rittenhouse stepped
through.

Randolph, with his curiosity aroused, followed Slocum's gaze. Not far from the gateway with a huge live-oak with low branches well foliaged. Beneath stood a car with, at the moment, a single occupant. Between car and huge trunk was the lank newspaperman, Morrison. His straw hat was pushed back on his head. He looked hot, perspiring and possessed of a beautiful bun. He weaved a little as he stood, shifting his feet but going no place.

As Rittenhouse stepped swiftly toward his own car, Morrison's mouth gaped. He took an uncertain step forward. "Hey," he called, "just a moment, Mr. Ritt—"

"Slocum," Randolph said sharply and loudly.

Slocum turned a sour face toward him.

"Recognize that fellow in the car under the tree?"

"I made him all right," he growled. "That damn' punk, Slinky Trasker, an' if he don't beat it outa here pretty soon I'll burn an ear off him."

Rittenhouse's starter whirred, caught; gears meshed harshly and the big roadster shot away. Morrison came to a jerky stop, still beneath the tree. He raised a hand to his head in disgust, knocked off his hat but paid it no attention. He lurched a little as he turned slowly around to face the gate. Then he scowled his eyes into focus; a grin spread over his saturnine face.

"Hi, you big dumbbell!" he yelled.

Randolph backed a pace, drawing Beryl with him.

"Slocum," he said softly, "I've seen what you can do at four hundred yards. Now, look over at that live-oak. There's something moving on that lowest branch—something bright that looks like the business end of a tele-photo lens. All right. See, just above it, that round-shaped gray thing? I'm betting you a dollar you can't put a couple of bullets through it."

"Huh!" Slocum said with sudden satisfaction.

He whipped up the rifle, threw the bolt and took careless aim. Two reports crashed, one on top of the other. Slinky Trasker in the car ducked spasmodically from sight. Morrison's face, with dropping jaw and popping eyes, was a mask of incredulity.

Then the surface of the gray wasps' nest was suddenly darkened; the air around it was filled with small flying objects. A tall, sandy-haired man fell off the branch, flat on the ground, dug his toes desperately into the ground as he tried to rise. Morrison looked above him in bewilderment. Then abruptly he slapped his cheek and commenced to run.

There was the sound of the motor starting. The car jerked into gear, moved ahead. Scanlon got to his feet, with arms waving wildly and set out after Morrison, whose own arms were flailing like the wings of a windmill in a gale. Randolph saw that they had outdistanced the car, when Slocum shot again. Dust kicked up close to a rear wheel of the speeding car and Slocum turned his head toward Randolph with the nearest approach to a grin of which his hard features seemed capable.

Randolph slipped him a bill, caught Beryl's arm and drew her away. They started along the winding road. She was laughing chokingly. Abruptly she sobered.

"Thank God he's gone," she said in low, almost whispering tone, "gone, out and away and forever. Say—for thrills you certainly deal out a packful. Whew! This past half-hour beats anything in my young career. You don't suppose Slocum caught that, do you?"

"I don't think so," Randolph said and grinned. "If he heard anything, he's certainly forgotten it by now. He looked almost happy."

He glanced sidewise at Beryl. Her eyes, looking straight ahead, were luminous. Her lips were twisted a little in the delightful curve that he had found so provocative, although now they held an expression that seemed very much like self-scorn.

"Look," he said quietly. "I hope you don't feel too badly about all this. It's my fault; I shouldn't have gone ahead with it if I'd guessed it was that bad."

She turned her head toward him, and her eyes, ordinarily so reticent in expression, grew warm.

"Feel badly?" she repeated, in her deep, full throated tone. "I'm happy—gloriously happy. See what I've escaped. Your fault? *Thanks* to you. I never did feel right about it from the beginning, and my hunch was right. Damn these schemes of parents who think they know it all anyway." And with her volatile change of manner, "I'm free. Man, do you get it? I'm free again!"

She pirouetted, with flying skirt; then came closer to him. Her eyes sobered. "I don't know who or what you are," she said in lowered tone. "You came to me from nowhere; yet he, with his millions and his name, was cheap beside you. A rotter." She came closer still, looked up to him, with head tilted back. "Kiss me once—for yourself—Dick."

He took her gently in his arms. She pressed close. He looked at her as he released her, and his eyes were wistful; but he said nothing. She glanced at him, with that little sidewise tilt of her head. "So," she said, "we go on from here—and may the best man win. Let's pray for a peaceful afternoon anyway. I simply must catch my breath before you pull anything else. Say—are things happening around you all the time?"

He continued to look at her and smiled; and his smile seemed more mature, stronger, and still a little wistful.

"I sure think I must be a lodestone for trouble," he said lightly. "Seems to me I've been scrapping ever since I was a kid. And, honest, I don't look for it."

"You don't seek it," she said wisely, "but you resist it. Slimy things like Burke and Fraser and Wheatley and—" she nodded her dark head over her shoulder.

She was silent for a moment, then asked, "Don't you suppose we could go now—you and I, and take Barbs?"

"I'm afraid it's not so easy as that. They have our keys, you know. I was a little suspicious of that, and I'm more certain of it now. Burke won't give them up without being nasty. For several reasons—for Barbara's sake for one—I don't believe we should force him. My hunch, you know—things aren't finished just yet."

16

BEFORE THEY WERE well out of the woods Barbara St. Clair came along the winding road to meet them. Her eyes were wide with curiosity and apprehension, but when she saw them she broke into a smile, waved her hand and quickened her pace.

"Gee," she said, "it's good to be with you two again. I'm lost without you, and strange things happen. But first—what was Slocum shooting at—more loons?"

"You might call them that," Randolph said dryly. "Actually, he was picking off some insects; rather large ones with wings and a habit of having things pretty much their own way. Wasps."

"Oh, was that all! Everyone ran out, except Burke, and was curious and excited."

"It was enough," Beryl murmured, with a peculiar gleam in her eyes. "But what's your news, Barbs? You're bursting with it."

"Damnedest thing you ever heard of. Fraser cornered me by that clothesline at the right of the porch, where they hang the bathing suits, helped me with ours, then—believe me or not—proposed to me. Yowsuh. Wants me to marry him and sail for jolly old England Wednesday. Can you tie to that?"

"Continue," Beryl said. "You leave me breathless."

"Oh, I blushed my most devastating blush, told him I must have time for consideration. Seriously, I've been wondering if it isn't really an out. I'm through with mother; I've wasted Dad's substance for years, never have given him any reason to be particularly fond of me. Fraser doesn't seem a bad sort. He's intelligent, good-looking, amusing, well fixed and says he has real people on the other side."

"Quite a category of husbandy requirements," Beryl said dryly. "Well, Barbs, I don't like him. He's screwy somewhere. Look what he tried to do to our Jack last night."

Barbara looked at Randolph; her eyes were dark violet and troubled. "I piled into him plenty on that, with Burke's intentions assumed, in the background. He gave me the chance, don't you think so? He made quite a fuss over it; insisted there was not the slightest foundation of truth in it; vowed they'd kill him first, or he them— whichever way it was—before anything would happen to me."

Randolph smiled a little, said nothing.

"And you believed him?" Beryl asked.

"Oh, I don't know what to do," Barbara said disconsolately. "I'm really in a devil of a fix. I haven't a red cent—even to go to Chicago. Mother gets it all and doles me out what is necessary. I'm damned if I ask her for any." She paused in her walk and they stopped with her. "Gee, this thing has waked me up. I can see now how I was slipping—playing around with that grub, Gerald Wheatley. There's a specimen for you! And my steady for months."

"You're not the only one who has waked up, Barbs," Beryl said softly, and her eyes strayed toward Randolph.

"Well," he said, "you've all day and night to think it over, Barbs. And," he added, "I've an idea I'll know more about Mr. Stanley Fraser before morning."

Beryl looked at him quickly with eyes that frowned a little. "Don't you think I've been rather nice—"

"I hope to tell you," he murmured.

"That's the second quaint phrase of the South you've used in the past few minutes. I'll place you yet. Of course you had to say that; but I mean in the way of bridled curiosity. Very unwomanlike, I assure you. There were those two strange men out there—one of whom addressed you familiarly. Newspapermen, I take it. But I haven't asked. That telegram too. Likewise silence. But you've been hinting all morning of something in the air. Don't you think we're entitled to know that at least?"

"I've been guessing—mostly. But you can't know Burke without suspecting something more on the cards; especially as he hasn't played out one hand yet. And of course whatever he does involves Fraser, I suppose."

Beryl gave him a slow look which didn't particularly express satisfaction.

"There's another thing too," Barbara said as they started on. "I think Gerald Wheatley has gone bats. He's been moping all over the place, whenever I've seen him; and just now, when he caught me alone, he asked me the strangest thing. He wanted me to swipe your purse, Beryl, said that he wanted to get an address he thought you had, and didn't want you to know that he was interested."

Beryl's sober glance met Randolph's. He smiled.

"Wheatley's not hard to read," he said lightly. "I don't believe he could be really serious about anything. Just wants to make gestures so he can satisfy his conscience that he tried to do something. A dancer, isn't he?"

"A gentleman jockey, on other people's money," Barbara said with a smile that robbed the comment of some of its spitefulness. "In other words, a gigolo of the best class. But you're wrong on one count; I suspect friend Gerry could be right mean if he was in a corner."

"Thanks, Barbs," Beryl said. "I'll guard my purse like my life, and keep its secrets inviolate from prying eyes and fingers."

Barbara said, "But I've been talking so much myself you haven't told me how you made out with your unexpected visitor. From a discreet distance I observed his leonine entrance and his ba-ba exit. Looked to me as if someone had taken him for a trimming. How'd you make out?"

"Just that; out."

"No. Really? Can't you tell a fellow?"

"Not now. I'm still nauseated." Beryl glanced ahead, saw that they were nearing the end of the trees, and looked at Randolph. "This thing's getting me dizzy. What are our parts now?"

Randolph grinned. "Well, let's see. I guess the best bet would be that I'm not too downhearted. I'm trying to make you believe I've been framed; you're doubtful enough about it to be a bit sober, but willing to think it might be so. That way we won't have to think too much about it."

"Is that a riddle or something?" Barbara asked.

"Darn' tooting," Beryl said with tight lips.

Barbara sighed. "Some day will you make all things clear to me, sweetheart?"

"When we're at the sanitarium enjoying our rest cure after this dull week-end."

Their slow pace had brought them to the edge of the clearing. Randolph glanced casually at the lodge and saw several figures behind the screen on the porch. "How about Gordon?" He asked. "Did he cut up too?"

Barbara gave a mock shiver. She seemed entirely to have

recovered her spirits. "There's something dark and mysterious about that young man. I didn't see him and I think he's acted the most decent of the lot. But before Fraser began his wooing, Martha started to tell me something about Gordon. Said he was a gunman with a rep, as she picturesquely described it. I've an idea she's worried that Burke will try to push him too hard and call in her Steve for the pushing—and then, bingo—fireworks. She's not worried over what might happen to friend husband, but she says Burke has the tag on her and she's afraid of what could turn up if there was trouble and the police came in. Nice quiet place for a nervous woman. If I ever get out of here alive I'll recommend it."

Beryl said, "I wonder," half under her breath.

"What?"

"Oh, I suppose I shouldn't say anything. But I'm sure Dick knows something and won't tell because he doesn't want to worry us."

" 'Dick'?" Randolph said smiling.

Beryl's lips curved in what she probably intended to be a grimace, but it didn't go with them. "Just now I like you too well to call you Jack." Suddenly she laughed. "Honest, I never knew men could run so fast. I wonder if that car has caught up with them yet."

"More mystery," Barbara grumbled.

"Patience, my dear, until I recite to you my memoirs—in the psychopathic ward. And now, my children, it's lunch with His Oiliness. Brr! I've the feeling that I'm going on to an execution."

"Could happen," Randolph murmured, with his eyes on the porch.

Beryl gave him a quick sidewise glance. "I could go for a drink if it was safe around here."

"Well, I'm not taking a chance," Barbara said with emphasis. "Do you know, they're quite puzzled over what really did happen last night. Thank God, we haven't *that* to look forward to. Although"—a startled look grew suddenly in her eyes, clouded them—"I haven't even thought what he might cook up over his destroyed evidence."

Randolph's silence, as she glanced at him, might have been significant; but they were close to the porch now.

The screen door opened, and Burke came down a step. One foot, in his tight patent leather shoe, held the door back. He glanced inside, then included the three at the foot of the steps in his smile. "Come," he said, "let's all be happy the rest of the day. Miss Rogers, I want to see you smile; and, you, my dear Miss St. Clair. We have a gorgeous lunch waiting; and then— into our bathing suits and out on the lake in the launch. We'll make an afternoon of it."

He raised his head to glance around at the sky, and a lock of dark hair dislodged itself, exposing the baldness beneath. He lowered his head quickly, patting the recreant lock into place. "Looks as if it might make for a shower later, but we'll have our fun in the sun first, eh? Come, my dears. I'm sure you're hungry."

Mrs. St. Clair appeared at his shoulder. Her eyes were large, staring in frightened distress. Her face, in spite of its careful make-up, was distorted with the same emotion. She looked more nearly her own age than she had at breakfast.

She said, "Excuse me, Mr. Burke," and started down the steps. "Barbara, I want to speak with you a moment."

The blond girl turned her shoulder. "Come, Beryl. Let's see if our suits are dry." She smiled up at Burke. "Don't wait for us. We'll join you through the back way." She caught Beryl's arm, and they started off alongside the lodge.

Mrs. St. Clair stopped short, stood uncertainly. Burke rubbed his hands together. "Come, Mrs. St. Clair; we're not to bother over anything now. If you please." He gestured toward the open door. "Right now Stanley is making something very special for you, I'm sure. Thank you," as she turned and, without looking at him, went inside.

Burke continued to hold the door back until Randolph mounted the steps; then laid his free hand on Randolph's arm. He glanced inside and in the direction the girls had taken.

"I've telephoned since our talk, Mr. Rittenhouse. We won't discuss it further now, or today. But tomorrow morning before you leave, it is imperative, for your interests of course, that we come to some agreement."

Randolph nodded without saying anything, and stepped on to the porch. Burke followed him and let the door swing closed. From the room beyond there was the sound of a cocktail shaker in active operation. Gordon lounged against the door-frame, a cigarette between his lips, his eyes squinting in the smoke.

"What was the shootin'?" he asked, around the bobbing cigarette. "Slocum on the warpath again?"

Randolph faced him with his meaningless smile. "Driving out some hornets. He's good with a rifle."

"That's the beauty of this place," Burke said from behind him. "It's Sunday, isn't it? Yet rifle shots don't disturb anybody. No one around to hear."

"Yeah," Gordon said. "That could be handy sometime."

"Heads up!" Fraser called from the room beyond. "Cocktails a-pouring. How many customers?" He glanced past Randolph and Gordon, as they came in, looked faintly puzzled as he saw only Burke following them. "Where's everybody?"

Burke pushed forward to the drink wagon. "Serve us here, Stanley," he said. "The young ladies will take theirs at the table, I think."

Fraser scowled slightly as he filled glasses for Mrs. St. Clair and Wheatley who stood close beside him. Randolph strolled slowly over to the davenport table and picked up a magazine while Fraser poured drinks for Gordon and Burke. Fraser glanced toward him. "How about you, Rittenhouse?" he called.

"Not your kind; thanks," Randolph said, without looking up.

Fraser filled his own glass, took it up and walked over beside Randolph. "You still seem to be harboring your strange hallucination," he said in a low tone that was ugly.

Randolph tossed down his magazine and looked at him with a faint smile. "Curious, isn't it, Fraser?"

"Don't s'pose it's occurred to you that you might have drunk too much, eh?"

"Still up to your kid tricks, huh? Why don't you grow up a little?"

Fraser held his glass in his right hand, a little raised. He made a slight movement with that arm, as if he were about to dash the liquor in Randolph's face. Randolph was poised easily, on both feet. His eyes were very alert and hard, although his lips were twisted in faint amusement.

"Try it," he said very softly, "and see what it buys you."

With an almost impatient gesture, Fraser raised his glass and drank the contents at a swallow. "Damn it, Rittenhouse," he said, "I don't want to quarrel with you. Only I didn't like your passing the insinuation on to Miss St. Clair."

"I haven't spoken about it," Randolph told him. "When I'm ready to, I'll discuss it with you, Fraser."

Fraser shrugged impatiently. He turned a little, sending a quick, casual glance over his shoulder. Then he set his glass on the davenport and took out a cigarette case. He extended it and Randolph shook his head.

Under cover of lighting up, Fraser spoke in a low tone:

"There's something about last night, old chap, I haven't got quite clear. Mind telling me what the row was all about in the middle of the night?"

Randolph shook his head. "Nothing to tell you, Fraser."

Fraser looked at him with speculative eyes narrowed against the smoke. "Woke up this morning with an idea everything wasn't quite on the up and up last night. Put a pretty bee in my bonnet. That's a ripping fine girl—Miss St. Clair—both of 'em. And I'm not such a rotter as you seem to think, Rittenhouse."

Randolph's smile broadened, but it was more sarcastic than amused. "I shouldn't think you were ordinarily so slow in getting an idea."

Fraser flushed, then laughed a little. "You're not going to get my wind up, old fellow, 'nother time I might take you up on it." He turned to flick the ash into a tray, and the movement gave him a glimpse of the cocktail drinkers. "Don't mind telling you th' old chap is acting up, for some reason you can probably guess better than I. When he's particularly suave and friendly, he's cookin' up some deviltry. Had a run-in with him after you left him this morning. He's bearing down on me and he's set to put the lot of us over the hurdles."

He made another motion toward the ash tray, and turning back, leaned closer to Randolph. "I'm telling you so's you can keep an eye out for our two young friends. From the signs, I've an idea tonight will be a honey. Will try to get another chance to talk with you."

"Coming, Stanley and Mr. Rittenhouse?" Burke called pleasantly. "Lunch is waiting, and so are our guests."

"Righto!" Fraser answered heartily.

"I'll find the chance," Randolph said, as they walked slowly after the others. "I want an answer to that question I asked last night."

"Oh—the hypothetical one?"

"Only so far as it concerns a friend."

Fraser gave him a sharp, probing glance. "I say—could his name by any chance be Randolph?"

"Hers could," Randolph said slowly.

Fraser peered around the door-frame into the dining-room. He nodded his head and smiled warmly. His expression changed. "Er—just a moment, Ross. You start things. I'll mix some fresh ones for the young ladies."

"No, thanks," came Barbara's voice. "Not while the sun is high," Beryl's echoed.

"Then for us," Fraser said, and turning his back on the room, got busy at the drink wagon. "Now, Rittenhouse," he said in barely audible tone.

"Fifty thousand was sent to your house by a certain lady—in securities. She wants them out. I've agreed to get them. I'll have them back if it's a question of wrecking the outfit and everyone in it. I mean it, Fraser. You'd better make me believe you'll play fair on it if—for one thing—you want to get away this week."

Fraser capped the gin bottle, reached for the vermouth, with his eye on Randolph. "Whew!" he whistled softly. "So it was you visited the office. By gad! I suspect you have a left. Webley says Hennessy was out a half-hour." He put the top on the shaker, began to work it vigorously, while he studied Randolph with a puzzled frown.

"Snap it up, Stan, will you?" Burke called impatiently.

"In a little moment, old dear," Fraser drawled. "Have another yourself?"

"Wouldn't mind. But you're keeping us waiting."

"Coming up." He turned to Randolph, said in a low tone, barely audible to his listener above the rattle of the ice, "I'm damned if I make you, Rittenhouse. Not from that, the way you've carried on here and what he"—with a nod over his shoulder—"slipped to me a while back. It just doesn't jibe. But, tell you what; I'll see you through on those securities, if—"

"Mind giving me a note on that?"

Fraser frowned. He twisted the shaker top and began to fill the glasses. "It's already complicated. It means"—again the nod over his shoulder—"would have to disgorge."

"Can't he be eliminated?"

Fraser spilled a little of the cocktail as he shot a quick look at Randolph.

"If he was," he whispered dryly, "you'd then deal with me. But you better hear my proposition. Back me with Miss St. Clair and I—"

A chair scraped back in the dining-room; there was the sound of a step. Fraser caught up the two glasses, met Burke as he appeared in the opening. "Here y'are, Ross. A perfect frappé."

"What in the infernal hell's been keeping you?" he growled under his breath. "Makes me nervous to have men somewhere behind me. You know that."

"Take it, old dear, an' stow it. Mr. Rittenhouse insisted on watching me do it. I don't know why."

Randolph saw that the rest were seated in the same order as on the preceding evening, and found his chair as Burke, still sputtering, sank into his seat. Fraser came around to Barbara and held out his glass. "Burke rushed me," he said. "Afraid it's a bit too dry. A sip will do the trick, no?"

Barbara smiled up at him and as he bent over her, touched her lips to the brim. Fraser's eyes were very much alight as he took the glass back, raised it and drank with his gaze on her. Burke fidgeted during this by-play and when Fraser stepped away, pushed his own glass toward her.

"Sweeten mine too, my dear—please."

"I'm afraid it wouldn't work a second time," Barbara said coolly, and started on the melon before her.

Gordon laughed aloud.

Burke did not look at him, but as he raised his glass and slowly drank, his sidewise glance at Fraser was malignant. Then when he set the glass down and turned his watery eyes on Barbara, he was again suave and ingratiating.

"I see you like it, my dear. Rather a hobby of mine—melons."

Gordon's laughter still grated. "Better go easy, Fraser," he said across the table. "You took Burke for a ride that time on one of his pet hobbies."

"Cut it," Fraser said curtly, and turned his attention to Beryl beside him.

Gordon laughed again, almost challengingly. His eye was

clear; hand steady; but there was a recklessness in his manner that suggested that he might have been drinking excessively, or was bent on baiting his host.

"Gerry," he said to Wheatley, with a weak attempt to soften his hard tone, "I'd ask you to sweeten mine, but you've got such a sour puss this morning you'd turn it to vinegar."

Wheatley gave him a sickly grin. The fear that was riding him showed plainly in his nervous hands, his furtive glances toward the further end of the table. "Let me have it. I'll see what I can do."

"Nuh—uh. You'd keep it, and that's worse than wasting it. Well, Burke, here's hair on your chest."

"Don't be vulgar," Burke snapped at him.

"My dear Mr. Gordon," Mrs. St. Clair said, "your good spirits are a reproach to me."

Gordon bowed deeply to her. "Thanks for calling me that. I was afraid Burke was going to do it in a minute, although Rittenhouse comes next before me."

"Well, let's keep it at our end of the table."

"Sure, sure. That's an idea. Gerry, my dear, will you let me have the sugar?"

Barbara burst into laughter. "Oh, Mr. Gordon, you're so funny," she said, with a little mocking tone beneath her gaiety.

"Yeah," he growled. "Only Burke don't think so."

"It may seem strange to you, Gordon," Burke said unexpectedly, "but I do."

"Now ain't that nice. Then we're both laughing."

Randolph glanced covertly at Mrs. St. Clair. She was sitting very erect with head raised, looking at Gordon. But the smile she forced on her lips was stiff, her expression wooden, and there was a pallor on her face which make-up could not conceal. Her manner of bold, almost defiant relief at breakfast was shattered; had been, Randolph had observed, when she had burst from the porch and sought futilely to exchange a word with Barbara.

"I say, Ross," Fraser said, "if you and friend Gordon are finished with your entertaining repartee, can't you tell us what you've planned for the rest of the day?"

"Why to be sure. Huh? I thought I'd told you. Well—I expect we'd like to lounge about, say for an hour after lunch. And by the way, Stanley, suppose we take that time to run over your accounts again."

"But, I say," Fraser started to protest.

Gordon laughed loudly. "You asked for it, old dear."

"The irrepressible Mr. Gordon," Burke said in his oiliest tone. "It might be a relief to the rest of us if Slocum took you for a long walk this afternoon. You haven't seen the country on the other side of the lake. Most enchanting view."

"Yeah? Gunner Slocum and who else?" Gordon growled, with a dark look at Burke.

"Listen, my dear chap," Fraser said, laughing a little. "You know, you're sticking your jolly old neck way out. But the plan, Ross; the plan. I've something in mind for myself, but of course I won't run athwart the wish of mine host."

Burke was still looking at Gordon. His jowls and paunch shook with silent laughter. Beryl touched his arm.

"Won't you tell us, Mr. Burke?" she asked a little wearily.

"Of course, my dear."

"My Gawd!" Gordon grumbled. "It's coming around your way now, Fraser."

"And then, as I said," Burke continued lightly, "we'll go out on the lake; have our bathing beauty parade, so to speak."

"Er—Ross," Gordon said meekly.

"Yes, Mr. Gordon?" sarcastically.

"Are you entered in—"

A step sounded behind Burke. He started nervously; swung around. Martha appeared in the doorway.

"Why in the devil—" Burke began, in grumbling tone.

"Party on the wire," Martha said tonelessly. "New York. Insists there's a man named Randolph here. Wants to talk with him. Wouldn't take my no, and rang on again when I hung up."

Instinctively both Beryl and Barbara glanced quickly at Randolph, then hurriedly looked away. Fraser caught this, and stared at Randolph, with a puzzled frown and a growing light in his eyes. Burke too, faced partially around to his left, saw Beryl's swift raising and averting of her glance, and continued to look at her while he spoke to the maid.

"We can't be annoyed. Tell them— No. Wait a moment. I'll take it." He stood up, placing his napkin on the cloth. "If you will excuse me," he said, with a sweeping, comprehensive little bow.

"Perhaps I'd better go with you," Fraser said, as he also rose and started after Burke.

"Do you swim, Gordon?" Randolph asked casually.

Some of the color had left Beryl's face. Barbara's eyes were fixed absently on the spoon which she idly twisted in her strong slender fingers. Wheatley's face was a sickly, sallow mask. He fidgeted nervously, pushed his chair back slightly and glanced after the departing men.

"Sure I swim," Gordon said. "Thrown into the river when I

was a kid, and had to." He, too, looked toward the door. "Ain't he the pill! If he was half a man and would stand on his own, it would be a pleasure to slip him one. But you can't sock putty."

Randolph laughed. "He's just—Ross Burke. They don't come in duplicates, I guess."

"You said a big mouthful, brother," Gordon growled.

"Jack!" Beryl spoke a little breathlessly. "Do you remember what you did with the keys to the car?"

Randolph gave her a slow, unworried smile.

Gordon laughed. "He didn't do anything with them, Miss. They're all hanging on a hook where Burke can watch 'em. It's an idea of his."

There was a step in the living-room. Every pair of eyes turned that way. Martha appeared. Her eyes had lost their rather sleepy, impersonal look. She spoke to Randolph.

"Burke wants you to come up, Mr. Rittenhouse."

Randolph put surprise in his expression. "Wants me? Oh, very well."

Martha stepped back from the doorway, whispered, "O.K." Randolph strode to her. "Watch out for a phoney, mister. And keep your eye on Burke's right-hand drawer."

17

BURKE PLACED THE Continental phone carefully on the desk as Randolph approached it. "Will you please answer that, Mr.—Rittenhouse. We can't seem to satisfy Mr. MacArthur."

Randolph smiled easily. "Why of course, if I can do any good." His eyes, resting on Burke's, held just the right look of puzzled amiability.

He cupped the receiver close to his ear, still keeping the pleasant smile on his face and his eyes on Burke's very suspicious ones.

"Why... no," he said... "I don't understand... Try speaking a little slower and less loudly." He made a wry grimace, but did not lighten his pressure on the crackling receiver.... "There, that's a little better... No.... Rittenhouse... John... Rittenhouse... Yes, I was at the gate when Miss Rogers' brother was leaving... Your men?... Decidedly not. Slocum did not shoot at them. I can swear to it.... Suppose you keep quiet and let me speak a moment... He fired at a hornets' nest and some men who were concealed in the tree came tumbling out and ran away. It was really very amusing. But... See here; if you wish to do all the talking I'll hang up." He grinned amiably at Burke; and put his free hand over the mouthpiece. "This guy is quite hot under the collar," he whispered. "Yes?... I said Rittenhouse.... Oh, but see here; you can't publish anything on us.... Now, damn it, you, whatever your name is, listen to me. If you print one line about Miss Rogers and myself without my consent and if it varies one iota from the strict truth, I'll see your damned rag… No. I will not. If you'd been decent about it, I might have asked Mr. Burke but… Shut up, will you and listen!… As it is, I shall ask him to keep any representative of yours away from the premises during the rest of our stay here. Now go and have apoplexy if you want to."

Randolph's eyes had located the cradle. He slammed the still sputtering receiver on to it, and turned to Burke, while he edged further toward the back of the desk and its right-hand drawer.

"Whew! Who was that chap, and why d'you put him on to me?"

"That," Burke said slowly, "was MacArthur, city editor of the *Argus,* and no particular friend of mine. He described you very carefully and said your name was Randolph and that he had personally sent you here to cover this party."

Randolph's narrowed eyes held their steady gaze on Burke. "Did you ask him how I happen to be engaged to Miss Rogers and to have accompanied her here? That's funny," he went on quickly. "If it's as close as that, this chap should make a good alibi for me, in need."

"That's what I tried to tell Burke," Fraser broke in. "Miss Rogers makes it unquestionable. Looks to me," he continued, with an attempt at lightness, "like a clever newspaper gag to get a man in on you, Burke—pretending that one of your guests is a reporter and demanding to see him, for a chance to get inside."

Randolph's face suddenly clouded. "See here, Burke," he said a little roughly, "did you by any chance mention to this man anything of our discussion of this morning?"

The lids drooped slowly over Burke's watery black eyes, hiding meanwhile their crafty expression.

"If that matter gets into the papers," he said coldly, "it will be your fault." He turned to Fraser. "Perhaps you are right, Stanley. It would be like MacArthur to pull a trick like that—either way." He stepped a pace from the desk, still with his glance avoiding Randolph. "Well, let's rejoin the ladies. We left them rather unceremoniously. After you, Mr. Rittenhouse," he added blandly.

As the three men went down the stairs, Fraser was humming *The British Grenadier.* Reaching the lower floor, he broke off with a laugh. "D'you hear me last night, Rittenhouse? Seems to me now I must have been in uncommon good voice."

"It was one of my pleasant recollections," Randolph said dryly.

Burke, with his unctuous smile, entered the dining-room in the lead. "My apologies, ladies. It was nothing at all. A newspaperman trying to put a trick over on me." He took his seat. "However, Mr. Rittenhouse promptly spiked his guns. And now, Martha, be so kind—the coffee. I'm eager for my afternoon. You wouldn't believe it, Mrs. St. Clair," he said down the table, "I designed this place here for rest and enjoyment, and precious little do I get of either. But this afternoon must be a red letter one."

"Say," Gordon drawled, making his brows frown, "didn't some guy write a book about a scarlet one? You weren't thinking of that, were you, Burke?"

Mrs. St. Clair got very red in the face. "Really, Mr. Gordon, you are quite incorrigible."

"Why," Gordon said innocently, "what've I done now?"

"I think," Burke said in soft, oily tone, "I'll have to speak with Slocum about that walk, Gordon. We're all finished, no? Then I'll see him now. In about an hour, shall we say?" he asked generally. "At the boathouse?"

"Wait a minute," Gordon snarled. "Don't go to setting Slocum on me, Burke. We understand each other pretty well right now, but you could start a deal that somebody'd have to finish."

"Take it easy, Gordon," Fraser intervened. "Don't you know when Ross is joking?"

"Yeah, but it ain't a rib when he signs up that hair-trigger punk."

Burke bestowed his most gracious smile on the two girls and Mrs. St. Clair as they passed him, and started across the room toward the rear exit. Fraser was close behind the ladies, and Randolph followed him.

"Let's go on down to the boathouse," Randolph proposed, before Burke had left the room.

Beryl said, "All right," and turned to wait for him.

The door closed behind Burke.

"Hold on there, Gerry," Gordon called as Wheatley started to leave. He was still seated. "Martha's got some brandy for us."

"I gotta see Miss St. Clair," Wheatley said.

"Aw, you can see her better after a nip. Come on back here and sit down."

Wheatley retraced his steps and sank heavily into his chair.

Barbara had turned back with Beryl, and Mrs. St. Clair went on to the stairs. Just inside the living-room, Fraser caught Randolph's arm, turning him a little aside.

"D'you get the set-up?" he said barely above a whisper. "He's seeing Slocum, not on account of Gordon but about you. I believe he's convinced you've run a jigger on him. If I was sure, I'd tell you to get out of here before an accident happens. At that I could be wrong; but what do you say to my proposition?"

"I'll play fair, if that's what you mean," Randolph said. "Of course it depends on you."

"Righto, and thanks. I'll do what I can." He turned toward the two girls who were regarding them curiously.

"Where do the phone wires come out?" Randolph asked.

"Straight down the front wall, right of the porch." Fraser's eyes were very alert. "Better have a care."

Randolph pulled him over until the four were close together. "Come to the steps slowly," he whispered, "and do plenty of talking, will you?"

Not waiting for an answer, he strode on to the porch, gave a quick glance in the direction Burke should have taken to go to Slocum's cottage, then slipped softly out the screen door and hurried down the steps. When he reached the bottom, he had his knife, opened, in his hand. He turned the corner, saw the double telephone wires attached to the wall. At one point of exposure they passed through a short porcelain insulating tube.

Without disturbing the attachment, he slipped the wires a couple of inches from the tube and cut a short slit in the insulation of one. Bending it, he bared the wire, and opening the cutter blade on his knife, nipped off a little section. While he worked, he heard the laughing voices of Fraser and the girls in most animated conversation.

Straightening the wire, he pressed the slit hard and pulled the two wires back into the tube. There was nothing to indicate in the least that it had been disturbed. Replacing his knife, he pressed the tiny piece of cut wire into the earth, and stepped to the corner.

Beryl and Barbara were coming down the steps, balancing lithely on each tread before their sport shoes sought the next. Randolph joined them as they reached the last, and the four strolled on together.

A little further along they could see more of the shore line to their left and Slocum's cottage approximately two hundred yards away. Glancing in that direction, Randolph saw Burke's pudgy figure approaching the shack, and simultaneously Burke half turned and looked back over his shoulder.

"Did you have a bad five minutes when I was upstairs?" he asked Beryl who was walking beside him.

"Whooee! I'm aging by the minute. Can you tell me about it? Do you think—what does he think? Did you convince him or is he still suspicious?"

"Rather talk about it later," he said in very low tone. "He's a fox. Things are getting a trifle warmer but that doesn't mean they're any worse. Wish he'd come out with whatever he has on his mind. It's always better to have a fellow do something than to be guessing what he might do."

"Aren't you afraid he'll—"

A hail from behind interrupted her. All four swung around. Wheatley waved a hand from the porch steps. "Wait a moment, Barbs," he called. "Want to speak to you."

"Well," Barbara said, in a tone audible only to her immediate companions, "I'm not particularly anxious to speak with you, Mr. Gerald Wheatley."

"He seems harmless enough," Fraser said lightly. "A perfect type, I should say. We have 'em over there too."

Red spots showed on Wheatley's otherwise pallid face; his eyes were bright and harried. Within a dozen feet, he said, "Can I speak to you alone for a second, Barbs—if you others will excuse us."

"Say your piece, Gerry," Barbara said indifferently. "You and I haven't any confidences."

Wheatley scowled. "It's not for me," he said, a little pettishly.

"All the better then. What is it?"

"It's your mother. She simply must have a word with you. Don't be silly, Barbs. It's damned important."

"What is it, then?"

"She wouldn't tell me—only that it's of the utmost importance to you. Aren't we all of us in a bad enough mess now? You can't afford to be stubborn. Look; she's coming now. Sent me on ahead to stop you."

Barbara turned deliberately toward the lake. "I don't know of anything important enough to—"

Randolph laid a restraining hand on her arm. "I think I'd listen to her if I were you, Barbs. Things are beginning to shape up pretty fast. It might be something we should know."

Barbara looked up at him. "You're so darned persuasive—Jack. All right. But you and Beryl must stay with me. Mr. Fraser, will you excuse us a moment?"

"By all means. I too think he's right, Miss St. Clair. Come on, Wheatley. I'll show you where one of the workmen was drowned putting in the supports for that crazy boathouse."

"Thanks," Wheatley said sarcastically. "I'll go sit on a rock. Come on. Got a cigarette?"

While the three waited, Barbara continued to gaze steadfastly toward the water. Randolph, facing Beryl across the path, observed Mrs. St. Clair's approach without appearing to do so. Her color was high, but something new had come into her expression. She always carried herself with an appearance of haughtiness, yet now the erectness of her head gave an impression more of determination.

"I see," she said, when she had joined them, "that my daughter does not wish to speak with me alone. I do not exactly blame her, and for my part I am glad that you two have waited."

Her wide, somewhat staring eyes swept from Beryl to Randolph. "I am bitterly humiliated by what transpired last night," she continued steadily, "and by the interpretation which I understand has been put upon my own share in it. I shall not attempt to explain now, only to say—"

"It seems to me," Barbara said, in an unnatural tone, "that it's a bit late for all this. So what is it that you wanted to tell me?"

Mrs. St. Clair hesitated, until Barbara, still without looking directly at her, gave an impatient gesture.

"Burke tells me," Mrs. St. Clair said, "that he overlooked two of the letters and came upon them by accident when he was searching for other papers in his safe."

Beryl turned swiftly to Randolph. "That is what you were expecting." It was more of a statement than a question.

Randolph nodded soberly. "I suspected it."

"You suspected it!" Barbara cried, aghast. "Why?"

He shrugged. "Solely from what I've seen of this slimy crook. They all run more or less alike."

"And that's why you thought we should wait," Beryl said.

"He didn't offer to give them to you, did he, Mrs. St. Clair?" he asked.

"He did not. He told me he should demand the fullest payment without equivocation."

"Whatever shall we do now?" Barbara appealed to Randolph.

"Do!" burst from Mrs. St. Clair with explosive emphasis. "I refuse to pander longer with this situation. I shall have Gerald get our car out and we will return at once. Moreover I shall go immediately to Chicago and discuss the whole matter with your father, Barbara."

"I don't think it will be as easy as that, Mrs. St. Clair," Randolph said mildly, conscious of the repetition of the same refusal. "I believe Wheatley gave up his keys as I did. Burke undoubtedly intends to hold us all here until tomorrow, and it wouldn't get us anything to ask him for them now. Rather, it would weaken our position. As a matter of fact," he added, with a dry chuckle, "I shouldn't worry much about it just now. I've an idea that he's more concerned over me at the moment."

"You think then," Beryl exclaimed, "that he knows. Well, you're darned cool about it. I am not."

Randolph smiled at her. "Y' know, as Fraser says it, I've been hoping all along it would come around to this; so why should I be upset about it? Like the shower I've an idea we'll get before evening, it ought to clear the atmosphere. Here comes His Oiliness now, as Barbs calls him. Watch him play poker with us. It's funny."

"Funny like hell!" Beryl murmured.

"I'll go back, if you don't mind," Mrs. St. Clair said. "I think we might talk later."

She turned toward the lodge, while the others strolled on.

Burke came down the shore line, then swung over to the path. As he drew near, he took his watch from a vest pocket. He replaced it and beamed on them. "Only a half-hour more." They smiled mechanically, and he went on, with his short, quick step. Randolph followed his retreating figure with a speculative glance.

"I think," he said amusedly, "that our friend is about to make an important discovery."

Beryl gave a short laugh tinged with exasperation. "You are so darned mysterious, and then something goes pop. Couldn't we just be calm and peaceful for a little while, or must you go stirring things up?"

"I've always heard the best way to cure a boil is to bring it to a head, and this Ross Burke is a boil if I ever saw one. Come on, let's go sit on the rock with our erstwhile friends and look at the pretty water."

Beryl gave him a long, sidewise look as they moved on. Barbara seemed altogether occupied with thoughts of her own.

Fraser came to his feet as they approached, then sank down again as the girls seated themselves, and offered his cigarettes. Wheatley, with arms clasped around his knees and gazing moodily over the water, did not stir. Randolph stood between the little group and the lake. Facing them, he also faced the lodge.

"Here comes Gordon," he announced casually. Watching his approach, his eye caught a flicker of movement off to the right of the lodge's further end. He turned his eyes without moving his head and had a momentary glimpse of Burke's plump, bent over figure scurrying in the direction of the caretaker's cabin.

"Curious chap, Gordon," Fraser said dryly. "I've never before seen quite his type, even in this country. I'm blowed if I can make him out—good or bad."

"Aw, he's no different from the rest of us," Wheatley grumbled. "Who wouldn't have a grouch here!"

Randolph covered his watchfulness with a laugh and a casual

gesture of both hands. "Where do you get that 'rest of us' stuff, Wheatley?" he said lightly. "You're the sole possessor of an honest to goodness one."

"Sure you can preach," Wheatley growled pettishly. "You're sitting pretty." He glanced swiftly at Fraser, as if conscious of his slip.

Fraser smiled broadly. "Yes, we all know Mr. Rittenhouse has little to worry him." He looked up over his shoulder. "Hey, Gordon. We were discussing you. Have you a grouch?"

Gordon grinned. "When Burke's around I get one automatically." He seated himself, not too close. "When's this swimming party coming off?"

Randolph's wandering glance caught a flash of Burke as he moved rapidly through the scrub oaks, this time, however, in the direction of the lodge.

"A few moments ago," he said, "Burke told us in a half-hour. He'll probably come out soon and tell us when to dress." He stooped and picking up a flat stone, turned and sent it skipping over the water. Then he swung slowly about again.

A light haze, as yet hardly noticeable, was drawing across the sun. There was no breeze and the unruffled surface of the lake was like polished silver. It was very warm.

"Charming spot, this," Fraser remarked lazily, when no one seemed inclined to talk. He looked at Barbara's sleek glistening head. "A few days more, and I'll be on the big pond."

Gordon laughed sarcastically. "Having made your peace with the big boss, I suppose."

Fraser raised his blond brows. "I'm too comfortable to quarrel right now, Gordon. So let's not bring up anything so unpleasant."

From the corner of his eye, Randolph saw a figure step out of Slocum's cabin and turn in their direction. He gave a casual, all-the-way-round survey of the sky, letting his glance rest momentarily on the approaching figure. It was Slocum, with his ever present rifle cradled over his arm.

Almost as if he had waited for this, Randolph turned more squarely toward the group. His eyes were narrowed slightly, but he smiled as Beryl met his glance, and shook his head.

"You'll have to give me a handicap in the hundred this afternoon. I don't believe I can swim that fast again."

She did not reply in words. Her lips curved a little, in an expressive half-grimace. Then she dropped her eyes. She seemed curiously strained and nervous for her ordinarily well-balanced poise.

"You were in this morning, weren't you?" Fraser asked, and when Randolph nodded, "Sorry I missed it. How was the water?"

"Splendid. Cool enough to be refreshing. This lake must be deep."

Looking at Fraser, Randolph now saw Burke approaching from the lodge. He appeared in no especial hurry.

"Runs right off from here," Fraser said. "That islet out there is a single outcropping. Otherwise it seems to dip with the cliff, over to the left, 's funny," he went on. "Burke can't swim a stroke, yet look at that boathouse. Half over the water which shelves right off with this ledge. You can get into it only through that one door and the water side. Not even a window. He'd be in a pretty pickle if he slipped off the platform some day and no one around."

"That's an idea," Gordon growled.

Randolph smiled. "You might tell him about it," he said in lowered tone. "He's coming now."

"I thought I felt my grouch coming back."

Idly watching Burke's approach, Randolph heard Slocum's footsteps. He didn't turn, but a moment later the caretaker came within his range of vision and stopped as Burke met him. They were opposite the group and about ten feet behind it. Slocum carried his rifle across his left arm, with his right hand covering bolt and trigger guard—much as would a big game hunter in thick growth.

Burke smiled, waved a hand at the group and spoke to Slocum. "Plenty gas in the launch, Steve?" he asked casually.

"Sure."

"Hmm." He raised his glance and looked toward Randolph. "Oh, Mr. Rittenhouse, would you mind stepping here a moment? I was going to have Slocum take us out, but perhaps it won't be necessary."

Randolph was the only one of the group who remained on his feet. He nodded, stepped around those who were in front of him toward Burke and the caretaker. He was within ten feet, when Burke commenced to speak again. At the same time Slocum started to turn slowly toward Randolph, the rifle barrel swinging with the movement.

"I remember now," Burke said, "you had the launch out last evening. Then why can't you—"

Randolph saw the barrel come to a line with his chest and threw himself flat down.

At that nearness the report of the rifle was terrific. Shrill screams knifed through the fading discharge, rose above its echoes.

With a continuation of the same movement, Randolph dived forward on hands and feet. He came in under the barrel, grasped it with his left hand, twisting it to one side as he came upright. His right fist crossed over, with all the power he could put behind it, and crashed on the point of Slocum's chin. Slocum slumped face downward in his tracks.

Randolph was conscious of the hoarse shouts and shriller cries behind him, of Burke yelling frenziedly. He tore the rifle from Slocum's senseless fingers, whirled it once around his head and sent it far out into the lake. Stooping, he patted the unconscious Slocum's pockets, felt in one the hardness of metal and drew out a revolver. He hurled this after the rifle; then sprang upon Burke.

The fingers of his big left hand clamped around Burke's puffy throat, shutting off both his expostulations and his wind. Burke's right hand moved, and Randolph caught the wrist, twisted the arm savagely. Letting it go, he felt of Burke's back trousers pocket, pulled out a small automatic and hurled that into the water. He then whirled Burke around to face him.

Whether real or assumed, Randolph's face was twisted in dark fury. He shifted his grip from throat to shoulder, his strong fingers biting hard. Burke, his face purpled, choked and gasped and tried to turn away. Randolph held him in position.

"I saw that play coming," he said brittlely. "Damn you, Burke, talk fast. Make me believe you didn't engineer that deal or I'll throw you after those guns."

"No, no!" Burke gagged, then got a little of his breath. "I swear it! I swear it!" he cried, beside himself. Tears welled between his puffed lids, spilled down his mottled cheeks. "It was an accident, my poor Mr. Rittenhouse. The worst I've ever seen. You can't—you mustn't think such a thing of me. Oh, I'm nearly mad over it!"

"Yeah," Gordon said coldly, at Randolph's elbow. "Just the kind of accident your Steve pulled year before last. Only you weren't on the spot that time, Burke. Go on, Rittenhouse. Heave him in the lake. Drown the damned skunk. Here, let me help you."

Burke sank on to his knees, held his clasped hands up before him. "Gentlemen, gentlemen," he blubbered, "I beseech you. You must believe me. I—I couldn't do such a damnable thing. I—"

Randolph turned away in disgust. "Stay here, will you?" he called, and sped along the lake shore in the direction of the caretaker's cottage.

As he drew near, he saw Martha on the little porch, one hand on the railing, the other covering her lips. Her face was drained of color.

"Are you all right?" she gasped.

"As rain." Randolph stepped on to the porch.

"What happened?"

"Slocum accidentally tried to shoot me. He's sleeping it off now. We put it up to Burke. You must have heard him squealing his denial."

"He would, damn him."

"Martha," Randolph said soberly, "I want you to show me every pistol and gun Slocum has in the place."

"Will I!"

She led him inside, went from bureau to desk drawer and handed him an assortment of two automatics and a thirty-eight Smith & Wesson revolver. He took them from her.

His roving glance lit upon a double barreled shotgun standing in a corner. He moved over and caught this up.

"Is that all?"

"Every damned gun in the place. I'm sure of it. These and the rifle were all he had."

"They're enough," Randolph said dryly. "Now load my pockets with all the ammunition here."

She obeyed with alacrity, stuffing boxes of the several calibres into his pockets. Finally there was nothing left but two boxes of shotgun shells. "What will I do with these?" she asked.

"Stick one under each arm," he told her. "Wait a moment, will you? I'll be right back."

She followed him to the porch. "I don't know what you are going to do," she said, "but I wish you would blast hell out of those two—"

He grinned over his shoulder. "War's over now, Martha. I'll be right back."

"Sure I'll wait," she said, and stood watching, while Randolph clambered gingerly down the rock to the water's edge and laying down his load, threw one article after the other as far into the lake as he could cast it.

Her slumbering eyes were on him as he came back.

"Look, Martha," he said. "I found one pistol on Burke, a thirty-two automatic. You spoke of the right-hand drawer of his desk. Suppose you can get into that and see if he has another? Do you know if he has any more? I'll take any kick there is coming and won't let either one of them bother you."

"When he goes out," Martha said, "he hides the keys and always keeps the safe locked. I can't get into them, but I never saw any other pistol than that small one. He's always let Steve keep the guns—except that little one."

"Then don't take the risk. I want to get back when Slocum comes to." He started to turn away.

"Wait a minute," she said, and came close to him. "There's trouble with the telephone. I heard Burke tell Steve he was going to call some of the boys from town—his punks, you know. Damned hard gunmen. When he found the phone wouldn't work, he went nuts. He came running over here, but they put me out of the cabin and I don't know what they said."

Randolph considered this a moment. "How can he get word to them if the line remains out of order?"

"He can't—unless he sends Steve to the station in the car."

"Uh-huh." He moved toward the steps. "You're a brick, Martha. We'll get you out of here somehow!"

Color flushed into her cheeks. "You mean that, Honey?"

Randolph turned, gave her a slow smile. "Now, now, Martha. I said 'we.'"

"I don't care. I'll be a slave to you, or to that sweet girl of yours if you will only get me away from here."

"Well, I'll have to see to that punk husband of yours now."

18

AS HE APPROACHED the group, Randolph saw that Beryl and Barbara were standing a little apart from the men who were clustered around Slocum's still motionless form. When he came nearer, the two girls advanced to meet him. Barbara seemed nervous, with an air of disguising it by a flippant lightness of manner. Beryl watched him with lights smouldering in her dark eyes under lowering brows. She appeared very serious.

"My Gawd!" Barbara said. "What's next on the program—a little thing like an earthquake or something?"

"Our swim."

"What! You mean you're going on with it, as if nothing had happened?"

"Why not?" Randolph had slowed his stride but did not stop. He saw that the men, fifty feet further on, were glancing toward him.

Beryl laid a hand on his arm. "Did it come very close to you, Dick?" she said scarcely above a whisper.

"Too darned close," he said cheerfully, pausing beside her. "And was I scared!"

"You knew it was going to happen?" There was a little of reproach in her tone. "You saw that coming and just went on and smiled so unconcernedly? I was watching you. I knew something was up, perhaps just because you were smiling; but not that," she added huskily. "Not that. Oh, you couldn't have suspected that!"

"Well, you see," he said hesitantly, "I've boxed quite a little—for fun. In the ring you get used to watching a man—his eyes, his hands. You know just about when he's going to start something; a sort of sixth sense, I guess. Of course I had warning that something might be pulled off—through Burke. I cut his phone wire. While we were talking here I saw him sneak over to Slocum's, and then sneak back to the lodge. When Slocum came out with his rifle, the answer was simple. I did the only thing I could."

Beryl shivered. "Can you tell us what you've done just now?"

Randolph grinned. "Pulled all his teeth. Every kind of a gun I could find is now in the lake. I want to say a word to Burke, then I'll come back. Nothing to worry about now."

"Do you think you killed Slocum?" Barbara asked. Her blue eyes were very wide. "He hasn't even wiggled since you left."

"Nuh-uh," he said over his shoulder. "No such luck."

"I shouldn't mind if you had," Beryl said softly.

Burke turned from the prostrate caretaker as Randolph joined them. He made his eyes very sober. "You don't know how I regret this, Mr. Rittenhouse. I can't understand even now what happened. Slocum is used to firearms. I don't for the life of me see how he could have been so careless. The only explanation I can give is that from his very familiarity he was lightly fingering the trigger, not of course suspecting there was a load in the chamber; or else in turning, the trigger caught on a button of his coat."

Randolph eyed him steadily during the long speech. He did not make immediate reply.

Burke sighed heavily. "Thank God, nothing serious really did happen. It would have been the most deplorable accident of my life. I should have never got over it."

"Hell!" Gordon said roughly. "You ain't even fooling yourself, Burke. We ain't guessing what happened. We know. Slocum's a gunman, and no gunman lets off a rifle at another feller unless he means to. I don't know what Rittenhouse is going to do to him, but I know damned well what I would. But what we'd like to be sure of is how far you stood behind this."

Fraser stood a little back of the men, watching each speaker in turn but making no attempt to enter the conversation. His expression was sober; his eyes hard and bright. He had the appearance of waiting for some further development. Wheatley was beside him, his cheeks flabby, his mouth loosely open.

"But, Mr. Gordon," Burke cried, "such a thought is preposterous. I am sure Mr. Rittenhouse doesn't entertain it for a moment."

Randolph had not shifted his steady gaze from Burke who, under the relentless stare, was commencing to fidget uncomfortably. He said, "I am waiting to hear you talk a little more, Burke." He turned toward the senseless man. "Showed any signs of coming out of it yet?"

"He hasn't moved a muscle," Burke hastened to say. "We feared possibly—"

Randolph stooped, laid a finger on the side of Slocum's corded neck. He stood up. "Too bad. He's all right. Mind getting a bucket of water from the boathouse, Fraser?"

"With pleasure, old chap." Fraser turned with alacrity.

"I—I'll go with you," Wheatley said and started after him.

"Thanks," Randolph called after Fraser. "I'd go myself, but I want to be right here when he comes out of it."

"You—you're—" Burke faltered, "going to—"

"I am not so much interested in him as I am in you, Burke."

"But, Mr. Rittenhouse, you can't—you mustn't feel that way about me. There's nothing I wouldn't do to prove that I was just as surprised, just as horrified as you."

"As I told you," Randolph said coldly, "I'm waiting to hear you talk."

"Look here, Rittenhouse," Gordon growled, "I'm not copper-hearted, but if I were you, damned if I wouldn't send that punk up for a ten-year stretch on attempted murder. It's out and out."

"But, my dear Mr. Gordon," Burke said with most uncommon meekness, "don't you see such a charge wouldn't stand for a minute in court? In spite of what you all appear to think to the contrary, knowing Slocum as I do, I maintain it was an accident pure and simple."

"And I suppose you'd defend him," Gordon said with elaborate sarcasm.

"He's an employee; I expect it would be my duty, if"—he glanced up at Randolph—"such a charge were brought."

Randolph turned impatiently as Fraser approached, took the bucket from him and dashed the contents on Slocum's face and chest. He then stepped behind him.

Slocum spluttered, coughed, moved arms and legs; then his eyes opened. He shut them tight; then opened them wide, lifted his head and raised himself on one hand. He stared straight before him a moment through narrowed lids; then slowly his head turned in the direction where Randolph had stood when the rifle discharged.

"No, Slocum," Randolph said softly. "Sorry to disappoint you, perhaps, but I'm right here."

Slocum lowered his head, shook it, and got staggeringly to

his feet. His glance groped over the ground close around him. "Where's my rifle?" he muttered.

"If you want it, you'll have to swim for it, you damn' punk," Gordon told him.

Slocum slowly raised his eyes to Gordon, then turned all the way around and faced Randolph. He seemed still a little dazed, but his beady eyes were getting hard.

"I remember now," he said hoarsely. "Something set my rifle off, then you hit me with a rock. You can't do that to me and get away with it, mister."

Randolph held his two fists loosely before him, knuckles up. "I have two more right here, Slocum," he said softly. "And you're apt to get them again on short notice. All right, Burke."

Burke stepped a little closer. He drew his brows down, made his eyes serious. "Slocum, the gentlemen here insist on saying that your rifle did not go off by accident. I do not hold the same opinion, but I am in the minority and consideration for my guests comes first. I am obliged to discharge you. Come to my study at once for your pay and then leave the premises. You may take the small roadster and have it returned later. You may also send someone for your things." He turned to Randolph with a satisfied smirk.

"That's enough, Burke," Randolph said tautly. "That just about settles it. You stay here a minute, Slocum!" he said sharply, as the caretaker turned away.

Slocum scowled at him. "Who th' hell 're you to give me orders!"

Randolph gripped his upper arm, whirled him almost off his feet and set him back. "You stay here till I'm through, or I'll put you out for keeps."

Randolph's manner was completely changed. Theretofore,

except for instants of action, he had appeared smilingly affable, almost self-effacing in his quiet way. Now he was coldly masterful of the situation.

"That was just what I was waiting for, Burke, and you've about convinced me that you are really back of this attempt to put the slug on me. You're not sending Slocum away for punishment. You've got some other idea in your slimy mind. You're not sending him away at all. He stays right here where I can keep an eye on him, and you too."

He stepped closer to Burke.

"I shall not decide until morning whether or not I'll have Slocum up on an attempted murder charge, with plenty of witnesses to prove my case and with the knowledge that you sneaked over to his cabin before he came out with that rifle. If Slocum attempts to leave this place before then, I'll put the police on him immediately, and as for you, Burke, I'll be certain then you were in on it and I'll beat you to a pulp before they get here. Now give your orders."

Burke's mouth hung open. His expression was almost ludicrous between consternation and sly, baffled rage.

"Why—why, Mr. Rittenhouse," he stuttered, "I—I thought I was doing just what you wanted. I—"

"Did you, Burke?"

"Well, I certainly want to convince you. Slocum, go to your cabin. Martha will look after the dogs tonight. Don't leave that place until my guests leave in the morning. Those are my final orders. Go now."

Burke spread his hands, as Slocum, scowling darkly, turned and started to retrace his steps. "There, Mr. Rittenhouse, I told you I would do anything to please you."

"Burke," Randolph said softly, "don't get the idea for a moment that I'll not be watching you. And if Slocum makes a slip, it's you I'll get to first the next time." He stretched his long arms, grinned over at the two girls who were pretending not to watch them. "All right, fellows; how about our swim?"

Burke's jaw dropped in surprise. He quickly recovered himself, put a bright smile on his face and took a step toward Randolph. "You mean it, Mr. Rittenhouse? Then we can forget this unpleasantness and really enjoy ourselves? I am afraid I haven't appreciated you. But I shall try now to make amends. Young ladies!" His voice cracked slightly. "Let's hurry now. Time for our swim, you know."

Without waiting for a reply, that seemed loath to come, he turned and bustled toward the lodge.

Gordon gave Randolph a hard, up-from-under look. "I still think you're a sucker, guy."

"You may be right, Gordon," Randolph said lightly. "At least we've got all the guns in soak now and can enjoy ourselves, as our kindly host says."

Beryl and Barbara were coming slowly toward them.

"Kindly host hell," Gordon growled. He glanced up quickly, and his eyes were bright. "You know, feller, I'm beginning to think I haven't played out all my string with Burke after all." His glance turned slowly where Slocum was plodding sullenly on. "Yeah; let's get into the water. I guess I need it." He started after Burke, but showed no intention of catching up with him.

"I don't believe I'll go in," Wheatley said in disgruntled tone. "No sense getting into a bathing suit when I don't swim."

"Don't be silly," Barbara told him. "Burke asked us all."

"And I think you're right," Fraser said. "There's no question that he's got his wind up bad. If you want my advice, Wheatley, it would be to humor him. Do you get me?"

"Oh, I guess so. But say—I haven't a suit."

"Several at the lodge. I'll fix you up."

Barbara started on, and Wheatley fell into step with her. Fraser turned to Randolph who was waiting for Beryl.

"Sorry I wasn't of any use to you in that mixup, old chap. Fact is, I was stupefied. Didn't get a thing of it until that gun let go and frazzled my eardrums. Want you to believe me, if I'd suspected anything I'd have had a hand in it."

"Thanks," Randolph said, without expression. "What do you think, Fraser—was Burke behind it?"

Fraser's eyes showed the utmost frankness. "Pretty serious thing to put on a chap, isn't it? I hate to say it, but I don't know just what to think. You have the upper hand now, but don't forget you set him on his heels, and 's long as I've known the bounder he doesn't take nicely to that sort of thing. Now we'll have our jolly old swim, eh what, Miss Rogers?"

Beryl smiled, a little tightly, without reply, and Fraser hurried on after Barbara.

"What did he mean by that?" Beryl asked a little sarcastically. "To warn you?"

"Oh, he probably thinks it would be pleasanter all around if I didn't rub it into Burke," Randolph said unconcernedly. "Hey—don't tell me you're getting nerves."

"Say—don't you know you darned near got killed?"

"Whatever it was, it's behind us now. We don't have to think of it any more. Good thing it happened too. I was nervous all the time with Slocum and his guns and didn't know it. I'm breathing easier already."

"You and your damn' cheerful grin," she said with a note of exasperation. "Good Lord, what a time a gal would have if she really cared for you."

He glanced at her quickly, but she was looking ahead and the long lashes partly hid her eyes.

"Tell me," she said abruptly. "You look so darned smug; are they going to pull anything else?"

"What can they do?" he said blandly. "One thing, they haven't anything to shoot with."

"Do you know, I had an idea that you and I were closer than any two here. Don't you think you can trust me; do you want to treat me like a child or—don't you feel that way?"

"Just now," he said, "I got the suggestion that you didn't—how'd you say it?—really care. Do you, a little—Beryl?"

She turned her head and gave him a long, slow look, but her eyes were unreadable.

"Damn!" she said unexpectedly. "I got such a shock I'm still scared. Won't you tell me, Dick? I know there's something on your mind."

His eyes lingered on hers a moment, speculative, a little wistful.

"I'm really not worried any more," he said. "But I still want to keep an eye on Burke. You see he wanted to call out some of his men in town. The phone wouldn't work, and the only way he could reach them was to send Slocum out to phone them. By keeping Slocum here he is checked; and that's all we have to think about. That was what I meant when I talked to him just now, and he knew it."

She glanced at him in wonder. "How'd you ever think that out?"

He laughed. "Simple. Martha told me when I went to Slocum's cottage to get those guns. She even dug them out for me."

She shook her head in mock sadness. "They all come and eat out of your hand, even Fraser. Say—do you trust Fraser—absolutely?"

"I suppose so. It's diplomatic to, anyway."

"Uh-huh. Going secretive again."

He stopped and faced her. "There's only one thing I've kept secret from you," he said slowly. "Beryl, Beryl—oh, I guess I've no right to say it."

"There's one thing sure, Dick," she said in lowered tone. "This is a darned poor spot to say—whatever it is. Look; they're all waiting for us on the porch steps."

19

THE WHOLE LOT of them were gathered on the porch. Randolph, the two girls and Burke wore bathing-robes; Mrs. St. Clair, who had been persuaded by Wheatley to join them, was still in street clothes, while the three other men had on their bathing suits.

Fraser was stockily built, with thick chest and heavily muscled arms and legs; Gordon, on cleaner lines, appeared hard as a rock and scarcely less powerful; Wheatley, slender but tall.

Burke looked them over with envious eyes. "Poor little me," he said plaintively, "I feel as if I was in a bunch of prizefighters." He was smiling broadly and apparently in the best of spirits. He caught Barbara's hand. "Come on, my dear. Let's lead the way."

The launch, decked over forward, was broad beamed, with a commodious cockpit. Mrs. St. Clair was helped in and took a seat in the stern, Burke sat down near her, gathering his robe about his thin legs, while Beryl and Barbara clambered on to the little deck where Fraser joined them. Gordon and Wheatley got aboard, and Randolph cast off.

He started the motor and put a hand on the steering line. "Where to, Burke?" he asked.

"Go up the right-hand shore a little way. I want to show you my guest cottage."

Inside the dark boathouse, the air was comparatively cool, but when they shot into the sun it was hot.

Burke pointed along the shore. "See that landing, Mr. Rittenhouse? The cottage is right behind it, in the trees. You'll see it in a moment."

They skirted close to the shore line which, unlike the end of the lake near the lodge and the appearance of the further side, had a sandy beach backed by thick foliaged trees.

"Looks like a path in there," Gordon commented.

"It runs to the cottage," Burke informed him. "It's only a half-mile from the boathouse. A place to sleep, for some of my romantic friends when they want to get away from the crowded lodge and enjoy the moon on the lake."

"Your moon must rise in the north," Gordon said. "That shore is south, isn't it? If the sun is in the right place."

"Figuratively speaking," Burke said with a chuckle. "Yes, that's south, Mr. Gordon. The lodge is on the western end."

"It is really very lovely here," Mrs. St. Clair said soberly.

"The most charming spot I know," Burke said enthusiastically. He spoke carefully, very politely, seemingly eager to impress his guests with the polished side of his character. He was smiling, too; but Randolph, glancing at him from time to time, frowned slightly. There seemed something decidedly incongruous in this new attitude.

Burke waved his arm comprehensively. "I own the entire lake shore and for a considerable distance back of it all around. No one can trespass on my property from any side. I'm really quite isolated here." He sighed. "The only place where I know perfect peace."

"Yeah," Gordon rumbled. "I've observed how peaceful it is here."

"Ah—there you can see it now," Burke said quickly. "The top

of the roof just back of the landing. It's just a cute little love nest. Can't you go a little slower, Mr. Rittenhouse?"

Randolph threw the gear into neutral, swung the launch around the end of the landing.

"Got a rowboat there, I see," Gordon remarked. "Oars in it too. Somebody use it?"

"There is no one here but ourselves. As a matter of fact, besides the launch there is no other boat on the whole lake."

"Padlocked?"

"Yes, but the key is at the lodge."

"Think I'll come up for a row later. I need the exercise. Mind?"

"Whenever you wish, of course. The whole place is altogether at the disposal of my guests. Remind me to give you the key when we get back, Mr. Gordon."

"Thank you, Mr. Burke," Gordon said and grinned.

"Shall we go ashore?" Burke asked everybody. "The sand is very soft to lie on in the sun and the water is not deep. I come here often to splash and tan."

No one seemed inclined to accept the suggestion. Finally Fraser said, "I fancy we're all deep water swimmers, Ross."

Burke bowed almost ceremoniously which, in his bathing suit and robe, was not particularly impressive. "Very well, Mr. Rittenhouse. Why not take us back to the islet? Wheatley and I can sit on the rock, and I assure you the water there is deep enough to suit anyone."

Randolph threw in the clutch, swung the launch around in a large circle and headed back. He stepped a pace forward and leaned a hand on the combing of the little deck where Beryl and Barbara were sitting, with Fraser sprawled on his stomach, elbows propped and chin supported by his cupped hands.

The haze had cleared perceptibly, but in its stead clouds had banked and were slowly rising along the western horizon. There was no breeze except that of their passage. The air, when they were still, was hot, sluggish and oppressive.

Wheatley, who for some moments had been frowning severely to himself, with his eyes shifting from point to point with no one objective, seemed to come to some sudden decision. His lips moved as he muttered some expletive; then abruptly he left his seat beside Gordon and moved close to their host.

Randolph, lazily dividing his attention between their course and Beryl's lovely, half-averted face, listened expectantly.

"See here, Burke," Wheatley said, above the steady throbbing of the motor, "I've been thinking over the matter. You had me on the run, and you were all the time telling me what Slocum would do if I didn't fall into line. Now with Slocum out of it, seems to me it changes the whole complexion. I've still got to make a deal with you, I know that, but I haven't got to be rushed into it. I'd like to talk it over again."

Fraser, who caught some of the words, raised his head, frowning. He met Randolph's glance. "The damned fool," he muttered. Randolph nodded, increased the speed of the motor.

"I do not choose to discuss it now," Burke said with asperity. His tone was angry, badgered.

"Well, I do," Wheatley said hotly.

For an instant Burke's mask of polite amiability dropped. He stared at Wheatley with flaming eyes. "Then wait till we get alone on the rock." Wheatley began a retort, and Burke stood up, stepped up beside Randolph. The launch was nearing the islet.

Burke pointed. "If you will swing around it, Mr. Rittenhouse, you will find a little beach on the side toward the boathouse. You can run up on that and let us off."

Randolph nodded. "Grand place you have here, Burke."

"Thank you, Mr. Rittenhouse," Burke said with an attempt at cordiality, although his tone still held a vestige of his former anger. "I could turn it into a resort and make a lot of money if I wanted to. I thought of it once—but I have enough."

He remained beside Randolph while he turned the launch in a wide swing that brought it back on its first course, headed it for the sand at the base of the outjutting rock, and pulled out the clutch.

"Clear the forward deck," he called lightly. "Passengers ashore. You deckhand there, forward, stand by to get overboard and snub her."

"Aye, aye, sir." Fraser stood up and stretched his muscular arms.

Randolph reached up and swung the girls, one after the other, down into the cockpit. The little craft nosed in with decreasing speed. Randolph glanced ahead, then over the side.

"All right, forward. Overboard you go."

Fraser splashed into the water, put a hand on the stem and set his legs. The bow crunched softly to a light, jarring stop. Wheatley crawled awkwardly over the deck and down the side.

"Fifty yards anywhere off here," Burke told Randolph, "the water is very deep; twenty feet for that matter. I don't know if there is an anchor, but perhaps you won't need it. There doesn't seem to be any wind."

"We'll manage."

"Now do enjoy yourselves, young ladies," Burke said, with

plainly forced amiability. "I like to see people around me happy. Er—Mr. Rittenhouse, will you give me a hand up? A man gets a little stiff for want of exercise."

Randolph grasped him with both hands on his waist and lifted him lightly from flooring to the small deck.

"My God!" Burke gasped over his shoulder, with a quick frown. He felt his way gingerly along, sat on the combing and plumped down on to the meager beach.

Randolph stripped off his bathing-robe, stepped to the deck and sprang down beside Fraser. Before shoving off, he turned to glance curiously at the islet which was scarcely more than twenty feet across at its widest part. The beach gave to a short slope of sparse grass and then to bare ledge. On the right, as Randolph looked at it, the rock rose to a height of five feet in a rough pinnacle.

On the opposite side, another outcropping extended upward approximately the same distance, but was topped by a flat, smooth surface. Wheatley crawled up on this and seated himself, gazing down the sheer drop into apparently deep water beside him.

Two or three scrub trees had sprung up in crevices where earth had lodged. Randolph looked at the base of one and his eyes narrowed at the evidence of Slocum's marksmanship of the previous evening. Fraser, following his glance, chuckled dryly. "He'll get a bit out of practice now," he said below his breath.

Randolph saw that Burke was moving up beside Wheatley, and set his shoulder to the stem of the launch. As it started to move, he vaulted aboard and Fraser followed him.

Back in the cockpit, he smiled at Beryl's sober face, received one of her twisting little grimaces in return and put his hand on the lever. Reversing the propeller, he let the launch go astern a few lengths, then shifted into forward speed and pointed off to one side of the rock. Almost immediately he shut off the motor.

Getting on the deck, he waited until he was sure the craft had lost all headway. He stepped to the combing and went into the water with a flip backward somersault. When he came to the surface, he saw bobbing heads all around him and that Mrs. St. Clair was the only occupant of the launch. An impromptu race started, with all five keeping well abreast. As Randolph rolled in his stroke, he saw that Fraser and Gordon were to his right and observed that both, while appearing a trifle muscle bound, were swimming like old timers.

Fifty yards off the side, Randolph, slightly in the lead, raised an arm and twisted around in the water. The others turned obediently.

"Give you five yards, Beryl, Barbs. Go to it!"

The water was churned into five lanes as they shot back at swifter pace than the outward journey. Randolph worked his way to a corner of the transom, caught the edge with both hands, let himself out to a full arm's length and then shot upward and twisted lithely to a sitting position.

One after the other, he pulled the swimmers aboard. Then finding a short piece of rope, he made a short sling over the side. A glance to the islet between whiles showed Wheatley and Burke, side by side on their flat rock, apparently in very heated conversation.

"Want another race?" Barbs asked. "That water's just plumb gorgeous. Not too warm; a bit cold when you go down."

"How about some plain and fancy diving?" Randolph said. "We've got all of a three foot take-off."

"So, why not!" Beryl said. She was standing, sleek as an otter. Her cheeks were flushed; her eyes bright. For the moment at least, she seemed to have forgotten the day's unpleasantness.

"Follow my leader," Barbara suggested. "You go first—Jack. Anyone stumped is out."

After several minutes of this, Fraser suggested a halt and asked for cigarettes. Mrs. St. Clair offered her case and held matches for them. Beryl and Barbara took theirs to the little deck and sprawled at their ease, while the men remained in the cockpit.

"What a pity," Mrs. St. Clair sighed. "This is a perfect beauty spot. What a charming place it would be if it were not brooded over by that evil genius—"

She broke off, gazing toward the islet. Abruptly her voice rose in an incoherent scream. She pointed frantically.

Heads bobbed up as the others looked around.

Randolph saw Burke alone on the rock. He was standing half erect, starting to clamber down to the flat ledge. Wheatley was nowhere in sight.

"Look! Look!" Mrs. St. Clair cried. "Gerald—he's gone down."

Randolph saw movement in the water close beside the abrupt rock. A hand, threshing wildly, came into view. Like a flash, the three men went overboard.

Before the water closed entirely over his head, Randolph heard a sharp cry from behind him. It was not Mrs. St. Clair's voice, and it held a note of pain. But now he was intent on speed.

He was the first to the ledge. Reaching into the water, he got a firm grip on the back of Wheatley's bathing suit as his head sank beneath the surface. Holding him securely at arm's length, Randolph raised his mouth above water, turned on his back and swam toward the little beach. Wheatley moved his arms in desperate attempt, but very weakly and as if it were an unconscious effort of survival.

Fraser came up from behind, put an arm under Wheatley's body. Gordon swam close but seemed uncertain what he could do. After a few strokes, Randolph tried and found bottom. At once he caught Wheatley in his arms, raised him bodily above the water and carried him to the flat ledge.

Wheatley, gasping and choking, seemed, with his eyes closed, to have lost consciousness. Randolph rolled him on one knee, rid him of some of the water he had swallowed. Then placing him on his back, Randolph helped him with artificial respiration. He kept this up until Wheatley's purpled face assumed more normal color and his breathing became more natural.

Pausing in his kneeling position, Randolph turned a frowning glance toward the launch. Beryl was standing, watching. Barbara, seated on a thwart, was bent over so that he could see only the bright sheen of her hair, while Mrs. St. Clair was leaning above her daughter. Randolph came to his feet.

"How in hell did it happen, Burke?" Gordon growled.

"Why—why," Burke stuttered, "he was talking to me, then suddenly he slipped off the rock and went down. I don't know what happened. It was so quick I couldn't possibly catch him."

Randolph turned from his slow scrutiny of Burke's agitated face. "Seems to be coming around all right now," he said quietly. "You fellows look after him and I'll get the launch in."

He started to wade into the water.

"Why the hell didn't you do something to help him?" Gordon persisted. "He came damned near drowning."

"I couldn't," Burke said excitedly in denial. "I can't swim a stroke—and I guess he can't—"

Randolph took off in a flat dive.

When he pulled himself over the side he was immediately aware that something was amiss. Barbara was bent over, with both hands grasping an ankle. She looked at him with a wry grimace.

"Now I've gone and done it," she said ruefully. "Sprained ankle, if it isn't broken."

He took it gently from her grasp, felt gingerly of the already swelling flesh, flexed it slightly against her unconscious protest.

He shook his head. "Nothing broken, Barbs; but a darned nasty sprain. How come?"

"When Moms let out that ungodly screech, I jumped from the deck into the cockpit. I must have been half looking toward the rock and my foot struck that board there. It twisted under me and I went flat. It hurt like hell."

"What happened?" Beryl asked. "How is Wheatley?"

"Pretty narrow squeak; but he seems all right now. Hadn't come to when I started out. I thought something had gone wrong out here," he added with a glance at Barbara.

"What did he do anyway?"

"Well, Burke says he slipped."

"Do you think he—" Mrs. St. Clair began, when a sudden clap of thunder interrupted her.

They glanced hurriedly around. The storm was stealing upon them unawares. Already the western sky was darkened and scurrying clouds were shutting off the sunlight.

"Got to get you invalids in," Randolph said, with a smile at Barbara.

He started the motor, headed the launch around toward the rock.

Beryl stood beside him at the wheel; Mrs. St. Clair and Barbara were in the stern, and the noise of the motor rose between the two pair.

"Suppose Burke pushed him off?" Beryl asked.

"Could; but it might have been just an accident."

"Like Slocum shooting at you."

"Something like that. Wheatley will tell the world when he comes to, or, if it is true, he may be afraid. He was dumb enough to be riding Burke, which doesn't help matters all around."

"I expect the next thing will be he'll poison the lot of us."

"Pleasant thought, and I'm hungry." He made a little gesture with his head toward the stern. "Getting better acquainted?"

"Ve—ry penitent; and Barbs is always easy."

There was another dull peal of thunder.

Randolph threw out the clutch and let the launch glide in. Wheatley was still lying prone, but they could see that his eyes were open and he was moving his head. Burke was fidgeting around just behind him, glancing anxiously at the gathering clouds. "Can you hurry, Mr. Rittenhouse?" he called. "It's going to rain, and I don't like storms."

Fraser and Gordon caught the bow and eased the launch to a stop. Randolph went forward, knelt and took Wheatley in his arms as they passed him up. Randolph carried him back and laid him on the deck. "Feeling pretty bad?" he asked.

"Weak as the devil," Wheatley said hoarsely; then, as Randolph bent down to put a sweater under his head, whispered, "Tried to drown me, damn him!"

"Pass it up now," Randolph answered in the same tone. "See you later."

Burke and Gordon came aboard; Fraser pushed off, as Randolph reversed, and then hopped over the side. He came to the cockpit and looked at Barbara with sudden concern. "Anything happen to you, Miss St. Clair?"

"Sprained ankle. See how it's swollen?"

Burke, who had been watching the clouds, glanced around, where Barbara sat with the injured member extended, one of Mrs. St. Clair's arms around her shoulder. His eyes were wide beneath puckered brows with an expression of almost consternation.

"Why—why—my dear Miss St. Clair—" Thunder pealed and the echoes rolled around the lake. Burke broke, turned his head shoreward, glanced at Randolph, then looked back at Barbara. "You should have a doctor at once." He frowned and his eyes sought Randolph's broad shoulders in a quick glance. "I regret—my phone is out of order. But I can send Slocum out. It is the only thing to do. That ankle looks very bad."

Randolph measured the distance to the boathouse entrance, shut off the motor, and with a hand still on the wheel, looked slowly around.

"I know something about that sort of thing, Burke. We don't need a doctor, and Slocum stays here."

"Why, of course, Mr. Rittenhouse. Whatever you say. I thought only to do something to help. Can't you get us in a little quicker? This is going to break right away."

"Any faster and we'd smash," Randolph said coldly. "Fraser and Gordon, will you hop off and hold her? Then make her fast with those tie-lines. Guess you'll have to carry Wheatley up."

Fraser glanced at Barbara, then without a word got on the little deck beside Gordon. Dusk was fast gathering outside, but as the craft slipped slowly into the boat-house it was like entering a dark cavern. A flash of lightning illuminated the interior momentarily, but when it was gone, it seemed darker than ever.

Burke waited only until the side touched the canvas covered edge of one platform, then let himself awkwardly down and scurried for the lodge.

"Can you carry me?" Barbara asked. "I'm awfully afraid I couldn't make it, unless I hobble on one foot."

Fraser turned from securing his rope, but stopped when Randolph said, "Surest thing. Let me get them started first."

He lifted Wheatley, who was making no effort to help himself, and handed him over to Fraser and Gordon. Then he aided Mrs. St. Clair to the platform.

"Anything I can get ready?" Beryl asked, gathering up robes and sweaters.

"Martha might get up some hot water in a deep footbath. Throw in a half-cup of Epsom salts; best thing in the world for a sprain."

He held his hand toward her, but she vaulted lightly over the side and started on. Mrs. St. Clair said, "Bring her right to my room," and followed Beryl.

Randolph stooped, took Barbara's wet form in his arms, careful that the injured ankle swung free from the other, and stepped directly from the seat to the platform. She laughed a little and put one cool arm up around his neck to help ease her weight.

As they came through the doorway they felt the first drops of the advancing storm. The thunder was louder and more frequent.

"Heavy?" Barbara asked.

For answer Randolph raised her outward with both arms level with his shoulders. When he lowered her again, her blond head nestled a little against his shoulder. Her eyes were upturned, and he caught something of their half teasing, amused expression.

"Three—what was it—five thousand years ago the thunder banged and Æneas carried his Dido off to the cave? I'm just out of school and the story seems new."

He glanced ahead where Beryl was striding on with her lithe, springy step, and laughed. "Quaint thought. Does it hurt much?"

"So much it makes me foolish." She moved a little, and her arm drew heavier on his neck. He glanced down and saw that her eyes were on his, their blue deep violet. She smiled, showing white teeth. "Almost worth the darned ankle for this," and he couldn't tell now whether she was teasing.

Rain blotted out the western sky. They could hear it storming forward through the trees with the hissing, rustling sound of an advancing flood. Lightning ripped through the gray curtain, momentarily blinding them. Randolph swung into a fast trot.

"We'll get it now," Barbara said. The almost perpendicular wall of water swept over them. Barbara turned her face against his shoulder.

Randolph took the porch steps, nudged open the door. None of the others was in sight, either on the porch or in the big living-room as he pushed on, regardless of the water dripping from their wet bodies.

Barbara rubbed her eyes against his upper arm, raised her head and shook her matted hair. Randolph swung toward the stairs, groped for the first tread in the gloom.

"And now Sappho goes up," she murmured.

As they reached the first landing and he turned carefully to keep the ankle from hitting the wall, she twisted a little; her left arm stole up around his neck and joined its mate; her face slid up on his shoulder.

For an instant the muscles of his arms tightened; then he said, "If Sappho isn't darned careful, she'll get a bump. I can't see a thing."

"I feel so safe here," she whispered, then laughed unexpectedly. "It's such fun to tease you—Dick." The "Dick" was in a whisper.

Mrs. St. Clair had put a light on in her room, and the open door rescued the corridor from darkness. She had also placed towels on the bed, and when Randolph bent down to lay Barbara gently on these, he saw that her lashes were wet. Her hair was also, for that matter, but there was a mistiness in her eyes that did not come from the rain.

She looked up at him and smiled. "Thanks for the taxi," she said, and turned her face away.

"Call me when you're ready," Randolph said, "and I'll come in and fix up that ankle. It may keep you off your feet for a day or so, Barbs—but that has its advantages."

20

THE STORM PASSED, leaving an overcast sky, a light drizzle and an atmosphere that, while slightly cooler, was heavy and oppressive with moisture.

Barbara sat in a wing-chair. One leg of her flowing blue silk pajamas was rolled above the knee, and that foot was thrust into a deep basin which Beryl had requisitioned. Beryl herself, as fresh as a rose in early morning, sat on an arm of the chair, idly smoking a cigarette and watching proceedings with an outwardly casual but critical eye.

Randolph knelt beside the basin, gently massaging heel, arch and swollen ankle with strong, but expert fingers. His head was close beside the free chair arm and once Barbara reached out and ran fingers through his ruffled brown hair.

"You're pretty good, Doc," she said. "I think I'll have you regularly."

Beryl's eyes winced slightly, against the smoke rising from her cigarette. "Ah," she said. "A further discovery. He's a medical student."

Randolph caught up a towel, took the foot from the bath and patted it dry. "Nuh-uh. Only football."

Placing the foot in correct position, he wound it firmly with a roll of absorbent cotton which he secured with strips of surgeon's tape. When he set it on the floor, Barbara said, "It feels so good I think I can walk on it."

"Better not. Stay off it tonight and it will go easier in the morning."

"But I'm starved."

"I think we can persuade Martha to serve your dinner here."

"I'll be so lonely."

"I'll eat with you," Beryl said.

Randolph glanced over at Mrs. St. Clair who was sitting aloof by the window, frowning deeply at her thoughts.

He said, "I imagine she can serve three as well as one. Somehow I've an idea it will be pleasanter here."

"There he goes again," Beryl said. She reached over and mashed her cigarette on a tray. "More mysterious premonitions."

Randolph laughed. "Simple matter of deduction. Burke is sore at developments. He's on the outs with everyone here, and with the guns of his best bower spiked and the phone out of order, he is in a corner. A rat in a corner is not a nice, peaceable animal. He's sure to sputter and make everyone around him uncomfortable."

"Is that all? Honest to goodness now? You're not looking for any more near tragedies?"

He shrugged. "What more can there be? Of course there are one or two here who might try to take advantage of his position in the corner; not real rat catchers, but perhaps victims of the rat when he was free to roam. They might stir him up so he'll try to bite; but I just think it will be unpleasant—nothing more."

"Oh, yeah?" Beryl said softly. "Will someone tell me why I should trust this man! I know darned well there's another treat in store for us. Dynamite probably."

"Well, you won't be so near the explosion then."

"So that's what you meant by advantages," Barbara said. "I'd been wondering. You mean he can't—"

Mrs. St. Clair came abruptly to her feet. "The girls can eat here," she said, "but I think I shall go down. I want a final word with that man."

Randolph smiled placatingly. "I really think you might do it better in the morning."

Beryl said, "Damn it, he's smiling again. That's a sure sign of it."

"Well, you see Wheatley started to rag him this afternoon—"

"And darn near got killed for it. You mean he's dangerous."

"I mean he's pretty well stirred up and might be more tractable when he's cooled down."

"Oh, well; you'd better take his advice, Mrs. St. Clair. He knows something, but he'll be damned if he'll tell it; then something goes pop."

"Nothing but base calumny," he said and grinned.

Barbara said, "Hey, Doc. Suppose it would be safe to have a cocktail? Three cocktails?"

"If Martha takes 'em from the bottle. I'll go see about it."

Beryl's "You and your Martha," followed him out the door.

He went down the back stairway, chanced on Martha in the hallway and stated their wish.

She agreed without demur. "Better that way," she said. "Burke has been drinking and he won't probably notice at all. He started soon as the storm let up and he's drunk as he oughta be now. And when he's drunk he's mean as poison. He'll put on a show; you see if he don't."

"How about your Steve?"

"My Steve!" she said with utter disgust. "Say, you must 've handed him a cuckoo, mister. He's over there nursing a bad jaw and a grouch. Lucky you got rid of those guns, and I don't mean maybe. And say," she added, in a lower tone, "if he suspected I'd helped you he'd kill me. Don't forget your promise, Mister Man. I know damned well something's going to break tonight. I feel it." She looked around her, up the stairway, toward the rear door. "If those two ever get together tonight, they'll cook up something, guns or no guns."

"I'll tell you," Randolph said, "if he leaves his cottage, try to get word to me quick, will you?"

"Sure will. I got to take him his grub bimeby. I'll watch him, and you oughta keep an eye on Burke."

Randolph passed on the request for cocktails and handed her a folded bill.

"I don't want to take it," she said, "from you. But it could be handy for a getaway." Without troubling to turn away she thrust it into the top of her stocking.

As Randolph left Mrs. St. Clair's room after delivering his messages, he encountered Wheatley in the corridor. Wheatley looked a little haggard and drawn from his recent experience, but he also showed the effect of more recent indulgence in some liquor to which his weakened condition had not prevented him from gaining access. His eyes were bloodshot and almost feverishly bright. His manner was swaggering and assertive.

"Looking for you, Rittenhouse. S'posed you were in there doctoring Barbs; but those dames 've all turned the cold shoulder my way and didn't want to intrude. Now; Burke tried deliberately to drown me this afternoon. Pushed me off that rock with his elbow. I'm going to do something about it."

"Better take it easy, Wheatley," Randolph advised him. "You made a mistake getting after him anyway; and after all we don't want to get him cutting up while we're responsible for them," with a nod toward the door he had just quit.

"Hell! I don't know why I should think of them. They're not worrying 'bout me. 'Nother thing; Burke put the squeeze on me. I'm not afraid of that little guinea pig when his big snoozer isn't around, and I'm going to have it out with him."

"Oh, calm down," Randolph said wearily. "You haven't the only grief."

"Why the hell should I calm down? He tried to kill me. It's my turn now."

"Listen. I pulled you out this afternoon when you were making your last trip down—"

"Yeah; I meant to thank you for that."

"Don't mention it. But what I was going to say is this: I feel responsible for those ladies if you don't. We have Burke in a spot where he'll be inclined to behave for the rest of the time we're here, if someone doesn't start badgering him. Now, you lay off or I'll be inclined to drop you in where I pulled you out."

Wheatley glared at him with anger-ridden eyes. "Damn it, Rittenhouse, you've been against me from the start. You wouldn't pull in with me when I asked. You don't fool me a bit with your responsibility for the ladies. The thing is you have your own game to play with Burke and don't want any interference. And I don't see why I shouldn't look out for myself."

Sudden anger gleamed in Randolph's eyes. Then he smiled. "Hop to it, Wheatley," he said softly, "but just try to remember what I've just told you."

Wheatley gave him a mean sidewise look, muttered what sounded like a curse and strode on ahead. Randolph did not hurry his step. As he turned down the stairway he heard the murmur of voices behind Burke's tightly closed door. The fact that he heard them at all suggested they were raised above normal tone.

In the living-room he found Gordon sitting in a corner of the big sofa before the fireplace. A bottle of Scotch stood on a tabouret beside him, and he held a highball glass in which ice tinkled pleasantly. Wheatley had found another glass, ice and soda also on the tabouret and waited no one's invitation to prepare himself a drink.

Gordon turned his head as Randolph's step drew near. His dark, somewhat liquid eyes held an ugly leer. "Wheatley says you want us to lay off Burke," he said a little challengingly.

"I advised *him* to; not particularly for his own account, although it didn't get him much this afternoon."

"He was a damn' fool," Gordon said, scowling at Wheatley. "He says Burke pushed him off that rock. At the same time, if he did to me what he claims Burke did to him, I'll tell a man he'd be dodgin' bullets 's soon as I could get my hand on a gun."

"He would too," Wheatley blustered, "if I'd known where I could have found one."

"There you go shooting off your mouth," Gordon growled. He took a deliberate swallow. "You wouldn't shoot a fly, if the fly was looking at you."

Wheatley reddened. "Night isn't over yet," he muttered and raised the glass to his lips.

Gordon winked openly at Randolph. Then the mean look came back again into his narrowed black eyes. "What I was getting at, were you giving orders for the rest of us?"

"I don't know what you are making of it," Randolph said slowly. "I haven't anything to say about what you do or don't do. That's your lookout. Wheatley escorted two ladies here, friends of Miss Rogers. That makes it different where he's concerned. Since you spoke of it, I might suggest it would be pleasanter for the people upstairs if Burke wasn't stirred up any more without reason. If you have business with him, that's your own affair."

"I get you. Fair enough—'s long you don't start telling me what I can do." He looked at Wheatley with infinite disgust. "I have business with him, but I don't care whether I do it tonight or in the morning. I'll go easy on him this evening, unless he starts something himself. Wheatley will too. He only wants to shoot his mouth anyway."

Wheatley started to protest, then found it expedient to turn and stare toward the stairway whence came the abrupt sound of Burke's voice in loud, querulous tone. The slamming of his door followed, footsteps, then his voice went on again.

"I tell you, Fraser," he said distinctly enough to be clearly heard by those below, "this is my final word. Either you make over that half million to me or you go up for trial, when you won't be sailing this week or in ten years. I'll sign those acceptance papers in the morning; and that fifty thousand of securities stays where it is. I won't discuss it again."

They reached the landing. Fraser cautioned, "Sssh!"

Gordon cocked an eye up at Randolph. "Quite a storm we had," he said lazily.

Burke stumbled on the lower step, caught himself with a little difficulty. His eyes were watered and bleary, and his walk was uncertain. Fraser put a smile on his face as he came up to Randolph. His frank blue eyes held only polite interest.

"How is Miss St. Clair? Jolly nasty ankle she had there."

"I think it won't be so bad if she keeps off it tonight. The others decided to keep her company."

Relief showed in Fraser's face before he turned toward the drink wagon which, freshly served with glasses and ice, stood in its accustomed place beside the dining-room entrance.

Burke stopped close before Wheatley, fixed his unsteady glance upon him, and with hands clasped behind his back, commenced to teeter back and forth in most judicial attitude, even if his motions were like those of a boat at anchor in a choppy cross sea. Wheatley met the beady black eyes for a brief instant, then raised his glass and spent some time in swallowing its contents.

Gordon, who was watching amusedly, laughed aloud.

Rings rattled on the brass rod as the portières were thrust back. "Dinner is served," Martha said in her expressionless voice.

"How's for a cocktail?" Fraser said cheerfully.

"Safe bet we'll all have one," Gordon said, "except Rittenhouse. He's still in training for any more rescue acts he may have to pull."

Fraser said, "Four doubles, eh?" and got busy with ice and bottles.

Burke watched Wheatley step over to Fraser and stand with back toward him. He sneered and turned to Gordon.

"Don't believe you got anything more to say to me, Gordon." His voice had lost its sharpness and was becoming noticeably thick. "What I said stands 'n' nothing you could say anyway would alter it."

Gordon leaned forward, resting an elbow on his knee. His eyes staring hard at Burke, were smoky. "I got a hell of a lot to say to you, Burke; but I'm not saying it now. One thing, I promised Rittenhouse to be good; and for another you're getting too damned drunk to understand it."

Burke bristled angrily. He faltered a little as he attempted a quick side step, and Gordon laughed.

"That's deliberate falsehood." Burke sputtered. "I never drink so I don't know what I'm doing or saying. You're making deliberate pre—"

"Here we are!" Fraser called. "Come and get it, as they say in your bally old West, or I'll throw it to Wheatley. Come on, Ross," he added, when Burke did not move. "Let it go now. Drinks are waiting; dinner is waiting, and our guests must be served."

Randolph looked idly at a magazine while Burke stood up with the three other men. He drank his cocktail hastily, and its immediate effect seemed to brace him. "Ah, very good, very good, Stanley. Serve my double at the table." He set down his glass and clapped his hands, although Martha stood not ten feet from him and in plain sight. "We will have dinner, Martha. Come—gentlemen." He hesitated on the last word and gave it a slightly slurring accent.

Burke led the way, came to a halt with his hand on his chair back and looked puzzled when he saw the services all placed at his end. He glanced at the bare cloth beyond and around at Martha.

"Miss St. Clair can't walk," she explained. "The other ladies are staying with her."

Burke frowned, said, "Then we'll try to do without them," and apparently forgot the matter. He seated himself fumblingly, and Randolph took the chair beside him. Fraser brought in his own and Burke's second cocktail; Gordon and Wheatley carried theirs to their places.

When he had finished his, Burke turned toward Randolph. His head shook a little and he narrowed his watery eyes as if to help them to focus while he looked long and searchingly at Randolph's imperturbable features.

"Something 'bout you, I'm trying to remember," he said finally. "Can't seem to recall it. Le' see. You went in swimming. B'fore that, you hit Slocum. And b'fore that—yes, b'fore that—" He jabbed a finger in Randolph's direction. "Have it. It's your name. You aren't Rittenhouse. You're somebody else. Tried to fool me, damn it. I tell you no one can fool Ross Burke. Too damned smart for all of 'em."

Randolph smiled pleasantly, although it was somewhat doubtful if Burke was aware of the nature of his expression.

"That isn't it, Burke. You thought so for a moment. Now you're just thinking what you thought."

Burke looked puzzled. "Thinking what I thought," he repeated slowly. "Now just what does that mean? Yes, I b'lieve that was it. Thinking what I thought. That's Einstein, isn't it?"

"No; Hammerstein." Gordon clasped both hands to his head expressively; then continued with the food before him.

"Anyway, Rittenhouse," Burke said, "if you are Rittenhouse, you're only friend I have here. All these others hate me; damn it, hate me!" His voice rose. "But they're 'fraid of Ross Burke just the same—what he can do." He glared about him with malignant, if blurred eyes.

"Martha," Gordon said, with disgust plain in his tone. "Let me have that bottle of Scotch out there, like a good girl, will you? I don't want any of Burke's wine."

"Heh?" Burke said uncertainly. "Oh, Scotch. Yes, we'll all have Scotch, Martha. Serve it around, please. And make one for Mr. Rittenhouse. Insist on it, Rittenhouse."

When the bottle came to him, Randolph poured from it into a glass Martha set beside him, shot soda into it, then took up his water glass and touched it to Burke's.

"My only friend," Burke said, smiling broadly, and gulped his own.

By the time coffee was served Burke was almost incoherent; his mood had become sullen and morose. The black coffee freshened him momentarily and he made his faltering way with the others to the living-room. Fraser appeared unusually thoughtful for him, although his smile was friendly enough when he avoided looking at Burke. Wheatley had drunk copiously; whether sitting or standing, his head was bent, he darted furtive glances from left to right, under lowered brows. He seemed to be trying to make his appearance ugly and dangerous. Gordon was obviously disgusted. Altogether the atmosphere within was as dull and oppressive as that without.

Gordon yawned and turned to his host who was sitting in a deep chair, blinking his eyes in an endeavor to keep awake. "Hey, Burke; where's that key to the boat? I'm going for a row. If I stay here I'll absorb a grouch like the rest of you."

Burke opened his eyes, said, "Martha."

Gordon returned to the dining-room, came back with the key and started out. As he passed Fraser, the blond man said, "Better have an eye out for the dogs. With Slocum in his cabin, there might be one or two straying about."

Gordon tapped his left lapel significantly. "Then there'll be one or two less dogs."

Fraser raised his eyebrows, but made no comment.

Gordon had been gone but a few moments when Beryl came down. She hesitated at the foot, and Fraser stepped to her. "Please present my compliments to Miss St. Clair," he said, "and my wishes for a full recovery in the morning."

"With pleasure, Mr. Fraser." She walked on toward Randolph who turned from where he had been standing at the davenport table, leafing through a magazine. "Oh—Jack; that's what I'm looking for; a couple of magazines."

"For yourself or Barbara?"

"For both of us. Why?"

"I was going to suggest that we take a little run on the lake."

"Good idea. It's a little stuffy inside, and I'd like some air. Wait till I run up with these."

Randolph turned to Burke. "Mind if we take the launch?"

"Hey?" Burke opened his eyes wide. "Sure; sure. And Miss Rogers? I'll go with you. Make me feel better."

Beryl had paused on the first step. She glanced at Randolph, and he nodded.

Fraser was stuffing his pipe. He looked at the glowering Wheatley with an amused smile. "So that relegates me to a pipe on the porch and a book in bed. Wheatley, you're not exactly the most charming company I've known."

Wheatley stood up, yawned and stretched. "What the hell! Guess I'll turn in." He passed Randolph and muttered, "If you drop him in the lake somewhere, I'll try not to feel too bad about it. He'll cut up; you see if he don't."

Randolph laughed. "Don't worry, Wheatley. I'll check him in the boathouse if he gets too bad."

They were standing at the foot of the stairs. Wheatley went

up, while Fraser strolled to the porch, leaving a trail of fragrant smoke behind him.

Burke raised himself to his feet, with some slight difficulty, set his bearings and started across the floor. His course was a trifle erratic, and Randolph stepped to him and caught his arm. Beryl joined them and they started out.

"Cheerio and a pleasant trip," Fraser called as they descended the steps.

Randolph waved his free arm and grinned over his shoulder by way of reply.

A light breeze had come up, partially lifted the mist from the surface of the water and permitted the risen moon to shine wanly through drifts in the feathery clouds. Grass and bushes were soaked, but Beryl walked before them and Randolph guided Burke's faltering steps along the graveled path.

In the boathouse, Randolph remembered a flashlight on a joist at one side of the door, and with its aid got his two passengers aboard and cast off. Starting the motor, he sent the craft at slow speed through the opening. Once outside, he saw that visibility was not all that could be desired. He made out the darker shore-line easily enough, but could barely discern the islet a quarter of a mile away. He steered for that; had covered perhaps half the distance when an exclamation from Beryl caused him to look around.

"Look, Dick. He's gone to sleep on my shoulder, and I don't like that."

Randolph chuckled. "Ease him down on the seat, and we'll get rid of him."

He spun the wheel, turning the craft in a circle, and headed back. In the boathouse again, Randolph snapped the flash and set it on the deck. He took up the recumbent Burke, without awakening him, lifted him over the side and deposited him on one of the side platforms, close against the wall. He found a piece of canvas which he rolled and placed under Burke's head for a pillow. Not quite satisfied, he caught up a rope's end, looped it around one of Burke's arms and tied it to a staple in one of the upright joists. Stepping to the single door, he found the key on the outside, reversed it, closed and locked the door and dropped the key in his pocket.

"We'll give him a chance to sleep it off," he said as he hopped aboard, doused the flashlight and backed the launch into the open.

Once on their course, he came to the after seat to sit beside Beryl, trailing the tiller rope in one hand. They went past the islet for a short distance, and Randolph shut off the motor.

"Let's drift," he said. "I want to talk with you." He cocked an ear off the side. "There's Gordon rowing. You can hear his oars chocking. I imagine I can see him, nearer the shore and up ahead of us a little way."

Beryl said suddenly, "Dick! My—pistol! It's gone. Somebody must have taken it from my purse. It's not here now. I don't know why I didn't miss it before."

Randolph frowned; then said lightly, "I guess it won't matter. Perhaps it slipped out in the room."

21

SLOCUM SAT ON the porch of his little cabin, smoking and gazing surlily out over the dark water. From time to time, he threw a discontented glance over his shoulder toward the interior where Martha had retired to her own small room.

He heard the launch start out, although he could not see it. He frowned as he heard it return, pause and start out again. Five minutes later, he got to his feet, with a deep growling curse, knocked the ashes from his pipe and, entering the cottage, closed the door behind him. He turned off the light in the diminutive living- and dining-room and went into his own. In the darkness, he removed coat, trousers and shoes. He was about to get into bed when he heard the shot.

It was not a loud report. It sounded muffled; then in a moment of frozen silence he heard the echoes from the far shore of the lake.

In Martha's room there was the thump of her feet as she jumped from bed to the floor. "Did you hear that, Steve?" she called excitedly. "Sounded like a shot."

"Course I heard it," he shouted, wrestling around to locate his discarded things. "Damned right was a shot. Turn on that cursed light, will you? I gotta hurry."

Martha came from her room in a hastily donned skirt and sweater, and snapped on the light. By the time that Slocum, cursing everything in general and his missing weapons in particular, stood in shoes and trousers, she was ready to accompany him.

"Where d'you think it was?" she asked as he tore open the door.

"Come from the direction of the boathouse. Sounded like it too—sort of muffled," he called back from twenty feet ahead of her.

"Wait for me, Steve," she said imperatively. "You can't tell what it is, and I'm not going to stay here alone."

Grumbling, he stopped until she had groped her way to him. Clouds had scurried across the face of the moon, and it was dark once more. "Go slow," she cautioned. "No damned use to hurry, and I can't see a thing."

"Follow me then," he growled. "Wonder what the hell—" He broke off, stopped abruptly and she bumped into him. "Hear that?"

"It's the launch, isn't it?"

"Sure. Up above the rock an' headin' in. Come on. We gotta find out what that was."

"Maybe it isn't anything," she panted from close behind him. "Perhaps somebody shot at a mink. You said there were one or two 'round the boathouse."

"Yeah? An' who in hell's got a gun? Maybe Burke could've dug up another one, but 'cording to you he was drunk an' most like he's in bed. That's a hell of a crowd we got here this time, 'f you ask me. I wouldn't care a damn if any one of 'em bumped themselves off—'specially that damn' Rittenhouse," he added in a throaty growl.

"See," Martha said. "There's no light in Burke's room. Guess he's sleeping it off all right. Only the light in the living-room."

"Kinder funny that. They musta heard it too—unless they're *all* asleep. But we can't see them side rooms." He turned his head in the other direction. "Yeah; that launch's comin' in fast. Come on now. Just down this rock. We'll take a look in the boathouse anyway."

"Better wait, Steve. I'm scared. There might be—"

He reached the corner of the boathouse, went on.

"'at's damned funny," he growled. "Door's closed."

He put a hand to the knob, turned it and pressed inward. It did not give. "By Gawd, this is funny," he grumbled. "Somebody's locked it. Now what the hell!"

"The launch is almost in," Martha said from a corner of the building. "I think I can see two people in it. Yes—Mr. Rittenhouse and one of the girls. That would be Miss Rogers. The other can't walk."

Slocum came to her side, pressed gingerly forward on the sloping ledge. "Hey!" he yelled. "Know what the hell's the matter in here? Door's locked, and I heard a shot a few minutes back."

The motor was shut off. Randolph called, "We thought we heard one too. Wait; I've got the key. I'll run in and open up."

The launch glided slowly into the opening, and Slocum hurried back to the door. In a moment he heard the key in the lock, and the door was swung open. Randolph stood with the flashlight pointed straight down. "Better stay outside, Martha," he said very soberly. "Come in here, Slocum. I only got one quick look as I hurried to let you in; but it looks bad."

He pointed the flash toward the ceiling, stepped to the launch and extended his hand. "Come, Beryl; come ashore." He helped her over the side. "Wait out there with Martha, will you?" He swung the flash to light the entrance. Shivering a little, she strode quickly to the door.

Randolph turned, led the way along the platform, with the flash pointed ahead to guide them. At once they saw Burke's body lying crumpled against the wall where Randolph had left him. He was lying on his side, with his face toward the narrow lane of water where the launch now stood. He did not seem to have moved at all. His head was pillowed on the canvas. The rope's end was still attached to one arm. A crimson splotch showed on the left side of his white shirt and ran toward the floor until it was lost beneath his coat. He was dead.

Slocum came from his knees to his feet with a lurid curse. Even in the reflected light of the flash, now pointing toward the door, his eyes gleamed like those of a madman.

"All right, mister," he snarled. "What d'you know about this?"

"Not a thing more than you do, Slocum," Randolph answered steadily. "I do know how he got there. That's all."

"How in hell did he get there, then? Who put that rope 'round him?" Slocum was speaking with difficulty, as if his throat was constricted.

"He wanted to go out on the lake with us," Randolph said quietly. "We started. He passed out; went to sleep. We brought him back here and I put him where you see him. Thought he might sleep a little of it off in a half-hour. He'd been drinking badly. I put that rope on him, in case he came to enough to roll over and fall in. I locked the door and took the key, so no one would come in and fall over him. Are there any other keys to that door, Slocum? Where were they kept?"

"That's a special lock," Slocum said dazedly, replying almost mechanically, as if his mind was tangled with other problems. "There never was but just that one key, and no other key would open it." He broke off and stood staring hard at Randolph, with the same insane look in his eyes. "There's something 'bout this I don't just get—yet. You put him there, you tied him, locked him in and you say you went off and left him. I don't get it all—yet; but, by God, mister, I'm goin' to!"

He glanced backward over his shoulder.

"Can't touch a thing there, Slocum," Randolph warned. "You've got to leave that for the coroner."

"And maybe," Slocum muttered, as if unaware he spoke aloud, "th' coroner 'll have something else to look at when he gits here."

He turned abruptly—his glance sweeping Randolph like the cut of a knife—and started toward the entrance. Randolph followed more slowly.

A step sounded just outside the door, fell on the wooden threshold.

"What you got here?" Gordon asked coldly.

"Where the hell you been?" Slocum hurled at him.

In the light which Randolph turned squarely upon him, Gordon's eyes narrowed darkly. He shrugged. "Up the lake rowing, if you have to know," he said in the same tone.

"Where'd you leave the boat?" Randolph asked, turning the flash slightly aside, but leaving the three men in the reflected illumination.

Gordon gave Randolph a puzzled glance. "Up there; tied to the stake—and locked. Here's the key, Slocum."

"I don't want it," Slocum said savagely. "Then how the hell did you get here so quick? That's a half-mile, mister."

"Thought I heard a shot and ran down the path," Gordon said coolly. "What you got here anyway?"

"Burke. He's been murdered. Shot," Randolph told him.

"Whew!" Gordon whistled. "What the hell?"

Slocum abruptly pushed past them. "You go on up to the house," he said. He muttered something else they couldn't distinguish as he rushed out the door.

"Know anything about this, Rittenhouse?" Gordon said.

Randolph said, "No," shortly, and stepped outside.

He found Beryl standing beside Martha, and took her arm. "Let's get up to the lodge," he said, and led the way.

He felt Beryl's arm shaking under his clasp and tightened it. "Buck up," he said in low tone, bending down toward her.

"It's simply ghastly," she whispered.

Gordon and Martha followed in silence.

When they came to the porch steps, the door at the top was flung open. Fraser and Wheatley, in dressing-gowns, were silhouetted against the light from behind them.

"What's the trouble down there?" Fraser asked crisply. "I was dozing and thought I heard a shot."

"Burke's been murdered—shot," Randolph said succinctly, mounting steadily and helping Beryl.

"Good God! Is that true?"

"Absolutely. Did Slocum come this way?"

"Slocum? No. Where is he—Burke?"

"In the boathouse." Randolph reached the top, urged Beryl to go in and released her arm. He turned and looked off into the darkness; then he swung slowly back, glanced at Fraser's shocked features, and looked from him to Wheatley.

Wheatley's jaw hung slack with open mouth. His head weaved slightly; his eyes were round and staring. He seemed incapable of speech. Gordon came in with Martha, and all moved slowly toward the living-room, Fraser letting the door close gently and following them in.

A slow step sounded from above, on the stairs. Barbara came hobbling down on one foot, a hand on the banister, her other arm over Mrs. St. Clair's shoulder. Her face was startled; her mother's pale. "What has happened?" Barbara demanded.

Beryl stood at the foot of the stairs. "Burke's been shot," she said.

"Holy Mither of Moses!" The cry came from the further end of the living-room. Mary, the cook, stood there, her stringy gray hair in violent disarray; her cotton dress buttoned haphazardly. Her stout form commenced to quiver. She caught up a portion of her dress and began to cry in it.

Fraser came up to Randolph. His eyes were very keen, with a hard glint in them.

"You say he's dead? There's no doubt about it?"

Randolph nodded. "No possible doubt."

Fraser slashed the air with one hand. "We'll have to get the police on this of course. Sooner the better. But I ought to look at things upstairs before they come. There are certain things of Burke's there'd be no sense in letting get into their hands. You better put that phone in working order." He started to turn away. Randolph detained him with a hand on his shoulder.

"I'll come with you, Fraser. Leave the door open."

Fraser gave him a quick, hard look; then said, "Very well," and moved toward the stairs.

Randolph stepped to Gordon. "Do this, will you?" he said. "Take this flash. You'll find the phone wires running straight down the front of the porch. At the bend near the bottom, is a porcelain tube. Pull the wires out of that and splice the one that is cut. You can strip the insulation and put the two ends together."

Gordon looked at him curiously from the corners of his eyes; then without a word took the flash and started out. Randolph turned to Beryl and laid a hand on her shoulder. "I want to go up with Fraser. Please wait here with the rest. I won't be long."

She gave him a ghostly smile, and he turned, took the stairs three steps at a time.

The door of Burke's room was ajar. Randolph went in without knocking, closed it behind him. Lights were on in the study part of the enormous room. Behind the desk, Fraser had pushed aside an oil painting and was working on the dial of a wall safe. He did not look around.

Randolph saw paper on the desk, seated himself and taking a pen from its modernistic holder, wrote while Fraser read numbers from a slip he held and spun the dial. He was finished when he heard the bolt click, and stood up, leaving the paper flat on the desk. Fraser reached an arm into the surprisingly deep safe, drew forth bundles of elastic-banded folded papers, came over and dumped them on the desk. He seated himself in the swivel-chair which Randolph had vacated, and started to sort them.

Randolph leaned over his arm and laid a finger on what he had written. "Wish you'd sign that, Fraser," he said, "before you get too busy." He had an amiable expression on his face; his eyes were sleepily watchful.

Fraser suspended one hand which still clasped a number of the folded documents, and bent over Randolph's paper, with frowning brows. "It's only an order," Randolph explained, "on the Fraser Investment Company to deliver to Richard W. Randolph, on proper identification, the fifty-odd thousand dollars' worth of securities, standing in the name of Mrs. John

A. Randolph, entrusted to the company with no lien against them. It is to be signed by the president."

Fraser turned in his chair, gave Randolph a keen up from under look. "You know, of course," he said, "that you may not find yourself in a position to use this."

Randolph's smile widened, while his eyes looked even more sleepy. "Suppose we take a chance on that, Fraser."

Fraser turned more squarely toward him. "You don't want to give me a confession, confidentially, of course, in return for this?"

Randolph shrugged. "I don't see that it would do any good. I've an idea the authorities will iron the matter out, and we'll leave the findings to them. Meanwhile, suppose you sign it, Fraser. It won't do you any harm; it might save me a lot of bother, and it's what you promised."

"So I did; so I did," Fraser murmured. He reached for the pen. "I see now," he said while he wrote, "the deep significance of your remark concerning the elimination of Burke." He blotted his signature, shoved the paper over to Randolph, and shrugged his thick shoulders. "As you say, we'll leave the matter to the police. It is a terrific thing—murder; but I can't quarrel with you over it. I must admit, that regrettable as it is, it relieves me of a nasty situation.... Ah"—he was already busy in his examination of the purloined documents—"this is it."

Randolph folded his paper, placed it carefully in an inside pocket. Standing behind Fraser's shoulders, his eyes held an amused expression. "There must be one or two others, Fraser, who probably are in the same position as you."

Fraser said, "Hey?" absent-mindedly, and glanced around.

"Mrs. St. Clair, for one," Randolph explained.

"Oh, yes; of course. Miss St. Clair will appreciate it. I'll look immediately."

Fraser swiveled in his chair, snapped his lighter and set the flame to the paper in his right hand. He held it, burning, over a deep cuspidor, shifted it in his hands until it was entirely consumed; then dropped the fragments that remained into the receptacle. He looked around and up at Randolph. "I fancy it won't be too much to ask you to forget this, will it, old chap?"

"Not at all. Also two letters of Mrs. St. Clair's, and a little document concerning Slocum. I'm very curious to see that."

Fraser's blond brows drew down in a puzzled frown. He turned his head. "Wait a moment, and I'll see about it."

He took the cuspidor, walked over to the bathroom, and flushed the water. When he reappeared on the threshold, a bell tinkled faintly on the wall behind the desk. Fraser's eyes became alert. "Answer that, will you? It's the phone from the gate. Must be Slocum. See what he wants—and don't tell him I'm here. If he asks for me, say you'll have to call me."

The bell tinkled again. Randolph took the phone from its hook, as Fraser advanced slowly toward him. It made crackling sounds. A smile grew and expanded on Randolph's face as he listened.

"Ah," he said, "it's the ebullient Mr. Morrison.... Yes... Randolph..." The sounds in the phone became sharper. Randolph twisted his head around toward Fraser and grinned. Fraser seated himself on an edge of the desk. His expression was not amused.

"Now that's really too bad," Randolph said into the phone, with his eyes still on Fraser. "So you're shut in the gate house, it is cramped and hotter than hell, and a million dogs are running loose outside. My poor Morrison, you have my deepest sympathy."

The phone emitted a raucous squeak, and Randolph held it momentarily from his ear. "You don't sound even drunk, Morrison; and of course that makes it more unendurable.... Tell you what, old fellow; in my car is a pair of very stout corduroy trousers—yes, and a small strip of sheet iron. Would you like me to get them down to you?"

He again took the phone from his ear, and replaced it cautiously. "Ah, that is bad, very bad," he said after a moment. "Poor Scanlon up a tree and half of his pants gone?... And a cameraman too?... And the dogs are keeping watch on all you three, so you can't get away? What a predicament."

Randolph winked at Fraser; but Fraser turned his head away to glance down at the papers on the desk. He began to riffle through them, looking at the superscriptions on the back of each or the envelopes that contained them.

"Sorry, Morrison," Randolph said into the phone, "I can't do a thing for you; and you'll have to admit it was very injudicious of you three to climb over the fence.... Listen... But I'll give you something to help you while away your time... A bit of news.... Are you listening?... Then get this; Ross Burke was murdered a short while ago. Shot once, through the heart.... No; I really can't tell you anything more just now. Good bye, Morrison...."

He listened a moment longer; then turned to hang up the phone, after he had seen Fraser swing around toward him. The bell continued to tinkle frantically, and Randolph found a piece of paper and stuffed it against the metal, reducing the sound to a futile tapping.

"Do you think that advisable," Fraser said very seriously, "to break that to newspapermen, as I understand they are, before the police pass on it?" He shrugged. "Of course you know what you're doing."

Randolph chuckled. "Can you think of anything more exasperating, Fraser, than three newspapermen, figuratively and actually treed, at least cut off from all possibility of communication, with news of that sort breaking? I can't."

Fraser shrugged. "You amaze me. S'pose I should call you Randolph now, eh? You've amazed me all along. I'll say one thing; you have remarkable nerve. Fancy a man in your situation having the heart to joke." He shook his head.

Randolph came to the desk. "Have you come across those other papers?" he asked.

Fraser held out a thin envelope. "This I imagine will bring joy to Mrs. St. Clair. Will you give it to her, or shall I? On second thought, you do so. If she believes you came up here and took it, it will do you no harm."

Randolph identified the contents, and slipped the envelope into his pocket. "How about one for Slocum?"

Fraser looked further, held another envelope toward Randolph. "I'm not sure I should do this," he said doubtfully, "but I expect it will make little difference to the important matter if you satisfy your curiosity."

"None at all, probably," Randolph murmured, as he drew out a single typewritten sheet, with a notary's attestation of its signatures, and hastily scanned it. He thrust this also into his pocket. "I think I'll keep this a while, Fraser."

Fraser shrugged. "So long as you don't say how you came by it, old chap. I s'pose I'm really in charge of all these matters.

Doubt if Burke left any relatives. Still the police could make it disagreeable if they got the idea we did away with anything, no matter how foreign to the situation; and, y'know, I want to sail on Wednesday. Get the idea?"

Randolph nodded, without spoken reply.

"Here's one marked Wheatley," Fraser said, "and here, by Jove, is another for Gordon." He held them in his hand while he frowned thoughtfully. Then he glanced up at Randolph.

"Tell you what, old chap; I've thought you were a pretty decent sort all along. I shouldn't, but I'm going to do a turn for you; and I'll admit I've had no love for a man of Burke's type. I don't feel I owe him anything. Now these papers show a motive on the part of both these chaps. Enough perhaps, to take a bit of the burden off you. I'm going to put them back with all the others."

He slipped off the desk, arranged the disordered documents and shoved them carefully back into the safe. He closed it and spun the dial. Then he turned to Randolph with the faint suggestion of a smile.

"Thanks," Randolph said. "As a matter of fact, we all had what might be construed as motive; you, Mrs. St. Clair, myself, Wheatley and Gordon. Miss St. Clair only indirectly; Miss Rogers, Slocum, Martha and the cook, I presume, none at all."

Fraser's smile became a little more evident. "Which makes it all reasonably complicated. Of course these police chaps have a way of getting at things; but I'm inclined to believe, after a great deal of the usual pother, they'll arrive at nothing at all."

Randolph's expression became more serious. "I don't agree with you, Fraser. I think they'll find it all very simple."

Fraser clapped him on the shoulder. "You're wrong. Don't

worry, old chap. For my part, I'll give them no help. And now, don't you think you should give them a ring?"

Randolph stooped over the desk, took the Continental phone from its cradle. He held it to his ear, pressed the holder once or twice; then replaced the instrument. "The line is still dead," he said. "Gordon didn't do anything with it."

"Then we'd best go down and fix it." Fraser turned abruptly toward a window. "D'you hear that? Sounds like dogs barking."

"Morrison," Randolph said dryly, "said there were a million running loose."

"Then we should go down before they get up here. They're nasty beasts." At the door, Fraser paused to switch off the lights. "One thing you can be assured of," he said, "if things go wrong with you, I'll see that the ladies get home safely."

"Thanks," Randolph said flatly. "I should appreciate that—if necessary."

22

AH, YES; THE mystery!

23

BERYL MET THEM at the foot of the stairs. She clasped Randolph's arm, stayed close to him, as the three walked toward the fireplace end of the living-room where all the rest were gathered. Mrs. St. Clair and Barbara were seated on the couch; Gordon leaned against the chimney, a highball glass in his hand. Wheatley sat in a chair beside him. Between the two stood a tabouret with whiskey bottle, ice and glasses. Martha and the cook were a little aloof from the guests, just before the dining-room entrance. Fraser went on toward Gordon, and the tabouret, while Beryl pressed hard on Randolph's arm.

"I was worried," she whispered, "you were gone so long. And those dogs outside—they seem to be roaming everywhere."

"Will tell you something funny," Randolph began. "A little later. I want to ask Gordon—"

He broke off and turned his head as there came the sounds of the screen door being opened and hastily closed and steps on the porch.

Slocum came straight into the room. Beneath the brim of his hat, his black eyes darted from one to the other of the group clustered closely together before the fireplace. In his right hand was a pistol.

He came forward swiftly; stopped just beyond arm's reach of Randolph. He gestured with the pistol.

"You," he said to Randolph, "get over there beside those men. I ain't foolin', mister," he said harshly.

"Step!"

Randolph gave a quick glance down at Beryl, then walked over as directed, taking his stand at the left of Fraser, who was next to Wheatley. Slocum followed to the end of the couch, motioned Wheatley to his feet with an expressive gesture of the pistol.

"You women," he said, "get over there at th' other side of the fireplace where I can keep my eye on you. I don't know if I've got any business with any of you, but I'm not taking chances. Come on—move!"

Fires burned in Beryl's dark eyes as she raised Barbara to her one sound foot and, with Mrs. St. Clair on her other side, helped the blond girl across to a chair. Beryl and Barbara's mother remained standing beside her.

Slocum stood facing the four men at a distance of ten feet. He raised the pistol slightly. He brushed back his hat a little with his free hand. His eyes were both insane and murderous.

"One o' you four," he said hoarsely, "killed Burke. I'll let you all speak your piece, but I'm going to kill th' man did that job. If any o' you try a fancy move I'll shoot, and I don't miss at ten feet, 'nother thing; don't get a notion you can make a break for it an' get away from me. If you get outa this room, th' dogs will take you. Now, you, Gordon, there—"

"Just a moment, Slocum," Fraser said calmly. "You aren't the law. The law will take care of this. If you shoot one of these men, you'll burn for it."

Slocum gave a harsh, mirthless laugh. "You don't know your book, mister. A guy can't burn but once. I'm due for a burnin', and I'm goin' to take th' man with me who put that on me. I ain't so sore 'bout bein' shot out of a job. That ain't it, but Burke held a signed paper over me. That paper places me on the grid.

Burke told me that if anything happened to him out here—like what did happen—that paper goes to the police and cinches me for an old job. T' hell with this talkin'. You there, Gordon, take it up. Where was you when Burke got shot an' what you got to prove it?"

Gordon's eyes were cold, hard slits. He stood straight and his hands hung loosely at his sides.

"I told you once, Slocum. You must be off your nut if you forgot it. I was rowing, up the lake, when I heard the shot. I put the boat back and came down the path to the boathouse and found you there."

Slocum's pistol, which had been covering Gordon, shifted a trifle to center on Wheatley, although Slocum's eyes seemed on each of the four.

"You next there—what's your name—Wheatley. Spill it!"

Wheatley was shaking in every member, as if suddenly taken with the palsy. He opened his mouth, tried to speak, failed to utter a word, then swallowed.

"I—I," he stuttered finally, "was in my—room—upstairs. They—they—Fraser woke me up. I—I didn't know what had happened. I didn't do it, Slocum. I didn't. I swear I didn't."

The most of Slocum's attention seemed to hold a while longer on Wheatley, then moved slowly to Fraser.

"All right, mister. You're next."

"I don't like this, Slocum," Fraser said coldly. "You're making a—"

"I don't give a hoot in hell what you like," Slocum broke in angrily. "If you got anything to say, say it. You got your chance now an' your only chance."

Fraser shrugged resignedly. "If you force me— After dinner

I smoked a pipe on the porch. When the others left, I went to my room, prepared for bed, lay down and started to read a book. I must have dozed off. I was awakened by what sounded like a shot. I threw on my dressing-gown, aroused Wheatley, as he told you, and we came down together. When the others came from the boat-house, they saw me thus. They can tell you so."

Slocum's glance shifted to Randolph, and evil delight grew in his mad eyes.

"I was hopin' so," he said, and for the first time his voice was low, satisfied. "But you can shoot off your mouth before you take it if you want to."

A little of the color had gone from Randolph's face, but his eyes were steady.

"Thanks, Slocum. I'll speak my piece, but you'll wait till I'm done, won't you?"

"If you ain't too damned long, p'haps I will."

"In the first place, Slocum"—Randolph paused, cleared his throat—"you're a little dumb. You know the answer yourself, if you want to see it—"

"He was up the lake with me!" burst from Beryl.

Slocum did not shift his steady gaze a hair's breadth.

"Says you, Miss. Now shut up; I kinder enjoy listening to this guy—under th' circumstances. Go on, punk!"

"It's plain as the nose on your face, or that gun. You don't have to ask us. Each of us can tell a story that will make you believe it was one of the others. But you can prove it yourself."

"I don't see anything, mister, except you're on one sweet spot."

"I'll tell it to you then. But first, Slocum, I'd like to mention something else that I believe will interest you. I've seen a certain paper. I know just where that paper is this minute—

where you can't get your hands on it unless I tell you—where no one else except myself knows it is, although some others may think they know."

"What th' hell paper you talkin' 'bout? I ain't got a lotta patience."

"It begins something like this," Randolph said slowly: " 'In the matter of the wanton killing of John Cohalan—' "

"Stop!" Slocum yelled hoarsely. His fingers whitened on the grip of his gun. It seemed that he was on the point of shooting.

"Easy there," Randolph warned him. "I know where that paper is, Slocum. Would you like to have it?"

"You give it to me or I'll blast you now!"

"I can't give it to you now," Randolph told him. "I can tell you where it is. I'll make a bargain with you."

One or the other of the men at Randolph's right moved in his cramped position. Slocum's gun swept them, then returned on Randolph. Slocum's brows were knit in concentrated endeavor to think.

"Might make a difference; might not," he said uncertainly. "I ain't sayin' I'll let you off. What's your bargain?"

"You know that I know what is on that paper, signed by witnesses, attested to before a notary." Randolph spoke very slowly, very carefully. "You know that I wouldn't know it word by word if I hadn't seen it, if I didn't know where it is. All right, Slocum; I give you my word on this: I'll see that you get that paper—I'll do more than that. I'll let you prove to your own satisfaction who shot Burke—if you will hand that gun over to your wife, there, or to the cook."

Slocum gave a long time to a consideration of this. There was no sound in the big room, except that of breathing. Outside there was the occasional barking of a dog. Once, while Slocum thought on, soft footfalls pattered up the porch steps; there was the noise of sniffling at the screen door, a low whine.

Slocum's eyes were steady on Randolph. His gun had not wavered. Then he moved sidewise toward Martha, paused when close to her. "All right, mister. I'll take it."

"Pass it over then," Randolph said sharply. "I'm not giving you something for nothing, Slocum."

"I'll take th' gamble all th' way then," Slocum said, giving the pistol to his wife. "Hold that where I can get it in a hurry, Marty," he muttered, "if I have to."

Randolph reached a hand into an inside pocket, fumbled a little, came out with an envelope and a small, thirty-two automatic. He thumbed off the safety, held the weapon pointed toward the floor. Beryl gave a slight gasp. Randolph took the envelope with his left hand, leaving free the hand that held the pistol.

"Damn you!" Slocum snarled, beside himself with rage.

Randolph held up the hand with the envelope.

"I got one too," Gordon's voice sounded softly.

Randolph did not turn his head. "All right, Gordon. Keep it handy. It might be useful." He continued to look at Slocum, as he moved a pace nearer the wall.

"Here is your paper, Slocum. I should turn it over to the police, but I gave you my word. You'll have it in a moment. First I'll let you solve the mystery which really is no mystery at all." He turned slightly to include the rest in his audience, although his eyes seemed to be on Slocum alone.

"Now, Slocum; it is your turn to answer questions. Where were you when the shot was fired?"

"Me and Marty were in my cabin."

"What did you hear when you came out?"

Slocum looked puzzled.

"The launch," Martha said. "Up the lake."

"Yeah; that's what we heard."

"And who was in it when it came down?"

"You an' th' miss over there."

"So, you admit you were dumb, Slocum. Came very near making a mistake. And we both saw Gordon rowing a moment before we heard the shot."

"I told the damned fool he was nuts," Gordon growled.

"Keep your head up, Gordon," Randolph told him.

"I still don't see," Slocum said raspingly. "An' I want that paper, mister."

"Patience, Slocum. I have to keep my promise, even if it was at the point of a gun. To go on, Slocum; what did you find when you first got to the boathouse?"

"Not a damned thing. Th' door was locked."

"And who had the key?"

"You did. Damn it; get on with it."

"Then how could anyone get inside and shoot Burke who, unfortunately for him was lying helplessly drunk as well as tied by me; although if he hadn't been drunk he could have loosened the rope I put on him."

Slocum shook his head.

"I had the launch; Gordon had the boat," Randolph reminded him.

"Swum in then. Wheatley, damn your—"

"Wait a minute, Slocum. What happened this afternoon?"

"Wheatley damned near drowned."

"Why?"

"'Cause he couldn't—"

Randolph spun all the way to his right. The little automatic was pointed straight before him.

"Steady, Fraser. The hands down. I don't know how you ever imagined you could get away with it... And I believe that will be the police coming now, shooing away Slocum's dogs. My friend at the gate told me he had a pal outside in a car—a little sneak-thief called Slinky—who would be glad to do a favor for the cops."

RANDOLPH DROVE THE roadster slowly toward town. Barbara and her mother had already started on in their sedan, chauffeured by a much chastened Gerald Wheatley. That, Barbs said before they left, would be the last they would see of that estimable young man.

When the little way station came into sight, Randolph turned toward his companion.

"I believe it was about here—"

"Yes," she said, "it was just about here."

She lifted her head a little, as he bent over.

"And now in the cold light of morning," he said, "does what you said in the launch last evening still hold?"

"Like Dick Randolph," she said, "I never go back on my word even if given at the point of a gun."

"Which yours wasn't. You never guessed where the gun was. I took it with the idea I might find it more useful than you, and if I'd told you, you would have made me give it back."

"Anyway," she said, "I'm going to marry you." She glanced up at him, with that sidewise tilt of her head. "But you haven't told me a heck of a lot about yourself."

"That makes my romance perfect. You took me on trust. Well; let's see. I think I'll give up the idea of the ring and go into engineering with Dad; or rather go on with it. I'm on vacation now. An uncle of mine happens to be managing editor of a certain newspaper. I came up here to get back some securities of the family, and the first day I landed, that uncle of mine insisted that I try out a job on his sheet. They're that way."

"Yes; go on."

"That's all."

"But I don't know where you came from."

"Oh; the Randolphs of—"

"Virginia."

"Will that do for the register?"

"Well, we'll see what we can do about it."

An Interview with Joseph T. Shaw

Editor of Black Mask *magazine—by Ed Bodin*

THIS AFTERNOON WE have an enjoyable assignment. We are going to call upon one of the cleverest, friendliest and most popular editors in the all-fiction field— not only an editor and a gentleman, but an editor with a keen sense of humor—namely Joseph T. Shaw of *Black Mask* magazine, whose new book, *Danger Ahead*, released a few days ago has already found a fine reception.

We give the taxi-cab driver more than the usual tip as he fights his way through the tangled traffic of upper Fifth Avenue and shoots into Madison Avenue near 57th Street. We enter the Ley Building at 578 Madison, and an express elevator brings us quickly to the 11th floor.

The beautiful blonde receptionist of *Black Mask* and associated magazines, soon gets Mr. Shaw on the inter-office phone and nods her head as she says: "Mr. Shaw will see you at once— go right in."

As usual, the editor of *Black Mask* is up to his neck in manuscripts as he sits at his huge desk beside the wall where at least a hundred covers of *Black Mask* are trained and hanging in neat arrangement. They give off an atmosphere of virility and action.

Up comes Mr. Shaw's hand for a real handshake. No matter what he is ever doing, whether reading, dictating or talking to the President of the Writers' Union—he's never too busy to greet a guest with that uprising palm that bespeaks friendship and welcome. His grey-streaked hair and mustache add dignity to his middle-age appearance as he invites us to be seated.

"Mr. Shaw," we begin—"the readers of *Author & Composer* have come for a short visit this afternoon for a personal chat and message to carry back home."

"Fine," he smiles. "I always knew that real people like *Black Mask*—that's why we intend to keep the reputation it has gained as the leading magazine in its field."

We answer quickly. "You don't have to tell us—we know that *Black Mask's* fiction whether it is an adventure, western or detective story, finds its place in homes from the White House to the mechanic's cottage."

Mr. Shaw interrupts at this point. "Yes," he says—"I've always wondered what a composite picture of the *Black Mask* readers would look like."

"A typical red-blooded virile American—fit he-man comrade for the many animated women who also enjoy the thrill of *Black Mask* fiction."

But we soon get to the point of the visit and we put the first query: "What chance has the unknown writer to click with *Black Mask?*"

"Best in the world," replies the editor, "if he carries the *Black Mask* standard of craftsmanship as well as the story. You see— *Black Mask* demands fine workmanship. The names in the author list of our magazine, are found in the *Saturday Evening Post, Collier's, Liberty* and the best magazines in the country; but names don't mean much unless the story is there too. That's why leading writers consider it a distinction to be on *Black Mask's* contents page."

Then Mr. Shaw makes this vital point: "Remember—when I read a story by a new author, I don't read it from the standpoint of that one story. I read it also as an example of that writer's workmanship. He might not click with that story—but if he writes *Black Mask* quality, he will know about it—for I am always looking for the fellow with the flair."

When asked to mention names of his writers he most preferred, Mr. Shaw replied quickly: "This wouldn't be fair to the many *Black Mask* writers—for one never knows when one of the authors who write *Black Mask* quality, will step ahead with a story that is exceptional. All my writers are fiction masksmen—that's why so many writers who get their first breaks in *Black Mask,* soon appear in the *Post* and others, along with their *Black Mask* appearances."

We interrupt at this point and ask: "The best way, therefore, to know *Black Mask,* is to read a copy?"

"Not exactly—but rather study the technique of the *Black Mask* writers—not one issue, but a dozen—and suddenly you will feel that fiction punch that tells why their stories were purchased. You'll find that expert swing and delivery in every story in *Black Mask.* Until you can sense it and duplicate it—you are not quite ready to click."

"Now as to the best lengths to try," we ask. "We presume the short would stand a better chance?"

"Yes, *Black Mask* doesn't like novelettes over 15,000 words—and, of course, seldom does the new fellow hit the bull's-eye with that length. His best bet would be the 6,000-word story, or a little less."

THUS IT IS plain why *Black Mask* magazine holds such a high reputation in the all-fiction field. The editor is not just a purchasing agent of virile, adventure, western, detective or border stories that are usually found in such magazines—but a Judge of the Supreme Court of two-fisted fiction who knows quality as well as story substance and considers them with the eyes of his readers. As a popular author himself he has both the author's and the editor's vision.

So don't send ordinary material to Joseph T. Shaw. While he wants to be friendly and helpful—his judgment cannot be fooled by inferior quality of workmanship or weak stories. When shooting at *Black Mask,* you are shooting at as fine a market as there is in the magazine field—and Mr. Shaw intends to maintain that reputation for *Black Mask.* Don't overburden him, or impose upon his good nature. He will meet you more than halfway—but you've got to show him that you have the flair.